Annie McCartney is a former actress who has worked on stage, TV and radio. She was also a rock 'n' roll DJ in America for five years. She's a regular broadcaster on BBC Radio Ulster and RTE, and her first novel, *Desire Lines*, was chosen as Northern Ireland's book for World Book Day 2003. She has written ten radio plays for Radio 4, including the highly successful *Two Doors Down*. Annie is married with two children and lives in Belfast.

Also by Annie McCartney
Desire Lines

Your Cheatin' Heart

Annie McCartney

A *Time Warner* Original

First published in Great Britain in 2005
by Time Warner Books

Copyright © Annie McCartney 2005

The moral right of the author has been asserted.

A CIP catalogue record for this book is available
from the British Library.

ISBN 0 316 72963 9

Typeset in Bembo by Palimpsest Book Production Limited,
Polmont, Stirlingshire

Printed and bound in Great Britain by
Clays Ltd, St Ives plc

Time Warner Books
An imprint of
Time Warner Book Group UK
Brettenham House
Lancaster Place
London WC2E 7EN

www.twbg.co.uk

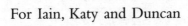
For Iain, Katy and Duncan

Acknowledgements

Thanks to Joanne Coen of Time Warner Books for all her help. Thanks also to Jay & Charlotte Paty, and Pam O'Dwyer, of Chattanooga, Tennessee, who kept my ear tuned to Southern voices. Plus all my friends and family who have listened to me gurning on for years now and are still my friends.

A big thank you to The Arts Council of Northern Ireland and The Tyrone Guthrie Centre at Annaghmakerrig – especially the wonderful women.

And Flossie, for sitting at my feet and keeping me calm – well, relatively.

And Mr Toad, of course.

1979

'Honey, you should have killed him, fat ole' Beefcake Buford, not this pathetic piece of white trash,' Sharla says calmly.

I say nothing. We both stare at the prostrate figure of Buford's 'baybay' doll – slut, mistress, former Miss Oogamooga County, Sue Lynne Crutchley.

'Well, am I right or am I right?'

'Sharla, you are right,' I mumble. For some reason my voice doesn't seem to be working properly. 'It's just when I saw her looking at me like that, her smug face all pink and shiny with triumph, and her pouting "Bee-stung" lips glistening at me, I couldn't stop myself, I pulled the trigger.'

That was true, I think, and for a minute after the gun went off, I felt my arm had jerked right out of its socket. The explosion knocked me clean across the room; I thought the gun had backfired and I'd shot myself. Even now, ten minutes later, my body is tingling unpleasantly, and my ears are ringing. But I guess I'm still in one piece and she's lying here dead as can be, and I'm wondering how long it'll take for the police to arrive. It seems like an hour since Sharla called them.

Sharla and I look at Buford: he's in a state right enough. He doesn't know what to be at. One minute he's lying over Sue Lynne's body, dragging her up and hugging her, giving her the kiss of life. Then he's flinging her back down on the floor with screams and wails that would put you in mind of a mad banshee. Next he starts pacing the room, getting redder and redder by the minute, his big wobbly gut swaying and bouncing, sweat flying off in droplets, calling me every low down name he can think of – and that's saying something. The foul language is pouring out of his mouth like effluent.

'You goddamm murderin' Aarish bitch. Yew've gone and kilt the lurve ah ma laafe.'

I'm starting to panic in case he has a heart attack and dies as well. One dead body is going to take enough explaining.

He makes me want to spit – Buford aka 'Big Boy' McConnell, *Mr Maple Syrup* himself. He, and his soon-to-be *fifth* wife, Sue Lynne, who is at present lying on my pale blue 'winter frost' shag pile carpet – one of Zollie's more useful trade-outs. I have to say it is a good backdrop for her body, and thankfully there's no blood to be seen, so I won't need to have it cleaned at least. She looks like a dead Barbie doll. She's even conveniently dressed from head to toe in Barbie pink. She looks as if she's faking death. Her make-up doesn't even look mussed, her long false eyelashes are lying like two little frills on her cheeks, her pink lips still forming a perfect shiny O – or maybe Buford was holding them open like that to get the air in better. God knows why. Her head is full of it.

Bloody Buford, I think despairingly as I look at him, what

a waste of space, what a blight on my life. Sharla and I look at him, our heads moving in tandem. He is, as my mammy would say, 'A sight for sore eyes'. His fat thighs are bulging in his blue jeans. His belly, seemingly with a life of its own, looks like it's straining to break free of his thick leather cowboy belt, explode and smother everyone in the room. He keeps lifting his cowboy hat to let the steam escape and to fan himself. I notice his remaining strands of hair clinging damply to his clammy head. I am utterly repulsed by him, but I am also scared – really scared. This is a waiting situation now. I fired the gun. Sue Lynne fell down. Sharla called the police.

It's been fifteen minutes now and I have stopped shaking but I'm numb, frozen. Even the words I speak are coming out of my mouth and bypassing my head; I am listening to them as if I am hearing for the first time. It's not every day you kill someone with the first shot you ever fired, let alone the first gun you ever held. I'm so glad Sharla is here.

Sharla is my best friend. She has always had impeccable timing. She's a girl who knows how and when to make an entrance. She arrived just after the shot had been fired, took one look at the situation and then went right into the kitchen; picked up some limes, avocados, picante sauce (Hot), fixed us a large bowl of guacamole, and opened a jumbo packet of tacos. Sharla loves Mexican food. Then she dialed 911. I didn't hear what she told them. I was, and still am, almost deaf from the explosion.

'Yep honey,' she says now, as she sashays out and places the tacos on the table. 'It's gonna be real awkward, on account of him having been here and seen it all.'

We both look again at Buford, but he is still sobbing and ignoring us both. We can't ignore him; he's making a noise like a whistling kettle and blubbering over Sue Lynne's body. I notice a glob of snot hanging on his moustache. I really did shoot the wrong person. The police and paramedics are on the way, but they are certainly taking their time. I think Sharla must have sounded too calm.

I'm feeling a bit queasy now; the fact I'm a murderer is starting to reveal itself to me. I hear the sob in my voice beginning. Sharla gazes at me reassuringly, fluffing her mane of blonde hair with her long, perfectly manicured nails.

'Oh Sharla, why did I do that? I don't know what possessed me, it's like someone else was inhabiting my body,' I blurt out at her, wanting her to forgive me. I know sure as hell the police won't. I'm a registered alien, and Tennessee still has the death penalty. I wonder briefly, would that apply to me? It's a chilling thought. I see the headline in my brain, engraved *National Enquirer* typeface:

REGISTERED ALIEN TO FRY AT DAWN
WILL HER LAST MEAL BE IRISH STEW?

People will assume it is something to do with UFOs. Anyhow, there is little point in speculation. Sharla absent-mindedly hands me a taco. I notice she has almost finished the bowl.

'Can you believe I shot her, Sharla? What made me do that?'

'I guess you had a reason, honey.'

'Yes, I must have. Mustn't I?'

'What did she say to you this time?'

'Nothing,' I sobbed. I try to remember precisely why I had pulled the trigger, though I hadn't known the gun was loaded. What was going through my head other than sheer distaste?

Contempt? Rage? Loathing? Revulsion? I can't remember. My brain feels cloudy.

Sharla gives me one of her searching looks – her green eyes fixed and glittering. 'Well, honey?'

'It was the way she looked at me,' I say haltingly. 'So triumphant when she said she and Buford were going to have a baby, it was so unexpected her being pregnant. Her mouth was fixed in that pout she does, it sent some signal to my crazed brain, you understand, don't you?'

Sharla nods sagely in between mouthfuls of tacos. 'Don't worry, baby, I know you were provoked.' (Sharla pronounces it preevoked.) 'I mean, I know that pouty look of hers, it's sickening, jest sickening, looks like they've just pulled her off a dick. I'd a killed her maself.' Sharla pauses as if something has just struck her. 'Pregnant? Are you shittin' me? I thought he had been fixed?'

'No, that's what she said. They're going to have a baby.'

'Hell, honey! Forgit Sue Lynne, baby, that means those ole' raaght to laafhers are gonna kill your ass – we need us a lawyer. We oughta call Big Billy Buchanan the third. He specialises in Murder One.'

My heart sinks. Big Billy Three, no less. This is gonna be some murder trial.

I'm not going to bother to quote Sharla phonetically from now on; it would be hard to get her down on paper anyway. You just have to hear her. She has one of those twangy east Tennessee accents that most people, even other Americans, don't quite believe. I can translate no problem now, but then it's been a long time, and we've been through a lot together. Besides, she couldn't understand me at first either, me being from Belfast.

1

Daytona Beach, Florida, summer of seventy-seven. It is sunny, glamorous, and full of college students, Vietnam vets, and crazed loons of surfers looking for waves. It's so different, so teeming with vitality, so tropical and exotic, so tacky and exciting, so unbearably hot and here we are, three milk-bottle white Irish girls traipsing the main drag looking for summer jobs. It's a far cry from war-torn Belfast, I can tell you, and *nothing* but *nothing* will make me go back there, at least not for a while. I have finished my finals and at present am awaiting the results of my degree. I have absolutely not a clue what I want to do with my life, despite my mother's fervent hope that the nuns will turn up a *wee teaching job* for me, even though, against their 'wishes', I did Social Anthropology. Well, this is as good a place to study another tribe as the next. I won't even allow my friend Patricia's endless whinging to dent my optimism. She's at it now.

'This is all your fault, Maggie Lennon. You told us it'd be

far easier to get jobs here, so you did.' Patricia sniffs loudly, self pity bubbling up in her throat. 'And I can't stick this heat; it's not natural for people from Ireland to live here—'

She pauses in the middle of her tirade to adjust her cork-heeled platform sandals. I bite my tongue. Maureen, my other friend, says nothing. She has learned not to interrupt Patricia's rants; it only winds her up more. I adjust the cheap sunglasses I bought yesterday for a dollar and squint back at my two friends. Their white legs look almost luminous. I feel so alien, yet I am deliriously happy to be here and feel the hot sun beating down on me. It is so bright and blinding, but Patricia has a point; we are in a bit of a fix right enough. We've been here almost three days now and not the slightest sniff of a job. I alone of the three of us am hopeful we'll get jobs soon. We had better. We have only about fifty dollars left. We are staying in a tacky motel well away from the seafront; three of us in one double bed. Not pleasant.

'Do you need another sticking plaster?' Maureen offers one to Patricia in an effort to placate her. Patricia sits on a low wall and attempts to get it to stick to her squelchy feet.

'And another thing – that fella in the chemist – you'd have thought I was speaking Greek. Imagine! *band aids.*' Patricia spits the word out. 'Why in the name of God would you call a plaster a *band aid*?' She steps down from her shoes and sur-veys her ruined feet. I don't point out that if she'd brought proper sandals this wouldn't have happened. We are outside a restaurant that overlooks the beach.

'Let's go in here and get a Coke,' I say. 'Look, it says it's air conditioned.'

Grumbling, they both follow me into Paesano's Perfect Pasta and Pizzeria. I order three Cokes and a waitress brings them to our table. They are massive and seem to be composed entirely of ice with a dribble of Coke. We sip them grate-fully. It is so cool inside, cool and dark; the temperature is practically freezing. I'm getting used to this. Burning up one minute, teeth chattering the next; it's interesting.

'Maybe we should have taken those jobs in Asbury Park after all,' Maureen ventures.

'Hmmm!' Patricia snorts with derision. She stares accus-ingly at me.

'Well, everybody else from Ireland was going to New Jersey; it seemed a good idea to come here. Anyway, we haven't met any other Irish people. I'm sure we'll be a rarity and get more tips.'

'A rarity, a rarity! Maybe we could get jobs in the zoo.'

'Do you think we *will* get jobs, Maggie?' Maureen sounds worried.

'Sure, maybe they need people here.' I hope I sound more confident than I feel. I get up and walk over to the waitress and ask her if there is a manager I can speak to. She tells me the owner will be back in half an hour. I go back to the table. 'The owner will be here in half an hour. I'm going to wait.'

'The place is half empty, I doubt if you'd make much working here.' Maureen sounds dubious.

'Wait if you want,' Patricia announces. 'I'm going to try the hotels.'

Two Cokes later, the owner arrives. He is a squat little peasant with a tanned, gnome-like face. He is solid, rather than fat, with very white teeth and the palest blue eyes. I go over to him. I am officially freezing now, my teeth are chattering.

'I'm looking for a job as a waitress.'

'No vacancies for waitresses.' The blue eyes stare unflinch-ingly at me – not offensively though. 'Where are you from?'

he asks eventually, adding: 'It's too late in the season to get jobs.'

'I'm from Belfast, Northern Ireland. How is it too late? It's only June.'

He shrugs. 'Season starts in May.'

'Where are you from?' I ask. 'You aren't American.'

For a moment I think he isn't going to answer. 'Everyone's an American – eventually.' He smiles finally. 'Greece via New Jersey.'

'I've been to Greece every summer until now,' I tell him. 'I love Greece.'

'What's your name?'

'Maggie Lennon.'

He indicates for me to sit down, and pours us both a coffee. It is bitter. It burns my mouth. 'Tell me about Greece.'

An hour later I have a job, and he agrees to see Maureen and Patricia. He says he'll fire some people. That's the way it works in America. You see something or someone you like better, you swap. Paesano has a friend who owns apartments. He rents them cheap to Paesano's staff.

Maureen is thrilled, Patricia less so. She has got her own job, thank you, working at the Ramada on the beach, but it doesn't have accommodation and it is waitressing during the daytime. Hence the chance of returning to Belfast bronzed and Goddess-like (as if) is slight. The summer is to resound to her whinging about how much better off she'd have been if she had stuck to her guns and taken the job at the Ramada.

I don't care; I am thrilled silly just being here. Belfast was never like this. Just the warmth of the sun alone is enough to make me feel exhilarated. Every morning it is still shining. I check first thing when I wake up. I feel as if all my muscles, which had been tense and cramped from hunching under grey, weighty Irish skies, have suddenly relaxed and allowed my bones to move more freely, and consequently allowed me to free myself too. It is intoxicating. Every day the sea is still blue. Blue and warm with the palest, whitest sand imaginable, and crazy rolling waves that fringe the entire Atlantic side of Florida. The clouds are white and wispy when they appear at all, and they never hide the sun, they float past it high in the sky like cheeky little frills to set it off. If you look out to the horizon, Daytona seems like paradise. Looking inward is tawdrier and trashed; lots of neon and endless tacky souvenir shops. So all summer long I look out when I can. Ireland is the nearest land to here. The same ocean touches both shores. It is impressive and it makes my heart surge. I am happy. The people are different from people at home, more assured, confident, they are larger than life. They demand more too, of course, but tipping comes easily as they appreciate good service. I learn fast. I make good tips.

Paesano's Pizza Parlor is open twenty-four hours and we work the afternoon shift. It would be better to work nights because of the tips, but we are on afternoons till we are 'trained'. The apartments are okay. Better than the motel, and at least we are earning now. We will get one dollar fifty an hour and we can keep all our tips. Last week I called my parents and told them I have a job. I made it sound brilliant because they feel concerned and are worried sick about me; although not as much as when I'm at home. The first two weeks fly by, waitressing is hard work but fun. I can't wait to move to the evening shift. That's where all the money is, and Paesano has promised me first vacancy on one. Then I'll get to work on my tan.

Maureen and I are walking home to the apartment. We have had a good day; there was a big crowd in for lunch and they were generous. We are comparing tips. Maureen has made over twenty dollars. She is an open-hearted, friendly Irish girl and the customers love her. The red hair helps. We arrive at the apartment to find that a virtual river is running freely out the door and down the steps. Even at six o clock it's still hot and steam is rising from the torrent. Maureen rushes to open the door and we view the devastation with horror. The floor is awash and there are clothes everywhere, wet, soggy ones. Even as we look, my purple and red tie-dye shirt is bleeding profusely into my new white jeans. There are no wardrobes, no chests of drawers in the apartment, so we have been living out of suitcases and these suitcases are completely flooded. The water is pouring through a large gash in the ceiling and Maureen's bed is directly under the torrent. It is saturated.

Maureen takes one look at it and her screams resound through the building. A girl of about our age hears them, and comes rushing down from the floor above to explain. I recognise her at once; it would be hard not to. She is barefoot and wearing an extremely small, shocking pink bikini. Her stomach is completely flat. I want to touch it. Her fingernails and toenails are painted the exact same shade of bright pink. She smiles at us, and introduces herself as our upstairs neighbour.

'Hey, ah'm Sharla – ah live upstairs. Ah sure am sorry,' she says in a languid southern drawl, pointing at the river running down the wall and the torrent under our feet, 'but ah've had a little ole mishap. Ma waterbed just burst – well, maybe an hour or so ago.'

Little old mishap? Are we hearing her right? A virtual Niagara Falls roaring down our walls a mishap? Her waterbed has burst? I have heard ads for waterbeds on the radio but have never actually seen one. She repeats the apology.

11

'It's okay, isn't it?' I say to Maureen.

'It's okay? *Little* mishap? Excuse me but I don't think so! This is a bloody catastrophe. Everything is ruined,' Maureen snaps at her.

Sharla smiles back. She is slim, tanned and gorgeous, twenty-one or two, and a natural blonde with big hair and a dazzling smile. Easy, since she has at least four dozen sparkling white teeth. Her eyes are an unusual shade of green and she has the slightest hint of a squint, or a turn in her eye as my mother would have said. This has the effect of making you feel she is gazing intently at you. In fact, I find out later she is short-sighted and just trying to see better. She has smooth olive skin, the type that turns brown easily. It had taken all three of us barely two weeks to discover that we turn red, peel, and then turn white again. This is obviously not one of Sharla's problems. I try not to loathe her. I want to look like that. I can't take my eyes off her.

Sharla squints at me, possibly sensing I am more sympathetically inclined. I notice then that her eyes are extremely bloodshot and assume she's been crying. But, as I am to learn later, she is simply stoned out of her brain. She speaks slowly, very slowly, like she is just getting used to having a mouth.

'Ah sure am mighty sorry about the bed. I was trying to figure why we were just soakin' wet, and why we were just skidding on the bed like crazy.' She pauses and looks at us. We wait. Finally she continues, with a sort of 'silly me' expression on her face. 'I guess I thought Buddy was sweating a lot. He puts so much effort into satisfying me.' She stops as if some amazing thought has hit her. We both look at her expectantly. 'Though it occurs to me right now that the air conditioning works real well,' she adds.

It suddenly dawns on Maureen and me that this is the

explanation for the swishy, thumping water sound from upstairs that usually stops about five-thirty each day. They had been at it. And we had spent the first week in the Beachcomber Apartment Building thinking it was related to the plumbing.

Sharla extends a languid hand and smiles again, dazzling us. 'Well never mind the waterbed, ah sure am finally glad to meet y'all. Ah've been meaning to say hi to y'all before this here mess. Ah'm Charlotte Emily Anne Williams and ah'm from Bristol Tennessee. Ah'm a Cosmetics and Psychology of Selling major at ETSU.'

'Oh,' I say brightly. 'Your parents must be Brontë fans.'

She looks puzzled at this.

'You know, the Brontës, *Jane Eyre*?' No response. '*Wuthering Heights*?' I venture. She smiles hopefully. Perhaps she thinks I'm speaking Gaelic.

'Come again?'

I realise quickly that an explanation would confuse her further. So I don't bother. After a lot of unravelling we find out that her name is Sharla Emma-Lea Ayn. Names are like that in America.

Our immediate problem is what to do with a soggy apartment. The water has slowed somewhat but is still cascading down. Maureen is sniffling and picking up her bits and pieces. We arrange them on the grass outside. The grass is thick here, tough and rubbery; it doesn't feel real.

Sharla helps in a sort of distracted fashion. She does re-assure us that the landlord, another gnome-like little Greek called Mr Stanisopoulos, has been told, and he will be fixing up for us to move to another apartment later on. This is fine. The clothes will dry and Patricia doesn't like the apartment anyway. The shape of the toilet seat has made her constipated. It is very tall and narrow and she has short legs and is a bit tubby, so she has to clench her buttocks too hard to balance on it – hence constipation. For the last two weeks she hasn't had a crap. Not as much as a rabbit pellet since the day we arrived. Her tummy has become hard as a rock, and in between serving customers she has been groaning in pain and drinking senna pod concoctions. Not even a fart has resulted. Just as well, the atmosphere in the apartment is poisonous enough.

I am really glad Patricia has gone to the drugstore for an enema on the way home from work; she would have ruined Sharla's sweet explanation by screaming abuse at her. Patricia has been locked in an ongoing row with our landlord about the cockroaches, the badly functioning air conditioning or lack of it, the fact that there are only two cups, and various other things. She hates him and thinks him a fat, greedy, Greek peasant, but Sharla has obviously seen qualities in Mr Stanisopoulos that have passed Patricia by. They've passed me by too, for that matter.

Sharla fixes us again with her crooked gaze. 'Lil' ole' Mr Staniswhateverpolos, ain't he such a honey?'

We say nothing, Sharla continues. 'He wanted to take me out to dinner 'cos he could see I was real upset. But I told him I wouldn't feel like eating till I was safely moved into ma new place. I think he understood that. He was real, *real* understanding.' She nods her head as if she is agreeing with herself and moves closer. She grabs Maureen by the arm and talks straight to her. Maureen freezes. 'I called him in considerable distress and why honey he dropped by at once. Held my hand and comforted me, and now he's gone to get him a plumber, I believe.'

She smiles serenely, confident of her charms. She reaches out and clasps my arm this time. I think Maureen's rigid stance has unnerved her slightly. 'But hell, right now why don't you guys come upstairs to the porch and meet Buddy? We can smoke a jay and forgit this here mess.'

Maureen refuses on the spot, and had she known the number of the narcotics bureau would no doubt be on the phone to them now.

'I'll come,' I say. I am curious. I follow her upstairs and leave Maureen in the flood.

Sharla's apartment makes ours look sparse and unlived-in. It is draped with silk scarves and smells heavily of incense. The walls are covered in Day-Glo posters. The largest of these features a sort of Hell's Angel type of guy with a machine gun. It says: Yeah, though I should walk through the valley of death, I will fear no evil for I am the meanest motherfucker in the Valley.

Sharla catches me looking at it. 'Don't that just crack you up?' she says.

I agree, glad that Maureen passed on the invite. I look around. A lava lamp bubbles quietly in a corner. There is a guy sitting beside it looking at it fixedly. He says nothing. The floor is awash and a large deflated waterbed is quietly seeping onto it; oh, so that's what they look like. I wonder briefly why Mr Stanisopoulos has gone for a plumber. A mop seems more appropriate. I offer to clean up but Sharla shakes her head.

'Forgit it, honey, it'll soon dry out. Anyways, we don't have a mop.' She goes to a drawer, takes out a joint, lights it and offers me some. I decline graciously. But we sit on the swinging chair on the upstairs porch and chat. I've never encountered anyone like this. Her accent and crazy logic are mesmerising. I am hooked.

Buddy, the boyfriend, isn't exactly a contributor. He spends all of the time staring at the lava lamp, listening to Lynyrd

Skynyrd, laughing to himself and playing the air guitar. It is weird and somewhat unnerving. I look at him quizzically a few times but he doesn't respond; Sharla notices my gaze.

'He's real mellow right now. Sex and drugs always does it for him,' she informs me. I nod, knowingly I hope.

A lot later that evening, Stani, as Sharla has nicknamed him, arrives to move us to our new apartments. He only has two available at short notice. Each apartment is for two people. If we want one to suit three people, we'll have to wait another week. It is a dilemma. They are much nicer apartments though, and a lot nearer the beach. But there are three of us.

Sharla has the answer. 'Why don't you move in with me, Maggie? I'd love a roommate and you'll be right next door to your friends here.'

It seems a really daring thing to do, but what option do I have? Patricia isn't speaking to me anyway at this stage, you'd think I'd burst the bloody waterbed myself. And although I have come to the USA with Maureen and Patricia, they are the best friends – I am always the gooseberry. I feel I need a shot of adventure; I want to do something a bit different, so I might as well move in with Sharla. I can always move out if it doesn't work. So I agree. It does seem a much better arrangement all round.

And that is it. My life has changed – forever.

There are three things that Sharla converts me to within weeks of our meeting. One, I start to shave my legs; Americans have a horror of women with body hair. They simply can't cope with it. I had already started to remove the hair under my armpits (in the summer anyway). But up until now, I had seen no real need to shave my legs. The hair was blonde

16

anyway and hard to see. But Sharla can see it glinting in the sun as we sit on the beach a few days later.

'Y'all need to shave your legs, honey,' she says. 'You look like a lil' ole' fuzzy peach from where ah am.'

Later that day, in the shower, I do, and quite enjoy the new sleek feel of my tanned (well, pink) legs.

The second and even more important thing (though only just about by Sharla's reckoning), I lose my virginity, quickly and enthusiastically, with a large, blond, stoned surfer friend of Buddy's. The third thing is that I am stoned too – for the first time.

I meet Jay at the restaurant where Sharla works when he and Buddy – Sharla's boyfriend – arrive to pick up some left-over pizza. Jay is from Gary, Indiana. He is tall with sun-streaked hair and an easygoing personality. I like the look of him. He seems the sort of all-American type I had envisioned spending time with when I was planning my trip to the States. The reality is that up until now I have only been asked out by one or two obese rednecks who come into the restaurant regularly, and Calvin, the buss-boy, who has no teeth.

Jay is more like my idea of a boyfriend. So when Buddy brings him in I chat him up a bit. He starts dropping in regularly after that. He is funny. He likes to hear about Ireland. His ambition is to hitchhike round Europe. I suppose I flirt with him a lot. At first I think it isn't getting me anywhere, and then about a week after we first meet he arrives round at the apartment without Buddy. He asks me if I want to go and watch him shoot basketball on the Boardwalk. He plays bas-ketball for one of the big college teams, despite being only 5'11" and white. I don't know whether this is a big deal or not, but I take him at his word that it is. It is my night off and I am happy to go out with him. He has teeth and looks normal; well, good-looking actually. He is amiable and undemanding.

He smiles a lot, probably due to the number of joints he smokes, but I don't care. His sunniness is infectious and he cheers me up. And besides, Sharla spends a lot of time with Buddy, heaving away on the waterbed – they have mended the hole, turns out you can fix it like a bicycle puncture – and I am beginning to feel a wee bit left out. I have actually phoned home twice in the last two weeks. My sister Sinead thinks I need an American boyfriend and here I am going out with a surfer – how much more American can I get?

The Boardwalk (I have never been until now) is a sort of permanent funfair. There are lots of stalls full of tacky little prizes, the usual old rubbish. Three of them give you three shots at a basketball hoop for a dollar. The star prize is a teddy bear. The teddies are awful-looking things: the body is plaid, or check as we call it back in Ireland, and they have big googly eyes. Jay wins three at the first stall, and then the guy says he can't play any more. He gives them to me. I am touched by these awkward, tawdry gifts. I am living the American life, with my boyfriend shooting basketball on the Boardwalk. It is exhilarating. I want people to look at me, see my happiness, my sudden sense of belonging. We repeat this at two other stalls, until we are staggering about laughing our heads off and clutching nine check teddies. No one else on the Boardwalk will let Jay near a stall. We bring them home to the apartment. I feel very warm towards Jay. It's not every day a girl gets a present of nine ugly check teddies.

'Maybe I could sort of spend the night here and we could make out?'

'Well, you could have a beer,' I say, having the idea of a cuddle in my head. This is a first date, after all.

Jay takes out his little box and starts to roll a joint. I don't mind. I quite like the smell of it.

'Here,' Jay says, holding out the joint. 'You have some.'

'I can't do it, I don't smoke.'

'Whaddya mean, you don't smoke?'

'I don't like tobacco,' I say.

'But this is grass. It's different.'

I shake my head. 'I don't think I'll like it.'

'You'll love it, babe; look, hold on a minute. Open your mouth and suck this in, and swallow it.' He takes a long draw from the joint and then blows a large jet of smoke into my mouth. I do what he says. I suck like crazy. I love the proximity of his mouth.

'You call this a blowback,' he tells me. 'Just tell people you can't smoke and they'll do this for you. It works just as good.'

It feels glorious; sensual and sexy. Suddenly I love him. He is my real live check teddy, and so talented, a sharpshooter no less. He begins to kiss me. He has a soft, warm, melty mouth. Five minutes later we are totally naked on Sharla's waterbed (not hard since we are in Florida and had been wearing very little to start with), rolling about in ecstasy, making love till I am seasick. I am deflowered at once. All the nine check teddies look solemnly on. It is the seventh of the seventh seventy-seven. It has been ordained.

Sharla comes home early next morning. Jay and I are fast asleep on the waterbed. I tell her what has happened and she almost passes out with enthusiasm. She is busy cracking vitamin E capsules on to her nipples at the time to keep them supple.

'Maggie, honey, that was real smart. I am so proud of you. You really needed to unload that baggage. I'm sure you feel normal now.' She studies me critically. 'Why I believe you look better already, and to do it yesterday especially. The magic date. It's apocrital.'

I think she means apocryphal, but I'm not sure.

I'd almost given up the virginal state earlier that year. I went on holiday to Southport for Easter with an English boy from university. Myles was his name. His mother ran a B&B there. We'd been going out all term. Despite the earnestness of his passion, I had refused to give up my virginity on Irish soil. But I had agreed in advance that we would do it that holiday. I had decided it wouldn't be a sin if I did it away from home.

One morning, before breakfast, Myles came to my room looking for action. We fumbled around a lot; even though I had already decided to surrender, I wasn't going to hand it to him without a fight. However, just at the height of our passion, when I was finally swooning into agreement, his mother shouted up to ask if he would put the fish fingers out to defrost for lunch. It was all downhill from there. In the end, he seemed to get his willie mixed up with his pyjama cord, and I left Southport a virgin.

The surfer, fortunately, is not a great man for pyjamas. Being naked suits him. He spends a lot of time that way, or trying to *get nekit* as he calls it. I fancy him rotten. His life consists of surfing, eating and fucking in that order. He isn't much of a conversationalist, probably on account of the pot. But I am comfortable with him. He is undemanding.

Sharla unfortunately shares my good news with Maureen and Patricia. She thinks they'll be pleased. They aren't. They corner me in the toilet at work.

'Sharla told us what you've been up to. God forgive you, Maggie Lennon. No self-respecting boy back home will ever look at you again. Soiled goods, that's what you are,' Maureen tells me piously.

You could say neither Maureen nor Patricia had heard of Germaine Greer. They are appalled when, under

20

questioning, I admit that I have thoroughly enjoyed losing my virginity.

'You're not supposed to enjoy it,' Patricia snarls at me. Part of me hopes they don't go home and tell everyone I am a fallen woman, but the weirder thing is that I feel I am actually doing what I want to do for the first time in my life.

So now I have experienced the sex and drugs, and with Sharla's prompting I stumble into rock and roll.

My accent already goes down a treat with everyone. I had figured out after a mere week working in Paesano's that the fact that I talk *funny* is a great tip-booster. Maureen and Patricia do this too, though not so flamboyantly. Bob, the manager at Paesano's, cashes in on his Irish waitresses too. He encourages the customers in the belief that we are political refugees from the conflict in Northern Ireland.

Sharla, however, has bigger and better ideas for me. My accent is a vital commodity waiting to be exploited. Not squandered on mere waitressing. She has plans; she thinks I should be on the radio. There is a great rock 'n' roll station called WA1A that we all listen to.

'You should be on the air, honey. Your accent is so cute, and WA1A has no female DJs. They need them one.'

Sharla encourages me to phone and ask for an interview. She has a car; we drive out on my day off. WA1A's DJs talk eloquently about the station being on the beach with the Atlantic waves lapping outside its door. Such a romantic image, I am really looking forward to seeing it.

The reality is anything but. When we finally locate it we find it's a converted lock-up garage in the sticks. The closest water is a mosquito-infested swamp, and the place is about as far as you can get from the ocean. Once you have this inside

knowledge and listen carefully, you can hear the frogs croaking during the quiet parts of 'Us and Them'. WA1A plays good music though. And I am getting used to things not being as they seem. After all, we aren't too far from Disneyworld.

Zollie V Follie IV, the station owner, is sitting behind a humongous desk in one of the small rooms. He is wearing a large cowboy hat and matching boots, a check shirt and denims. He looks about thirty something and he stands up to shake my hand, grinning broadly (more teeth). He is tall, and reasonably handsome in a louche sort of way. I am not sure what to expect. He speaks with a lazy drawl.

'Ah'm real pleased to meet you, Maggie. I'm Zollie V – for Virgil – Follie the fourth, and I'm from Tennessee, the Volunteer State. In other words' – he thumps the desk loudly – 'I'll volunteer for most things.' He follows this statement with the laugh of a crazy person, but I take an instant liking to him anyway.

'I'm Maggie Lennon,' I say, 'from Ireland, and I wondered if you need any more DJs?'

For a minute he says nothing. Just looks at me with a bemused look on his face. I blab on.

'I mean, I'd like a job as a DJ if there is one. Anyway you need a lady DJ, it's an oversight not to have one.'

Zollie fixes me with his large grin. 'An oversight, huh? A lil' ole' ladee DJ, huh?'

'Yes, I think I'd be good.'

'Well, ma'am, you're British? Right?'

'Yes, well, Irish, but from the North. I suppose British. Ish.'

'Irish? How come you speak English so good? You talk like the BBC.'

'Thank you.' Immediately I reappraise my Belfast nasal.

'Have you met Pink Floyd?'

'No.'

'How 'bout Led Zeppelin?'

'No.'

'You related to *John* Lennon?'

'No, I'm afraid not.' I feel fairly useless being related to no one. Then I hit inspiration. 'I might be a cousin of his,' I say. 'I've got fifty-two first cousins and some of them live in Liverpool.' This is true and I add for good value: 'My cousin saw The Beatles in Belfast in 1964 and got me their autographs.'

'You did? Hellfire, sheeeit! I'm impressed! You have them with you?'

'No, but I can copy them from memory.' (I really can.)

'You got a social security number?'

'Yes.'

'Hell, you're hired. I just lost me a DJ 'bout five minutes ago.'

He had just fired the all-night man for getting too stoned and breaking FCC regulations by saying 'Mother fuckin' sonofabitch' on the air. So it is fate. I have come at the right time. To quote Sharla it is apocrital.

Zollie gives me a tour of the station. We start with the studio, where I will work my shift and play the records. He introduces me to Bilbo, the engineer, who is small, dark-haired and sort of tubby. He seems a sweet and shy guy, and says he will give me a crash course on how to turn a turntable.

Zollie calls it the studio but it is a joke of a place. A small, poky room, three walls of which are covered with lots of egg-box-shaped soundproofing which is made from fibreglass. I find this out to my cost; I touch it and get a splinter in my hand. The other wall is covered in shelves for the carts. A cart, I learn, is a sort of tape thing, and these are all loaded

23

with the individual songs which saves playing vinyl. All the vinyl is kept in Zollie's office; Bilbo explains it is locked away from the Kleptos, so called for their ability to rip off any LP left lying around. Only Bilbo and Zollie have keys. If I need a certain album I am to ask Bilbo, and he will get it out and give it to me. The entire current play list is already carted up. Mainly Bob Seger and Fleetwood Mac, I notice. *Rumours* is a hot album this summer, along with Steely Dan's *Aja*.

The studio seems a bit claustrophobic, but I guess that is usual enough for radio stations. WA1A has no windows at all. It consists of three rooms – the studio, the office and the back room where the station Kleptos/groupies hang out. I think the building is only a thousand feet square – Bilbo tells me it was once a mushroom farm. It does smell odd, but then so does he.

I agree to start the following evening, and go back to work my last night at Paesano's. Zollie assures me he will spend the next day advertising my arrival to listeners. He will give me a big build-up. I am in bits with excitement. I float out of the station on a high – a natural one. Sharla is waiting outside for me.

'Well? How'd it go, babe?'

'They've offered me a job! I'm starting tomorrow night.'

'Didn't I tell you your accent would make you famous, honey?'

I hope they don't find out in the foreseeable future that there are at least half a million more people with exactly the same accent in Belfast.

We drive back to the restaurant delighted with the whole adventure. Paesano is just as excited as we are at my big break. It is slowing down anyway and he will be laying off staff. He gives me an extra day's wages and says I can have as many of the leftover or uncollected pizzas I want tonight. We usually have about six of these a night, from the people who call in and order and then get too stoned to remember where to pick them up. It is balanced some nights by those who have been too stoned to order, or who think they have, and come to pick up pizzas someone else has ordered. Jay lives on them.

I can't wait to start. I go through the evening in a haze. Funnily enough, I make more tips than ever. I will be taking a dip in wages but I don't mind. My head is already turned by the prospect of becoming a DJ.

We play Radio WA1A in the restaurant. We turn it up loud. The customers like it like that anyway. It is such a thrill to hear Zollie keep his word and give me the build-up he promised. We all listen, Maureen and Patricia with their mouths open in disbelief. It's obvious they both think I'm insane. But I bet they're impressed really.

'WA1A is real, real proud to introduce to all of y'all the one and only real authentic British person on the aayer in Florida – Maggie Lennon, a close personal relation of Beatle John. She'll be playing for y'all night-time listeners the records of many of her close personal friends – all of which speak funny like her. You know whom I'm referring to folks! Yes, y'all do! Here's just a few names for starters: The Beatles, the Stones, Pink Floyd, Yes, Genesis, The Moody Blues, Led Zeppelin and many, many more! Yessir, remember only here on Dubya Ay One Ay, the station with the Atlantic waves breaking outside our door, can you hear the close personal friend of British groups play non-stop ass-kicking British music from midnight till dawn. Be sure to tune in.' This is screamed loudly in Zollie's Tennessee sharecropper drawl to backing music of '19th Nervous Breakdown', Zollie's all-time favourite British hit.

25

'And you'll be up all night?' Patricia asks me. She hasn't stopped gurning at me since I told her.

'From eleven to five in the morning?' Maureen echoes.

'Yes, I don't mind the hours.'

I reason that I can sleep all day on the beach. I will buy a little fold-up sunbed and lie just exactly where the waves hit the shore, and the breeze takes the pain out of the sun. I will cover myself in Hawaiian tropic coconut oil and hopefully get a tan just like Sharla's.

2

So here I am, twenty-one, Queen of the Airwaves in Daytona Beach, Florida. WA1A is an AOR station. That means Album Oriented Rock, and its audience is mainly college students. Daytona is full of them in the summer: just about everyone you meet, regardless of ability, seems to be at college. You can study anything in the States. A degree in beauty skills is perfectly acceptable, no intellectual snobbery here. I don't know what they'd make of Punk though. That's what's happening musically at home. But I soon take to the AOR sound; it fits in with the good weather and easy lifestyle.

It is surprising how fast you get used to a totally new way of life, 'cos let me tell you, working for Zollie, I soon find, takes some mind adjusting. He is crazy – in the truest sense of the word. Everyone he surrounds himself with is crazy too, a cast of fools and lunatics, all except Bilbo. Bilbo is the first workaholic I have ever encountered. He doesn't appear to have a life outside the radio station and he almost lives there.

Trouble is, it is hot and stuffy in that place and, delightful as Bilbo is, he has what I quickly learn to call a hygiene problem. I guess his weight doesn't help. He is a little tublet. Nor does the fact that everything he wears is man-made. He crackles with static, like those old nylon sheets that were so fashionable years ago. We all pretend not to notice – all except Zollie. He isn't what you would call the soul of tact about it.

Zollie comes in early on my first day here (I am in getting a turntable lesson from Bilbo), sniffs a bit and then hollers at the top of his voice: 'Goddamm, Bilbo! Has something died inside your armpits? You got two skunks up there? Hell fire! I need to get me some kind of deodorant trade-out.'

Poor Bilbo moves as far away from Zollie as possible. He remains impassive.

Zollie begins again. This time his voice is quieter, almost pleading. 'Have you heard about plastic surgery where they remove your armpits? You need to read up on that, buddy.'

No response. Then finally: 'Godammit, Bilbo, baby! How can I eat my donuts with that aroma round me? Call Eckerd's now! I need to get me a trade-out for Sure.'

I am almost dying of embarrassment, but poor old Bilbo had obviously heard it all before. He slinks into the loo and sprays something that smells like air freshener on top of his already humming armpits. We spend the entire day with the air conditioner on so low that our teeth are chattering.

Yes, you could say it is an unusual environment.

Over the following weeks I get to meet the cast of weirdoes who hang around the station. The most mindbendingly insane of the lot have to be Chance and Vance Prince, or Vance and Chance Prince. Twin brothers, who look like famine, and the cause of it.

Vance is 5'6", easily 350 pounds. His skin and hair and eyes

28

are pinky red (though that might be directly attributable to the dope). There isn't a lot of his hair either, just a few seaweed-like strands clinging vainly to his round, pink head. He has sort of smooth, girlie skin which is always covered in a thin, shiny film, though he smells okay, which is a relief.

His brother Chance – his twin – is so different. Chance weighs about 130 pounds and is over six feet tall. He has long, jet-black hair which he wears in a braid down his back, black beady eyes, and a long, untrimmed beard. He looks like a roadie for ZZ Top. They have opposite voices too. Chance has a deep, growly voice, and when it emerges people always look at the wrong guy. Vance has a thin, effeminate voice.

Zollie knows the family. They hail from Possum Creek, Tennessee. Zollie has a theory, not as preposterous as it sounds, that their Mama, who goes by the name of Evangeline Oreya Prince, had been fertilised by two different sperm the same day – possibly by two of her own brothers. She was fond of the drink, apparently, and to this day their Daddy isn't in evidence, so he could have been any shape at all.

Not having made it to Vietnam is a constant source of anguish to Vance. He spends hours telling us what he 'Woondo to them Gooks over thar'. That is, had he only been given the chance. He'd applied twice to go to Vietnam (or *Can*bodya) which just about convinced the military he was crazy. I mean, every sane American male of draft age was in Canada during the Vietnam War. Here it is 1977, the ghastly war is over, and he is still calling the draft board volunteering like crazy. He certainly was taking the fact he came from Tennessee seriously. I don't think he knows the war is over yet, though he's been told often enough. Hell, he thinks Nixon is still president.

The Prince Twins are regular visitors to the station. I meet them the first day on the job. I wonder why they hang round there so much; they don't appear to do anything but get in the way. It is several weeks before I realise that they are Zollie's drug dealers. They also supply stuff to Big Al, the morning drive jock, and Art, the afternoon DJ. At this point, the trade is mainly pot and Quaaludes. Later, with dire consequences, they progress to cocaine.

Vance has a sort of notion of me. After the first week or so I get used to it and learn not to find it offensive. We have the same chat about every third night. He waits till I put on a long track, or three in a row (which is one of our 'features') and sit down with my coffee. I wait for him to sidle over.

'Whur you from Maggie?' he asks.

'Ireland, Vance. I'm from Ireland.'

'Yep, that's raaght, I believe you already tol' me that.' He pushes his strands of hair back and his pink cheeks flush with the effort of remembering. Then he gives up. 'Where d'you say Ireland was at?'

'It's in Europe, actually.'

'Is Europe y'all's hometown?'

'Sort of.' (I mean what's the point?)

'Shit, Maggie, how come you speak American so good?'

'Picked it up, Vance. I'm a fast learner.'

'Damn raaght!' He pauses. You can see the wheels go round. 'They all talk like you thur?'

'Yes they do, Vance.'

'Well, ain't that cute. Can they all understand each other?'

'Yes, no problem.'

'Well, hell, you know I'd like to go thur sometime, meet your folks. Maybe me an' Chance'll drive back with you at Thanksgiving. Or maybe Chance and me'll go thur some weekend, go fishing or something. Good fishing there, raaght?' (I have told him that the first ten times we had the Ireland conversation.) 'Whaddya think Maggie?' He then beams at me, showing his bottom row of decaying teeth, and two ill-fitting, yellowish crowns on the top row, which seem to belong to someone else's mouth. I wouldn't be surprised if he had robbed them from a dead body. I fix a smile. He has to be tolerated. I like this job. In the background Bilbo rolls his eyes. 'You like a ride home t'see yur folks?'

'Sure I would,' I reply, 'sounds great.' I found that this was the least painful reply. When we first had this conversation, I had vainly attempted to explain to him where Ireland was geographically, but I realised he is completely a moronic git. So now I humour him.

'Well, howja say we give you a ride home some of these here weekends?'

'Soon as we can organise it, Vance,' I reply.

'Fantastic, thet gives me a reason to live, baby.'

'Great, Vance. Me too,' I lie.

'Want me to eat your pussy?'

'No thanks, Vance. It's not an Irish custom.'

'Raaght, well it sure is here.'

I wasn't familiar with this custom, and not being local I hadn't heard the term. I thought at first they were going to eat cats, but Zollie was quick to apprise me of the fact that they were referring to the male prowess in performing cunnilingus. Americans have oral fixations I think. I take a decision fairly early on in the job not to be shocked about all this tacky talk, because as I quickly learn it is purely talk. They are so courteous to me otherwise. Zollie has begun to introduce me to his friends with the line: 'This here's Maggie

Lennon, she's Irish, and she thinks that oral sex is talking about it,' and then we all laugh and that is it. Zollie is very proprietorial: if he sees any guy getting too chatty he intervenes, and he manages to keep a lot of unsavoury types at bay. He needs to; this station attracts loonies and misfits. Not all are as hard to take as the Prince Brothers. Some are a delight. Maybellyne is, for sure. She is the secretary cum accountant cum sales person cum everything. I meet her on my second night on the job. She is about twenty-five, has a very pretty face, a sunny smile and nice, wide-open grey eyes, but she is extremely fat. No, that's wrong. She is actually outrageously fat. I try to look as if this is normal, but a small gasp must have sneaked out of my mouth, for she is easily three times fatter than I am, and she is about my height. I weigh 105 pounds, that's about 7½ stone. I have learned to say pounds 'cos stones confuse people here. Zollie introduces us.

'Maybellyne baby, this here is Maggie. She's Irish and John Lennon is a real close relative of hers. She talks funny but she's gonna be working for us on the midnight till five a.m. slot.'

Maybellyne looks at my mouth, which is hanging open in a sort of rictus. 'Yes, I know hon, I am gargantuan. I expect I'm the fattest person y'all ever met.'

'No,' I say hastily, choking at the same time. 'No, not at all, I've met loads of fat people.'

'But no one as fat as me, raaght?'

I smile weakly. 'Well, no actually.'

'Dead right, Maggie, ole Maybellyne here could git her a job in "Ripley's Believe it or not" museum couldn't she?' Zollie grins from ear to ear at my discomfort. Maybellyne doesn't stop smiling. Zollie keeps on. 'Boy, she can cook the best cheese grits I ever did taste though, and her ham is to die for.'

As it happens, Maybellyne and I become firm friends. She has so little sense of her own worth, and yet she is such a kind person. She quietly shows me how everything works. Nothing is too much trouble for her, unless it involves moving fast. She is too fat to drive, so a cousin/brother type (I never do work out what he is), rolls her out of a large van every night at eight, and picks her up and hoists her back in at about six a.m. I get accustomed to the loud honk and the shout from the relative: 'Maybellyne babe, your haulage truck has arrived'.

I spend a lot of time trying to improve her self-respect and helping her stick to her numerous diets. She wears a sort of rubber wet suit garment under her clothes and I even guard the loo for twenty minutes every hour for a week while she finds the opening to pee. Whoever sold it to her had guaranteed it would *Sweat off all that ugly flesh in just one week!* All she has to do to double its potential weight-losing power is perform strange crab-like movements four times an hour. These exercises have the effect of wafting a rubbery smell throughout the station.

'Goddammit! Maybellyne baby!' Zollie yells at her with his usual tact. 'You smell like a used rubber.'

Through the week she perseveres, the sweat lashing off her as she gets on with the job of answering the phone and doing the books. She looks like a bouncy ball climbing out and into the van in the nights and mornings. She must have emptied a ton of talcum powder down her neck in a vain attempt to stop the constant itching and combat the build-up of body odour. After ten days she has to be cut out of the rubber suit, and unfortunately the poor thing has developed an allergic rash from wearing it next to her skin. So now she is red and itchy as well as hopelessly fat, and she has only lost two pounds. It doesn't seem fair.

3

As soon as I begin working at WA1A my life takes on a new
dimension. Well, actually that's an understatement. I begin to
live in some sort of new dimension, as almost everyone at
the station seems to – most of it drug-induced. The station
has been in operation for one year and is, I suppose, a fairly
successful commercial venture. But maybe it isn't. I really
don't know if Zollie makes a lot of money out of it. Very
little money changes hands as the whole set-up appears to be
run on a kind of barter system where everything is freebies
or trade-outs. Zollie is out there every day of the week bull-
shitting from dawn till dusk, getting every little business within
a twenty-mile radius to advertise with us. He promises results
within days, and many of them buy into the hype. I quickly
gather the truth doesn't play too big a part in his selling, and
boy can Zollie V Follie IV sell airtime. That's where the money
is *supposed* to come from – advertising time. The whole station runs completely on the amount of ads sold. It is hard

for me, used only to listening to the BBC, to take this in. This is my first brush with commercial radio, and boy, are we commercial!

We advertise anything and everything. The commercials bear no resemblance to reality, since our chief copywriter, Merlyn, is always on acid, so I learn to write copy fast. One of our accounts is a dry-cleaning shop, Sanitary Cleaners. Their ad goes something like this: *What does Sanitary mean to you? Let us tell you what it should mean. It should mean fresh, soft and good-smelling. Well folks, here in Daytona we have finally found a haven for your clothes. Right here at Sanitary Cleaners your special garments are pressed and ready to go before you get back to the car park, and for an extra fifty cents Sanitary Cleaners make them smell like they'd been tumbled in a mountain stream. Gaze into a sunset full of peace and love, wearing clean clothes fresh from Sanitary Cleaners.* Yes. Yes, I know. Reading it, it's hard to justify. Why don't we abort the ad or napalm the copywriter? Hey, it's business!

Zollie has persuaded the owners of this particular business that their trade will boom once this ad hits the airwaves. They are a small concern and haven't got a big advertising budget, so they have traded the advertising out with us – $250 a week's worth. That means that all three DJs, Bilbo and Zollie can have up to $50-worth of clothes dry-cleaned every week. I don't own that many clothes so send everything, even my knickers, to the laundry section. Our jeans have knife-edge pleats, and there is so much starch in my underwear that it hurts to walk. Bilbo's man-made fibres, which still smell bad, are turning to plastic, and my bras have stiff points.

Zollie has also arranged a trade-out with the local funeral parlour, Green Glades. No one seems sure why. He met the owner on some drunken night out in a bar on Atlantic Drive and I guess he just can't say no to any chance of airtime. We use the trade-out just twice. Big Bubba, a beer-drinking friend of Zollie who doesn't even work for the station, has a pet monkey called Marmaduke who is shot by the police for biting a tourist on the nose. We give Marmaduke the equivalent of a state funeral, right down to the solid brass coffin in order to use up as much of the trade-out as possible. The music Bubba chooses as Marmaduke is being cremated is 'Heaven's Just Sin Away' by the Kendalls – some old country song. Chance begins laughing hysterically at that point and we watch in stitches as he is hauled out of the crematorium by two sour-looking attendants for showing disrespect. Zollie promises to cut them a new commercial to calm them down. It's me that has to do it.

Cutting commercials is the down side of the job. I already loathe it. Every day I come in to a tray full of bad copy, littered with spelling mistakes, bad grammar and clichés. I always have at least two to cut – my voice is popular because it is different, distinctive. 'Give it to the gurl who tawks funny to make,' they say, and despite my protestations about being over-exposed, Zollie obliges. It pisses me off. But I can't object too much, it comes with the territory and besides, I just love being a DJ.

My show, I think, is distinctive. No disco for starters, and it consists mainly of British acts. For variety I also have a little call-in quiz where I pitch my wits against the listener. If I fail to answer their rock 'n' roll trivia question they get a free album. Usually it's something like, 'What group was Rod Stewart with before he went solo?' Yes, there are people out there who really give a shit. Mostly people lose, so the staff get the free LPs that we have bummed from the record companies. The callers don't have a hope really, because we also have a massive rock encyclopaedia on the desk and Maybellyne looks it up, then Bilbo vets the questions. We have to; there are lots of crazy types out there listening during the night.

There is a problem though. It is now August and my return flight is for September 5th. As it approaches I am apprehensive. I really don't feel like going home just yet. I have passed my degree – a third, a shit degree – and I have been accepted to do a DipEd which will enable me to get a teaching job in a Catholic school, if I am lucky. Anyway, things are bad politically right now. Even my parents like the idea of one less child to worry about. Belfast is scary these days. Every letter my mother writes is full of woe and death and stories of someone else we know who has been shot or bombed, and of course the weather's crap. It is a major dilemma. Chance has fake phone credit card numbers which mean we can call anywhere in the world for free, so I have taken to calling home about once a week. I lie to my mother that the job pays for the call, but they still get all panicky at the cost. I am gradually convincing them I should stay on. They have no concept of the radio station anyway – I expect they sort of think I'm famous. My sisters enthusiastically send me punk singles but I haven't the heart to tell them that people here are still swooning to the Steve Millar Band.

Maureen and Patricia have given up on me too. They both graduated last year and have just passed their teaching diplomas, and are going back to teaching jobs. To be fair to them we have sort of patched things up, I mean they were best friends and I was sort of an interloper who needed chums to go to America with. They do earnestly try to point out the folly of my staying on, not least the fact that my return ticket is non-refundable. But I can't face returning. I have got some crazy urge to stay and I know that going home to Belfast now will finish me off. I guess I have seen something else of life. For all its flaws, America has given me the chance to reinvent myself, forge another Maggie, give in to the side of my personality that I have been repressing for years. Eventually they accept that I'm staying on and shut up about it – I'm a lost cause. Zollie throws a party for them the night before they leave and Patricia gets drunk and tells me she admires my nerve in staying. I promise to write, and phone with the 'funny' cards.

For quite a few days after they've gone I am seriously scared, and Sharla is going next. I am to take over the rental lease on the apartment then. It is a daunting prospect. As soon as Labor Day is over Sharla leaves, tearfully, but with a firm promise that she will be back for a weekend very soon, and if not, then I am to visit her in Tennessee at Thanksgiving. It is really hard to see her go. I am all alone. But I wave her off brightly. I have a new family now, all the crazies at the station.

Almost instantly, things in Daytona slow right down. It's a summer town where the students and tourists account for most of the population. We are into old people now, lots of them. Florida isn't called 'God's Waiting Room' for nothing, and you know what? These guys don't care much for rock 'n' roll. Even Andy Williams would make them agitated. By the beginning of October, Zollie is getting restless, very restless. He can't concentrate on anything, and I notice we aren't doing as much business either, which bothers him. But leaving that aside, he isn't his usual self. I mention this to Bilbo.

'Hell, pay no attention to him, he gets antsy in winter. He'll settle down eventually. He got that way last winter too. Apart from mid-term break, he doesn't really pick up again till spring.'

The commercials are starting to change too, from disco bars to rest homes. 'Happy Haven – the only place to spend your twilight years', was one of our big advertisers (no trade-out). It was a far cry from The Pink Pussycat, and Dewayne's Drink-Till-You-Burst Beer Hut! Things are about to change more drastically than that though.

4

Vance and Chance are directly responsible for the demise of WA1A. They had started out as two amiable potheads long before I joined the scene, but by the time I meet them, Vance and Chance are beginning to get heavily into other drugs. Not hard drugs at first, no needles, nothing too serious. It doesn't really bother me. They smoke a lot of dope, but then a lot of people do, and they drop Quaaludes, or lewds as they call them. Quaaludes are sleeping pills, famous for making you horny – which is American for sexy – or at least that's the claim. Vance and Chance claim they give them to all of the women they date. A wise move on both their parts because, let's face it, anyone would have to be on some kind of drug to even talk to Vance and Chance for longer than ten minutes. And as for sex with either of them, well, no one in their right minds would touch them with a barge pole. So they figure it is a good idea to make the woman as unconscious as possible, otherwise they will wise up and leave. I guess it has a certain kind of crazy logic.

The Prince Bros, I believe, drop acid as well. But essentially they are so messed up to start with that life must be like a bad trip for them most of the time. But all this drug stuff is pretty minor league till they start experimenting with cocaine. That's when it gets dangerous.

According to Bilbo, Zollie had been trucking right along smoking the odd joint, but more or less clean of any other drugs. Then about a month before I started, Vance laid him out a line of coke. He became an instant fan. It helps him sell, keeps him bright and breezy and full of meaningless chat. At first Zollie is shrewd, he just uses it for special occasions and he never uses too much of it. He keeps a little vial of it in the pocket of his suit. He doesn't exactly flaunt it – I am completely unaware of it.

The first time he offers me some is the night after Sharla's going away party when I come into work with a hangover. I didn't have too much to drink, but the party had started at three p.m. because I had to be in work for midnight. It was some party, and they were still going when I arrived home the next morning. I joined in again, so by the time I arrive at work that evening I am away with the fairies. Zollie comes into the station to see why I sound so goddamm depressing. He always checks out my show.

'Goddamm, Maggie, you sound like you are about to die! You may as well put Leonard Cohen on, do a giveaway for razor blades, and go home.'

'I'm really sorry, I haven't been to bed for twenty-four hours. I'm just sleepy.'

He breaks into song – Rod Stewart's 'Maggie May' which he thinks is hilariously funny. I don't laugh, mainly because this is about the fiftieth time he has sung it since I've met him. He thinks for a minute, then says. 'Have some coke, Maggie, that should keep you going all night, baby.'

'No thanks,' I say, 'Coke doesn't work for me, and besides we could get it free in Paesano's. I got sick of it.'

'Sheeeit Maggie, y'all got free toot at Paesano's? Why'd you leave?'

'Yes, as much as we could drink in fact. I think my teeth are rotten at the front from too much of it.'

'It rots your teeth? How does it do that if it goes up your nose?'

'Oh that coke!' It suddenly hits me.

'Hell yes, Maggie, are you acting the dumbass or what? Are you in rock 'n' roll or ain't you? I'm talking about cocaine, honey, ye oldie Colombian marching powder.'

I am genuinely shocked. 'Zollie, it's a dangerous drug.'

'Yep baby, you got it! It sure as hell is, it's a class A *narrcotic*, but it's nice, real nice, and it'll wake you baby, so you don't sound dull on the air. Try some, just a lil' ole tootski, a liddle pop.'

I don't want to, it's too scary. I'd made one leap, thanks to Jay, and was by now pretty relaxed about smoking pot. But cocaine? I don't know. Jackson Browne had a song out about it, so did Eric Clapton. It was one of Zollie's favourites, naturally. Coke, or toot, was the hip thing to do.

Zollie pulls a small brown bottle out of his pocket. It has a teeny little spoon attached to it. He swings it like a pendulum before me. 'Well? You gonna fall asleep on me baby, lose me all ma listeners are you, Maggie? Or you gonna try some? Well?'

I get a surge of recklessness. 'Well hell, why not?'

He gets out the gear and I am fascinated by it. I have become blasé; I have already decided pot doesn't count. But this is my first close-up of real drugs. His little kit is made of brown suede and looks like a small diary. It contains a mirror, a small silver straw, a spoon and a razor blade. I watch open mouthed as he does a bit of chopping, and lays out two even white lines, then he rolls up a twenty-dollar bill, clamps an index finger first to one nostril, then the other and has two noisy snorts.

'Goddammit Maggie! This is good snow. Peruvian flake no less!'

None of this means anything to me. I am a coke virgin. It is my turn now. He chops again with a flourish, lays me out two lines. I look at them and hesitate. Am I really going to do this? 'I don't think I will after all, I might get addicted.'

'Maggie, honey, you won't. Not with one lil' toot.'

You could say I should refuse, but I am curious. I sniff each line cautiously and wait. I look at the mirror and it is all gone. It must be up my nose. At first nothing happens, then suddenly I am alert, jittery but alert, and just a bit scared. 'Yes, you're right, I do feel more awake,' I say to Zollie after a few minutes and a greatly increased pulse. This is an understatement: my pulse is about two hundred and fifty.

'You betcha you are a *lert* Maggie. Be a *lert* what exactly is a lert?' Zollie cackles insanely, slapping his leg.

I guess we had lots of lerts at WA1A, and Zollie was lert Number One. Thank God Maureen and Patricia have gone home to Ireland. They'd die on the spot at this step too far, me snorting coke instead of drinking it. Doubtless the fires of Hell will intensify for this. Coke is, as Zollie says, a class A narcotic, a felony of high proportion. I am doomed. Somehow I don't think Zollie can trade this one out – it's expensive, $75 a gram. But that's where I am wrong. He does. Yes, he certainly does. Some bloody trade-out it turns out to be.

About mid-July, a few weeks before I had started to work at WA1A, certain South American friends of Vance and Chance had opened a new restaurant-cum-Laundromat. No, I haven't got that wrong. You can watch your clothes wash while you drink a beer, play pool, or have a barbecue sandwich. It is called Sudsy's. They needed to advertise and Zollie was keen to sign them up. So now we have a huge trade-out at Sudsy's. We, that is all the DJs plus Bilbo and Maybellyne, can eat there, wash our clothes there, and generally hang out. They must have a commercial on WA1A at every break. It is overkill. You literally can't hear anything but the Sudsy's ad between songs. Zollie cuts the commercial himself, in his usual over-the-top, hard-sell voice. It goes like this:

'You wanna party? I guess you do.
You wanna smell bad? I guess you don't!
Got that established folks?
Well, why not have a beer and munch along to one of the best barbecue sandwiches in town, while . . .
Sudsy's washes your clothes and folds them in a real nice pile.
Hell Folks! Sudsy's will even iron your undies while you wait.
So if you wanna have good clean fun, don't hesitate.'

At this point he cranks up the backing track and yells in his most deranged voice:

'Why not be mean, and stay clean. Eat and drink the night away. At Sudsy's on the Beach! Only ten dollars for all you can eat and drink plus laundry.'

I think Sudsy's accountants have taken the meaning of laundering too literally, but anyway, the place was a smash. Easily the most popular place on Atlantic Drive. Full of students all night long until Labor Day, and now – not a soul. I guess the ordinary residents of Daytona Beach have either got washing machines or they don't fancy swilling beer and having their ears blasted by Lynyrd Skynyrd while they do their weekly wash. We are still running the ads though, six an hour.

Maybellyne is troubled. There's no money coming in and she is starting to get the books together for the taxman. She takes her job seriously and wants it all in order by Christmas. Ostensibly, we are letting Sudsy's have $1000 worth a week of airtime, and what are we getting in return? Not a penny in real money, just the trade-out, and even though Vance and Chance had said the deal would be half-and-half, Sudsy's wasn't paying up. We can't fit that many visits to Sudsy's in if we tried, and Bilbo and Maybellyne have washing machines and are both dieting all the time anyway.

So it isn't one of our more successful deals. We'd got more use out of Green Glades Funeral Home. First Marmaduke's funeral, and then about two weeks ago Art, the afternoon DJ, his grandma died and Art is able to use up practically all the rest of the trade-out on a coffin. He swaps it for two weeks' wages. Zollie is delighted since Art is one of the highest paid members of the team, and Green Glades are more than happy to oblige. Art picks the grade A coffin, the one people are 'Dyin' to lie in'. He wants it delivered to Alabama for the funeral, but Green Glades don't do out-of-state deliveries. That doesn't deter Art. He picks up the coffin himself and comes by the station to show it to us all. It is most impressive, like something out of *The Godfather*. It is solid brass and lined with purple silk, and absolutely massive. You could fit a gorilla in it – his grandma had been a large lady. She had lived in a trailer but had become so fat that she hadn't been out of it for almost ten years. She died from diabetic complications. Art tells us they had to chainsaw the front of the trailer off to get the body out. Big Al, Bilbo, Vance and Chance help him tie it more securely on to the back of his pick-up.

We all wave him off. He intends driving all the way to Selma, Alabama, with it. About three hours after Art leaves, we get a call from a highway patrol station on I-95 just outside St Augustine. I take the call. It's Art. He is in hysterics.

'What's up, Art?'

'Oh hell! Maggie, I'm in a state patrol station, and they are ripping ma grandma's beautiful coffin apart.' A large sob escapes him. 'What am I gonna do, Maggie? I think they're searching it for drugs.'

'Is it clean?' I ask hastily.

'Yes ma'am!'

'Did they tell you why they are searching it?'

'Well Maggie,' the words come out of Art with difficulty, 'seems like some asshole has gone and stole him a big ole alligator from Gator World. They think I might have done had it in ma grandma's coffin.' He sobs again pitifully. 'Imagine what ma pore ole Grammy would think.' My heart goes out to him. 'It's all plain disrespectful, Maggie. Her funeral cain't take place till I arrive with the coffin and I jest cain't convince them to let me go.'

He sounds an emotional wreck. Zollie and I agree there and then to drive up. What else can we do? It takes us two full hours, Zollie drives like crazy. I don't know how we don't get a speeding ticket. We arrive at the highway patrol station, and are led into a room where we behold a sobbing bundle of emotion formerly known as 'Art the Coolest DJ in Daytona – cool as the waves that crash on the shore'. Well, he is anything but cool now. He falls into my arms and points out the window with a shaky finger. Exhibit A, the big brass coffin, is lying outside on the lawn. It is wide open with the lid lying beside it. They have established that there is no alligator in it, and although Art has explained that he is taking it to

47

Alabama to bury his grandma they are still refusing to let him go. They have searched it for drugs, but not just a straight search. This is the bit that broke Art's heart. He points to the beautiful purple silk lining. It has several large slits in it. Zollie and I look at it in horror. Is this the 'Top Brass', the pride of Green Glades, the coffin people are dyin' to lie in? Surely not?

'What happened?' I ask.

'Well,' Art says. You can tell from his expression that it is causing him pain to relate the story. 'They got a kinda knife thang and this here guy . . .' He indicates a fat red-faced cop with a hat who is watching us from the door of the station. 'Well, he made these slits and felt inside. I told them there weren't any drugs, but he still did not believe me, they didn't even apologise for ripping a hole in the lining.'

Zollie tells us to wait, and he goes off to talk to the officer in charge. Art and I go out to the lawn. The coffin lining is not only slit open and torn. It is covered in stains as well and has a large wet patch.

'What's that?' I ask him. 'How did it get all stained?' My question provokes a further bout of sobbing. I hadn't realised Art was so emotional.

'Well, Maggie, after they finished searching it by hand, they came back with a big ole German shepherd dog, a real nasty type of critter who jest crawled all over it, sniffing, showing jest no respect.' Art pauses, his voice choked with emotion. 'And Maggie, I think I done saw him pee on the lid.'

I look closer. I think Art done saw right. The smell assaults my nostrils, and I notice the dog has left drool stains on the purple silk lining as well. I hold his hand and mutter words of comfort. It is hard to know what to say under the circumstances. Finally Zollie emerges from the station, followed by two police officers. Zollie is smiling broadly.

'Looks like you can be on your way, buddy.'

They have contacted Art's local police station to check his story out. They now believe him. They are profuse in their apologies. They help him close the coffin and offer him a police escort to the state line. They say they will also radio to both Georgia and Alabama state police not to stop him.

Poor old Art, he had been getting more and more frantic that his ma would panic and buy another coffin, ruin his big gesture. We say goodbye, and Zollie and I head back. I wondered what Zollie had said to get things moving so quickly. It turns out he had just given them all a box of records from the trunk of his car, and a pile of WA1A T-shirts. It did the trick.

Art phones us from Alabama the next day. He sounds a bit more like himself. The funeral worked out fine in the end. Everyone loved the coffin, and once she was in it you couldn't notice the mess. It took six of his family to lift her into it and even then they had to bend her arms backwards. But it was worth it, Art said, she looked fantastic. Better than he'd ever seen her look in her whole life. He paid a professional beautician to do her make-up. She had long, false eyelashes and green shiny shadow to match her green sparkly dress ''Cos of her Irish blood', he informs me proudly. Jesus, I think, that Irish blood sure travels. But I know he expects me to respond. 'That is really touching, Art,' I say dutifully, with no irony creeping into my voice I hope. 'I'm sure she would have loved that.'

'Yes, Maggie,' he continues, 'I knew you'd be impressed. I sorta did it for you.' He had polished the brass coffin till it shone. He said the family was reluctant to bury it, it looked so good. He felt he had given her the best send-off possible.

49

The coffin had been worth more than her trailer, which was now irreparable.

Yes, every trade-out is working well except Sudsy's. Maybellyne is really troubled. By mid-October, Sudsy's owes us over $18,000 in food and laundry. The station isn't making that much money; we can't afford to keep running the trade-out. We can't make a dent in it either, unless we all move in to Sudsy's or have a party every night for a month, and we are crowding the airwaves with the bloody commercial. People are starting to complain.

Maybellyne decides she'll speak to Zollie. Unusually, he doesn't seem to want to sort it out, doesn't want to talk about it. It isn't his account. So she speaks to Vance and Chance; after all, they'd set it up. Maybellyne suggests they could maybe cut the ads down to five a day or something like that. The guys say they will check with Julio and Felipe that very evening.

I am on the air when they come back, well after midnight. I put 'Layla' on – it is the longest track to hand – and go in to see what has happened. They have obviously availed themselves of some of the free beer and are both somewhat the worse for wear. They seem rattled, twitchy, like they are coked out of their heads.

'Well?' Maybellyne wants to know. 'Can we cut the ads?' They shrug. Vacant expressions all round; so no change there. 'Well?' Maybellyne insists, unusually firm for once. 'Can they stick to the deal? Trade out half and pay us the rest?'

Vance and Chance mutter in unison, the pitch of their voices clashing discordantly. Apparently not. Julio and Felipe say they need the ads more than ever now that the students have left. Business is bad, so advertise more.

'Raaght? You havta admit they do have a point, Maybellyne,

honey,' Vance eventually manages. He smiles uneasily at us. 'We jus' left there. There wasn't one of the machines turning tonaaght. It was spooky in there, real, real quiet. No business worth a damn.'

'That's raaght, Maybellyne, honey,' Chance echoes, 'they done got them no business.'

'But we can't use the trade-out up!' Maybellyne tells them. 'So there's nothing in it for us. Right?'

Wrong. Julio wants to talk to Zollie. Seems he has a proposition to put to him. I don't like the sound of this, but Derek & the Dominoes are just coming to an end, so I have to leave. I have that old gut-wrenching feeling, as if something bad is about to happen. This whole business smells bad. I hope Zollie can sort it out. But even he couldn't sort this one out. By the time I realise that, we are on a night flit to Tennessee.

5

One of the things Zollie is most proud of is WA1A's van, The Crazy Wave Cruzer. It is a huge psychedelic thing that Tim has customised for the station. Tim is a really talented hippie guy who lives in a boathouse out on the North Halifax River. He is a gentle soul who spends his days painting and lacquering and doing a lot of work on Harley Davidsons.

I was out there with Vance once, after he had scratched the van and was getting a quick touch-up before Zollie found out. There were at least a dozen Harleys parked about the place. Each was more fantastically painted than the next, an assault of colour with swirling rainbows, fantastical dragon-flies and every mythological creature one could conjure up. It was obvious that Tim had more work than he could handle, so when Zollie had wanted his van painted in exchange for some advertising, Tim had quietly refused him. But Zollie desperately wanted a sample of Tim's work. He has to have the best, and Tim is the best, so Zollie paid for it – cash, apparently. I guess even Zollie knows when the trade-out won't work.

The Crazy Wave Cruzer is one of the most distinctive vehicles I have ever seen, it is just unbelievable to look at! It looks like a big acid trip on wheels. It has every rock 'n' roll legend imaginable painted on the sides. Jimi Hendrix, Clapton, Robert Plant, The Beatles (the *Sergeant Pepper* cover), The Stones, and best of all as far as I am concerned Van the Man in a white, flowing kaftan, straight off the cover of *His Band and Street Choir*. It had been one of the first things I'd noticed when I first saw it drive past Paesano's long before I even worked at the station – Van on the Van. I was dead chuffed, him being from Belfast and that. The back doors are black, painted with a perfect prism, straight off the *Dark Side of the Moon* album. Everywhere it goes, The Crazy Wave Cruzer draws a crowd. I feel so important riding round in it.

Suddenly, the night after his meeting with Julio, Zollie wants it sprayed black. All of it. And the rainbow prism obliterated. Sprayed black? He can't be serious! Something is up, something strange. We are called in to a meeting in the office. It is Wednesday. Thursday is pay day. Zollie looks grim-faced and nervous. There is Maybellyne, Bilbo, Big Al, Art and me. Zollie asks us to sit down. There isn't enough room for all of us to sit, so we arrange ourselves haphazardly on the three available chairs, expectant, fearing the worst. He clears his throat.

'Well, folks, there's bin a major, and I mean *major*, fuck-up here, and I can't say what it is, but I am going back to my home state, Tennessee, real soon.'

'You're going when?' Big Al's famous growl could be heard for about a mile.

Zollie shifts uneasily. Al is over six feet, and volatile, very

53

volatile. 'Well, Al, I'm goin' tomorrow as a matter of fact, well, tonight really, as soon as the paint on the Cruzer is dry. The van will be ready at four a.m. Art is going to follow me in my car. I'm going to record my shift now, and the station will be on automatic for the next forty-eight hours.'

No one says a word. We can't think of anything to say. Not even Big Al. This is surreal. Zollie continues as if on auto-pilot.

'Vance and Chance are gonna run things for a few days till the new owners settle in. I'd like y'all to record your intros and outs of all the records. I'll pay y'all one week's wages, and I'm real sorry, folks, but this is out of my control. I've sold the station as of Friday and none of y'all can work here anymore.'

We are stunned. I certainly am. Just when my career is flying and I am having the time of my life, I am out on the street.

'What about us?' I finally manage. 'Well, Zollie? What about us?'

'I'm sorry, Maggie, I guess it's hard for you, not having folks here and that, but I need to get my ass outa town soon.'

I am on the verge of tears. My mind is racing. First thought: Paesano would probably have me back, but what a come-down! Serves me right for thinking I was an amazing DJ. Second thought, which is nearer the truth, it is October, Paesano is down to skeleton staff for the winter, and maybe I can't get my job back. I have no return ticket. I have a Social Security number at least, but my J1 work visa is also technically expired. I pay the rent monthly and we are halfway through October, so I have two weeks left, one week's wages to come. Not much in my case, in anyone's case actually. Zollie being the trade-out king that he was, pays us in hair

54

appointments, free meals (in at least five different restaurants), free dry-cleaning and free gas – if you have a car, which I don't. Oh, and free burials of course. I think Green Glades is the only trade-out we all feel like using right now. It is truly depressing.

I don't know what makes me do it, but I suddenly blurt out 'Can I hitch a ride with you to Tennessee?'

Zollie looks at me. 'What on earth would you do there, Maggie?'

'I can stay with Sharla,' I say. 'She's in Johnson City, are you going near there?'

'Maybe, maybe not, lemme think about it. Do your shift and record tomorrow's.'

Recording is easy. You just have to say things like: 'Hi, this is Maggie Lennon, and you're listening to WA1A, the much more music station. You've just heard "Josie", a track from the new Steely Dan album, *Aja*, before that you heard "Night Moves", Bob Seger, and we started the set with "Doctor My Eyes" by Jackson Browne from his album *Late for the Sky*. I'll be with you right through the night with your favourite rock 'n' roll tunes. And now this is Fleetwood Mac with "Rhiannon".' Then you press a tone button and that tone trips the next record. Then you rattle off some other spiel about the last three or four songs and that's it, on and on and on and on. It is possible to record a four-hour show in about thirty minutes, so it's a wonder there is any live radio around. A lot of stations are automatic since it's a lot cheaper. It means a DJ can do up to a six-hour, even an eight-hour shift, in a short time. You can run a station with only three voices, and the DJs can be out selling advertising slots while they are also on the air. The only thing you can't do is tell the time or, in Florida at any rate, mention the weather. It tends to rain in the afternoons, but not every day. Zollie has frequently pre-recorded his show and remarked on the bright sunshine during a particularly violent rainstorm.

Up until a month before I arrived in Daytona, WA1A had been an automated station and Zollie had been making money. Then he got ambitious. He had decided to go All-Live. He hired three extra DJs and gave himself the early evening slot so he could still sell advertising during the day. The station's popularity increased but so did his running costs. He is cash poor. I didn't know any of this at the time. I found it all out on the long, tiring, twelve-hour drive to Tennessee.

Black Thursday, I come off the air at five. I record my show for the next two days, feeling lousy, trying to sound chirpy and up, feeling anything but. I am finished by six. I usually love the dawn. The air is still and soft. The only sounds are the songs of birds, exotic, unfamiliar birds, and the thrum of the ceaseless ocean way in the background. The colours of the sky on my walk home after a night cooped up in the box of a station are uplifting. Long streaks of fiery red and gold, soaring through the azure. Clouds stretched out like dreams.

This time it is different. The dawn is as sombre as our mood. No uplift. Bits of the night linger. Zollie has left to collect the Cruzer. Big Al has followed me into the studio and is doing his show. I push open the door on to the morning. Even in October it is already warm at this time. Bilbo follows me outside. His mood isn't any livelier than mine.

'What's going on?' I ask. 'I know Zollie has told you!'

Bilbo looks on the verge of tears. 'Maggie, I cain't really say, but I've packed all my things and I'm off with Zollie. My folks live in Mentone, Alabama, anyways. He can give me a ride to Tennessee and my brother Lee is gonna come get me there. There's no point in me staying here.'

'What are you going to do there? Why don't you stay here and get another job?' I ask.

Bilbo shakes his head. 'I never go to the beach. Anyhow, I cain't swim and I hate water.'

I can't disagree with the last bit. 'But what about your apartment?'

'It's paid through October, that's all. I save any money I earn. Eat only trade-outs, as you know. I only got about one case of clothes. I got no friends here, 'cept at the station.'

That is all true. But it is true for me too. Maureen and Patricia are long back in Ireland and Sharla is in Tennessee. I am working all night, sleeping most of the day, and I haven't bothered to make any new friends. It hasn't seemed important. The station life is still too new and fresh for me to be bored yet. Jay, the surfer, left a few weeks earlier in search of fresh waves. Lynyrd Skynyrd has nothing on me. I am free as a bird. The words of the song 'all gone to look for America' float tantalisingly through my addled brain. If I had any money I could go and see the place, but I am broke – all those trade-outs, all those fucking trade-outs.

We sit miserably staring at the dawn. The red streaks spread like dreams, the day is going to be warm. A large van pulls up. It is matt black and smells strongly of paint. Our hearts break at the sight of it.

Zollie gets out carrying two bags of donuts. 'Any coffee, Bilbo?' Bilbo doesn't answer. We are both looking at the black van, mesmerised. All Tim's lovely work wiped out, annihilated, just like that. I have goose bumps. I rub my arms while Bilbo goes to get us some coffee. I try not to have it in the mornings usually as it tends to make it harder for me to get to sleep, but this is different. I drink it eagerly and wolf a few donuts. Bilbo eats six. So his appetite is unaffected, I think. We sit in silence. Eventually Zollie says:

'Well, Maggie, I've bin thinkin', and I guess y'all can come with me, since you're only a poor abandoned Irish girl. My momma will love you, and I'm gonna stay with her till I get me another station.'

And that was that really. Nothing else to say. No time to change my mind. Maybellyne isn't coming though. She will follow on to Tennessee when Zollie gets settled. She needs her special van to drive her, and her cousin/brother isn't available. She plans to lose weight in the meantime so she can catch the Greyhound. Some chance of that! I promise to call her as often as possible. We are both in tears. I'll miss her big, cuddly body, and her self-effacing, wry humour.

We go by my apartment – I am already saying go by, instead of call in to. It tickles me. I pack everything I have in ten minutes, only one suitcase full of clothes, but I also have a few bits and pieces I have got from various trade-outs. I have a good stereo system as we advertised Sound Blasters a lot and the guy there liked my accent, hence the extra good stereo. I have three lava lamps that the old hippie warehouse, Planet Zog, had traded for some ads about their flying yogi gatherings, and I now have my own bed linen, which I had to buy from Sears. I also have a pile of dry-cleaning at Sanitary Cleaners so we stop by there as well. Poor old Mister Skidelsky is distraught at the idea of us leaving. He had enjoyed the craziness of advertising on a rock 'n' roll station. I expect he got vicarious thrills from removing the little cocaine bottle from Zollie's suits and pinning it by the little spoon to the lapel every time Zollie forgot to go through his pockets before bringing in his clothes. And that is it. I decide to skip saying goodbye to Paesano. He doesn't come in this early anyhow. I'll send him a card.

So Zollie, Bilbo and I hit the road. I haven't quite got my thoughts together as I am totally exhausted from being up all night, and have so many emotions about leaving so quickly. It is barely nine o'clock. I should be tucked up in my bed now, the air-conditioning unit blasting away. But no, here I am, beetling up the I-95 towards Jacksonville with Zollie at the wheel, singing along with our radio station. Bilbo is slumped in one of the back seats, overcome by fumes from the brand new paint job no doubt.

Bob Seger's 'Night Moves' is blasting away. Every third or fourth track, the ads cut in and I hear myself extolling the virtues of Sudsy's On the Beach, Paesano's, Pancake Pete's, and then Zollie comes on, doing his quiet TV missionary voice about sending your loved ones to the Lord via Green Glades and so on. I feel heartsick. I will miss it desperately. Surely this isn't the end of my radio career so soon after it has begun?

'Maggie? You look too goddamm morose, honey! You need to lighten up! Here!' Zollie hands me a little bottle and a big bottle. 'Have a lil' pop, or if you want to crash, have a 'lude.'

That's it really, I have two choices: wake up, or pass out. I decline both.

'Okay,' he says, 'we need us a big ole joint to lighten your mood then. I wouldn't have brung you if I'd thought you were going to be this dismal! Bilbo buddy. Roll us a big one, y'hear?'

Bilbo, although he doesn't partake himself, does what he is told. It is amazing how much more relaxed the journey becomes through a haze of dope. I start to enjoy it. By mid-afternoon, we are on the ring road round Atlanta. Two hours later we still are. All Zollie's nonsense about being a better navigator on dope was bullshit. Automatic pilot my arse. We pull into a Cracker Barrel. We have the munchies now anyway. After a massive stack of pancakes and country ham we are off again, this time in the right direction.

By the time we hit the I-24 into Chattanooga I am starting to feel excited. We have driven up the interstate I-75 with all these signs *Visit Rock City*, *See Ruby Falls*, *Fireworks For Sale*, *Buy Pecans*. I'd discovered a pecan was a nut and not a bird as I had originally thought when I first read it. Closer to Chattanooga the billboards are urging us to visit the Choo Choo. I ask Zollie to stop. I want to see it.

'Hell, honey, it's only a Hilton Hotel now got all red brothel bedrooms. You'd hate it!'

Tennessee looks beautiful though. It is green and lush, all trees and mountains and much more like home than Florida. I haven't travelled down through America before, I'd flown with Maureen and Patricia from New York to Daytona on an Eastern Airlines special that had somehow worked out cheaper than the Greyhound, so this was my first journey through the States.

We decide that Bilbo and I will spend the night with Zollie's mama. I can call Sharla and take it from there. Zollie's mama, Annie Mae, lives in a clapboard house with an all-round porch near Nickajack Lake, which is between Chattanooga and Nashville. She is a big, comfortable woman with twinkly eyes and a huge smile who makes me feel at home from the minute I meet her. She tells me her kin had been Irish, family name of Foley. Zollie changed his second name from Foley to Follie because he thinks it sounds good on the air. He also added the IV – he thinks that makes him

60

sound like he is from an old family. I can't stop thinking about his choice of 'Follie'. It seems apocryphal somehow.

Annie Mae has been expecting us and accordingly she's been cooking all day. I have never seen so much food! She has made baked beans (not the canned variety but her own recipe), broiled spare ribs, baked potatoes, a huge salad, and warm corn muffins. It is my first meal in a real home since I arrived in America and it is exquisite. I think I am about to explode from overeating when she produces cherry pie and cream. Bilbo and Zollie are in heaven. Zollie sits there, despite all his troubles, beaming like the crazy person he is, and every now and again saying, 'Well Maggie, don't you just love my momma?' While he talks, he keeps patting her hand and giving her hugs and kisses. I have never seen a man display so much affection before. It is quite affecting. She just beams back at him with pure pleasure. I decide that no matter what he's done, I will always like him for that.

That night I sleep in a huge, soft bed under lots of sweet smelling linen and a beautiful patchwork quilt, which Annie Mae has made herself. It is bliss, and we stay a couple of days. I phone Sharla and she says she will drive down and get me at the weekend, assuring me that I can easily get a job working as a waitress in Johnson City, maybe even as a DJ at the College Station, but she'll sort something out.

On Saturday morning, Bilbo's brother, Lee, who looks just like him, comes up from Mentone to get him. He seems more driven than Bilbo, a lot thinner, ferret like. Not as nice either, a bit shifty, I think. His car is a flashy Trans Am. He is a businessman, he tells us, says he is thinking of opening a ski resort in Alabama in December and Bilbo – or Bill, as he prefers to call him – could work there in the meantime. Skiing in Alabama? It sounds fairly deranged to me, but hey, what do

61

I know any more? Craziness works in America. Who am I to knock it?

I leave reluctantly with Sharla on the Saturday afternoon. I pile all my bits and pieces in to the trunk of her car with a large lump in my throat. I hate leaving Annie Mae. She has baked me three pies to go, and I have put on about a stone in the three days I have been here. She cooks non-stop and seems to constantly clear the table and reset it. We must have had six meals a day. Zollie is eating too. He is obviously off the cocaine. His mama would have thought it strange if he hadn't been eating a lot – she doesn't take no for an answer as far as food is concerned.

Zollie says he'll be in touch with me as soon as he gets another station, maybe in a month. I am not feeling too hopeful, I am desolate. I get in the car with Sharla trying hard not to cry, and when we drive off I am thinking I'll be lucky to see any of them again.

6

I'd been in Johnson City with Sharla for barely two weeks when the call comes. Zollie has bought another radio station. It is a former gospel station located in Suck Creek outside Chattanooga. The owners have skipped town after the listeners discovered their 'Hundred Dollars to Heaven Concert' turned out to be a scam. They had asked all the listeners to send in a one hundred dollar bill. In exchange, Brother and Sister Precious Love, the station owners, assured them that the Lord would personally guarantee them a straight entry to heaven on their death, and while they still trod this vale of woe they'd get a pair of tickets to a concert with Kenny Rogers, Dolly Parton and Crystal Gayle. Then, about two days before the concert was due to happen, the fans were told over the air that the concert had been cancelled and the ticket money was going straight into the Precious Love Fund to purchase them all double bonus certificates which guaranteed them and another family member direct entry to heaven.

Well, they sure had underestimated their listeners – it seems God hasn't the same pull as Kenny Rogers or Dolly. Two irate Christians showed up at the station with a sawn-off shotgun looking for their money back plus their guaranteed entry to heaven certificate. When neither was forthcoming they almost blew the brains out of the unfortunate engineer who was playing the reel to reel gospel songs. When word got out, Brother and Sister Precious Love disappeared fast. So, the station is up for grabs, and Zollie lucks out. He gets the license dirt cheap.

'We're gonna be automated for eighteen hours a day, Maggie, with two live shifts. I'm doing morning drive, and you're doing afternoon drive. Sound okay?'

It sounds fantastic. Nice as Sharla and everyone have been, I feel in the way. They are students and I am a working girl. Sharla's friends are delightful, but all they think about is men, well, boys really, and their lives are dedicated to preparing themselves for possible dates. They spend most of the time rolling their hair and rubbing their bodies with creams and exfoliating and debilitating, removing hair, or whatever it is called, and they douche with strawberry-smelling stuff. Douche with it! I am appalled. Why? I hadn't even known what a douche was before I came. French for shower, I thought. The bathroom smells like a candy store. It is so unIrish. They are driving me crazy with all this endless obsessing about their bodies, and are making me homesick for people with greasy hair and dirty jeans. But worse than that, I am so bored. I have a waitressing job four nights a week in a hamburger joint, but I am not making any money because the town is all students and they are lousy tippers. Sharla and her roommates, Angelina and Connie, won't take any rent, which is sweet, as their parents pay it for them, but I feel I have to cook more in return,

64

and they are all slobs, so I do most of the housework as well, and I end up feeling like the Irish maid.

Zollie's call lifts my spirits. To be fair to Sharla, she is thrilled for me. She knows I haven't been happy, even though I have become a bit of a celebrity purely due to my accent and the fact that she has told everyone I am John Lennon's cousin. I mean, I can't let her down in front of her friends, can I? So, I play the part, even down to speaking fondly of my Great Aunt Mimi whenever appropriate. I quite enjoy that aspect of it. One night, after a few joints have been passed around, I find myself railing with indignation about the fact that Yoko has caused so much family stress by persuading John to pose in the nude. Even Sharla is convinced. She asks me if she can come with me next time I visit John. She has always wanted to meet him. I tell her she can, of course. He'll love her.

The radio station will be ready next week and it is getting new call letters, Zollie explains. 'W' something, I suppose. All stations east of the mighty Mississippi have 'W' and all stations west of the river have 'K' at the start of their call letters. Like KLOS in LA and WNEW in New York. Our station was to be WQQQ on the frequency ninety-two. Therefore we would call it Q92. There are probably loads of Q92s all over America, so you tag the name of the city afterwards, like Q102 Tampa. But this is the only station broadcasting from Suck Creek, you can be certain of that. We will pretend that we are broadcasting out of Chattanooga though. I mean, would you listen to a station based somewhere like Suck Creek?

I am to start in three days. Zollie has arranged an apartment for me in the same block as his and he tells me he'll pay the first two months' rent. I am to sell advertising as well as do a shift, which I hate the sound of, but at least it is better than waiting tables, and I'll get commission on everything I sell. It also means I have to get a car. The thing is, I have never learned to drive. Zollie doesn't seem to think this will be much of a problem.

'Hell, Maggie, they drive funny over there in Britain anyways, don't they?'

'No, they just drive on the other side of the road.'

'That's 'zactly what I said, funny, like they talk. Can you imagine what that would do to traffic here if they all decided to move to America? Goddamm Armageddon!' Warming to his theme he continues, 'Now if you had bin drivin' you would be at a *disadvantage*, but seein' as how you weren't, you have the *advantage*.' I must sound unconvinced. 'Let me tell you, Maggie, drivin' is real, real easy. It's like shootin'. Everybody in America can shoot a gun and everybody can drive a car. You can learn real quick.'

So once I arrive in Chattanooga I learn. No gears anyway, you just have to start the engine, press the accelerator and steer. Zollie trades me out some lessons from the AYBEECEE School of driving, and Bilbo and I spend every night for two weeks driving round a K-mart car park. (Bilbo has also been re-recruited by Zollie.) Round and round and round. It's good fun. Then Bilbo takes me along to the Highway Patrol and says I had had a British licence, which I had lost. They make me take a Highway Code test, a 'press the button' sort of thing, guess the answer. It works. It is all fairly obvious. Then I go outside with a pompous little twerp called Leon. I fix my face in a reverential smile and nod humbly at all he says. We get in the car, I drive around a fixed course and manage not to hit anything, and he signs a form, shakes my hand and I go back in and they give me a driver's licence. I am thrilled. I drive to the station with Bilbo sweating profusely beside me, and crash the car into the entrance door. It is broadcast all over Tennessee. Zollie is on the air at the time, and he announces to all the listeners that Maggie, the mad Irish DJ, has literally driven all the way to work, right into the studio. I wait for them to call up from the Highway Patrol place and demand the licence back, but they don't. I am a real American. I can drive.

7

The new station is the clean slate Zollie needs. Over dinner the first week back together, he more or less admits to Bilbo and me that Sudsy's owners, Felipe and Julio, were drug dealers, and in a *major*, major way. They had been supplying Vance, Chance and Zollie with loads of cocaine at inflated prices in exchange for the advertising. The food trade-out was a smokescreen. The trouble was that the Prince Brothers had noses like vacuums. They were going through a ton of the stuff, and Julio was getting more and more pissed that the advertising wasn't paying off. He needed customers, not to make money, but to keep up a front for his drug business. All very sordid. These were hard men and they had called in the chips. Zollie was lucky to get away when he did. He had a friend in the police who tipped him off that some really heavy stuff was about to happen, and if he stayed he could well find himself involved in a major drug scandal, or dead, so Zollie sold Julio and Pedro the station. They gave him a fair price apparently, although they had to buy it through a third party because they weren't US citizens.

Financially it wasn't all that successful a venture anyway, and Zollie had been hankering to return to Tennessee for a while. He moved to Florida in the first place because he had been married to a girl from Tallahassee called Sherilee, known to us as Sherilee the witch because she'd upped and left him and gone back to her mama before I started working there.

Maybellyne and I chat on the phone a lot. She tells me she hasn't been out of the house since we all left, so she hasn't seen Vance and Chance, and there is no answer from their apartment. I miss Maybellyne, but she plans on joining us at the new station. She is sticking to her diet, she tells me, and should be here by New Year. I hope so. It all looks hopeful so far, and I think I prefer it here to Florida. Despite it being so far from the sea, the landscape is more interesting. I like the tree-covered mountains and the width and sweep of the Tennessee River as it meanders through town, and I like the clearly defined seasons.

This will be my first Christmas away from home ever. My parents want me to come back to Belfast, but I told them I honestly can't afford the fare, and neither can they, so we were just going to have to wait until I make it. This new station is really going to launch my career, I have high hopes for it.

'You know, Maggie,' Zollie says, 'I reckon the Lord has given me a second chance. No more chemicals will enter my body. I am going straight. No more toot, no more 'ludes.' I must look unconvinced. 'Well, maybe just a little ole toke of a joint now and again, because that baby is organic!'

69

I hope he means it. I expect he does. But he shouldn't have changed his second name to Follie.

There is to be a grand opening the week before Thanksgiving, which, incidentally, I am to spend with Sharla's parents and her brother, Brother. Yes, that is his name. At least that is what they all call him, though his real name is James. All the years I live in Tennessee I never get used to the way people are known as Brother or Sister. A regular exchange would go something like this:

'I'd like you to meet ma husband, Brother Walls, Maggie.'

'Sorry? Your brother?'

'No, my husband, Brother.'

'Your husband's brother?'

'No, ma husband, he's called Brother.'

'Your husband is called Brother? Why?'

'Well, honey, Brother is his name, well that's what his family call him. His name is really Arnold. You see, he was the second child so his sister called him Brother, then his baby brother called him Brother, then his momma and poppa joined in. It happens a lot.'

Of course, it's obvious really! Why did I take so long to catch on? But I think it's a stupid old tradition. Even Bubba or Buddy is a step up from it. Every other man appears to be called that. But silly things like that apart, I love Tennessee, and I am excited about the new station.

Zollie plans to make an instant impact, grab as many listeners as possible. We are on FM, which means that the mountains sort of get in the way of our signal, so people will have to know we are there to tune in and pick us up. I am dispatched to the local paper to give a lifestyle interview. It is all pure bullshit. Zollie's old buddy, Ed, works on the features section and he sets it up for us. Zollie has told

70

him I am a direct import from the BBC and Zollie had heard me on the air on a European tour and 'headhunted' me. That is the word for stealing an employee from somewhere else. Ed reproduces this bullshit word for word. They take cutesy photos, and talk a lot about my 'lilting Irish brogue'. I am glad no one from home will read it, it is monstrously embarrassing. But I tell myself it is all in a good cause. We have to attract listeners. I just hope I won't be too big a disappointment to them. Zollie has also called in favours from a friend who owns the local TV station. I can't quite grasp the concept of someone owning a TV station, but they run wall to wall ads about the new non-stop Music FM Q92 all week.

We kick off at noon on November 17th, 1977 with Springsteen's 'Born to Run'. We are, as they say, 'happening'. The phone lines open and we invite listeners to call in. Our first call is from a woman of seventy-six from Possum Creek who had been getting into a worshipful mood for church on Sunday and had tuned in to her old faithful station to relax in the arms of Jesus. She was unaware how high she had left on the sound and had been knocked out of her armchair by Robert Plant singing 'Whole Lotta Love' at mega decibels. Bilbo talks her down and offers her one of our fifty star prizes: a weekend's skiing for two in Alabama at Christmas. She accepts with alacrity, and praises the Lord, of course.

I am slowly getting my bits and pieces together. My rented apartment is already furnished, albeit in 'Early Motel' style, but I feel a good bit lonelier than I ever was in Daytona. I call home a lot, even though I have to pay for it now. My sister Sinead promises she will visit soon. Also, another thing that isn't helping my frame of mind is that it is winter and my clothes are all wrong. I have nothing warm to wear.

71

Zollie is sympathetic to my plight. He comes in halfway through my shift just a week after the launch, waving a contract triumphantly. 'Maggie, honey, you're gonna be the best-dressed gal in Tennessee.' He has just traded out $500 of women's clothing from a store in town, and I have to cut the commercial. They are going to run $1000 worth of ads, half cash, half trade. We are on our way, back to business! I can't wait for my new wardrobe so I go there first thing next morning.

Unfortunately, Mamie's Modes isn't exactly my scene. It specialises in clothing for the 'smart woman about town', in other words Crap Clothes Inc. Had I wanted to wrap my body in silver lurex dinner dresses or one hundred per cent polyester suits I would be in seventh heaven. But I don't. All the assistants look like Dolly Parton and I want to look more like Stevie Nicks. They are so wonderful to me though, and I spend the entire morning there rejecting all their attempts to dress me. I drink their coffee, eat their proffered chocolate chip cookies, confident for once that they aren't laced with hash oil.

This is a recent paranoia of mine, suspecting that all chocolate chip cookies contain hash oil, and understandable given my experience of the previous week.

The third day we were on the air, Zollie had a packet of chocolate cookies on his desk and I took one to eat with my coffee. I was unaware at the time that they contained hash oil. Midway through my shift I developed a co-ordination problem, both with my speech and movements. I talked incessantly right through the intros of all the songs, played 'The Pretender' six times in a row and confessed to the listeners that I want to snog the face off Jackson Browne. My tirade went down surprisingly well, actually, and it made me think that maybe just a bunch of stoned hippies are listening to us. Zollie phoned the station to ask why I was running my goddamm mouth off so much, and after a bit of detective work traced my garrulous behaviour back to the cookies.

But back to Mamie's Modes and my winter wardrobe. There is definitely no hash oil in Mamie's cookies. No sirree! She has baked them herself, from her momma's recipe. A pity really. You would need to be on drugs to buy the clothes. At lunchtime, after trying on virtually every stitch in the place, I leave with the only item in the store made of natural fibres, a bright, cobalt blue cashmere sweater costing $90. It is the most expensive piece of clothing I've ever owned. I promise 'the girls' I'll be back for the other $410 worth soon, and that I will have a good look for 'Rhinestone Cowboy', the Glen Campbell record they want me to play. But there is no way in hell we have a copy of any country song. No chance. Zollie plays frisbee with anything that isn't 'balls to the wall rock 'n' roll'. Later I call them to explain we don't have it, and I play Andrew Gold's 'Thank You for Being a Friend' instead. They are touched since they had spent the whole morning telling me how cute my accent was.

Zollie is mad at me when he hears I've only got a sweater 'Goddamm Maggie! How in the hell is anyone going to take us seriously if you look like you do? You need to get you a new hairstyle. People expect the stars of Q92 to look the part. You look like shit. You need to wear make-up and braaght colours – not that goddamm hippie look.'

I wear a lot of denim. I like to dress casually. Power suits aren't quite my image, in my own head that is. I understand his concern but I need a store which caters for the under fifties. Mamie's Modes just doesn't fit the bill. He eventually sees reason, and agrees to give the rest to Annie Mae for Christmas and find me somewhere suitable.

He is working hard to get the station off the ground, out all day selling airtime, chatting up the proprietor of every little store for miles around Chattanooga. He won't let up on the way I look though. He has a real thing about my appearance. If I am going to be the star female DJ, I have to look the part.

I think I look okay. I am slim, my hair is long and straight, and a lot blonder than usual after a summer in Florida. My teeth are white, and I have large eyes. Attractive enough, not knockout, not a raving beauty, but it has got me thus far. Zollie's idea of female beauty is way on the trashy side. He has fixed himself up with some kind of a secretary cum salesperson that I think he is paying in drugs and sex. Sue Lynne is her name. She seems to think he is the stairway to her future. I am not too struck by her. I am prepared to swallow my distaste and like her at first, but when I hear her tell a friend over the phone that all she had to do with Zollie was 'wave ma pinky and it was real easy to git thangs from him,' I decide to loathe her instead.

She looks like a Barbie doll but Zollie thinks she looks classy. Shows you what he knows. She has an IQ roughly the same as the size of her waist, but she does all the typing and filing and, more importantly, she keeps Zollie out from under our feet. I console myself with the fact she'll be leaving when Maybellyne arrives. Sue Lynne has one of those breathy baby voices, like a girl rabbit from Looney Tunes. She wears a ton of make-up and dresses in bright, tight, polyester suits. She has that big hair that is currently in fashion, and somehow the comparison with my long, straight hair drives Zollie crazy.

74

Eventually, fed up with him droning on about my hair-do, or lack of it, I let him fix me up with a hairdressing trade-out. It changes my life. I get to meet Herman.

There is a salon on Racoon Mountain called Herman's Heavenly Hair Haven, and Zollie tells me I can get my hair done for free there. The owner is going to advertise with us, so off I go to be transformed. Within minutes of meeting him I can see why Zollie thinks he is a soul mate. Put quite simply, Herman is barking mad, but adorable. He is a talented hair-cutter and he looks after my hair like it was his pet rabbit. His philosophy is total hair care. I don't know what this means but this is the first thing he tells me when I have my one hour full consultation. You have to do that before he will allow you to make an appointment.

He tells me he is violently into health products, vitamins and drugs. He just loves drugs. That's an understatement. I don't think he could function without them. He rarely cuts hair until he's smoked about two joints and snorted a few lines. Then he expounds with enthusiasm about his ancestry. Like all Americans, Herman knows by heart all the various mixtures that have gone into the delicate gene pool that has produced him. I am getting used to hearing the phrase, 'Oh I'm part Irish!', and learning not to say, 'Which part?', which only confuses them.

Herman is part Austrian, part Cherokee, part English, part Dutch, and hails from Kentucky. He is tall, thin, and has dark black, glittery eyes, and long, dark hair that he keeps tied back in a braid. His facial features are pointed and he looks more Middle Eastern than Cherokee, but he certainly looks exotic. His manner is rather effete, and he speaks with a pronounced Southern drawl. He talks incessantly, and most of what he says doesn't make any sense, but it sounds good. It seems to be mainly about our hair being made up of various proteins and vitamins and chemical elements, and how we are composed of water and the same elements as the ocean. When he finishes this speech, he puts on 'Quiet sounds of womb and shore', a piece composed especially for him by a musical friend, and talks about trace elements in hair, or some other monologue about drugs. I never quite figure it out. It doesn't seem to matter as it is the ambience of the place that counts. Going there is an experience unlike any other.

He has a little machine in which he places a single hair that he then winds round two pins, stretches it out, and turns a handle. If it breaks, which in my case it always does, then that means your hair is 'fucked, baby'. He says the whole nation of America's hair is a cause for concern and he is dreaming of the day when a single hair will remain unbroken. I watch him break down almost in tears when he tells me this, so I venture ideas as to how this day will come about, but he is inconsolable. So I suggest how he can avoid breaking all the hairs he tests. I tell him not to wind it so tight, but he says that would be cheating. He prefers to practise preventative haircare to treat the atmosphere. Saturate us with vitamins. Strengthen our living protein. Revitalise us all.

He is a great hairdresser, though, and gives me a brilliant Stevie Nicks cut. He perms my hair, streaks it, and cuts it all shaggy. It looks great, and everyone at the station is really complimentary, except Sue Lynne who grimaces and says nothing. Bitch.

A few days after my first visit to Herman, we are doing a live broadcast from a local mall. I drive there in the Cruzer and I must admit I am scared. I have only had a licence for a few weeks, and driving my new, pale mint green VW Rabbit, which I had bought on some hire-purchase scheme, was one thing. Driving something that feels like a jumbo jet is another. The van badly needs a new paint job, or for the underneath to be re-exposed. This is out of the question, although Zollie lives in hope. He hasn't quite got the money or, for that matter, someone as talented with a paintbrush as Tim, so in the meantime it's known as The Big Black Box. It has Q92 in large stick-on silver letters on each side but it doesn't quite have the same effect on the crowds as The Crazy Wave Cruzer did.

I reach Northside Mall where the broadcast is to happen, and drive with extreme care into the parking lot. I circle for a while, looking for somewhere to park. I need a real big space but there isn't one. Finally, after driving round for ten minutes, I spot what I think might be a big enough space and start to reverse in. After about six attempts I am in tears and the bloody thing is still parked crooked and just about inches, no *centimetres*, away from a very shiny new, silver Porsche. It looks like a Tonka Toy beside the van. I just about manage not to mow it down, but I have effectively trapped it against a wall. I am afraid to back out and straighten the van in case I bang against the Porsche. I turn off the engine, still sweating from the exertion. There is no way the owner will be able to get out. I am completely frustrated and raging at my own inadequacy, and though I hate admitting defeat, I know I haven't the skills to park the thing.

I decide to go into the mall to find Zollie, Bilbo and Rick, our new DJ. I have arranged to meet them at Hits for Less Records where the show is being broadcast. I have all the equipment in the van though, so they come out with a trolley to fetch it. I mention to Zollie that it isn't particularly well parked, an understatement, and he is tickled. He just loves seeing me so flummoxed over a simple matter of parking. We arrive back at the van just as the Porsche owner realises he can't get out. He is just sitting there and he doesn't seem particularly fussed by being trapped, but I go over to him to apologise.

He is gorgeous. Simply put, he is a large hunk of prime US male. He has floppy light brown hair, piercing blue eyes fringed with dark lashes, a long, straight nose and of course he has white teeth, dozens of them. It looks like someone has drawn him and he's jumped off the page. He is almost too good-looking, and he obviously knows it. He has that easy way that good-looking people have, of just being. He is wearing a short-sleeved blue shirt, in December, though in fact it is dry and sunny, and his arms are brown and muscly. He probably has a shite personality, I reason, but I don't know that yet and hell, maybe he hasn't.

I fall madly in lust at once. Suddenly, I realise that since the exit of Jay the Surfer I have not been practising my new-found sexual technique. I have been celibate, and for what? All those little white pills I pop with such efficiency each evening are lying inside me, altering my hormones, not being put to use. I am polluting my body for no just cause. I stand there, all this flashing through my mind and I can't think of a thing to say, for a minute at least.

Zollie knows him, of course. I am beginning to think Zollie knows everyone in the entire State of Tennessee. 'Well if it ain't Nate Gilmore! How're you doin', buddy?'

Nate stops appraising me and turns to Zollie. 'Fine, Zollie, I'm doin' just fine. Nice to have you back in town. Bin listening to the station. Sounds real good.' He raises an eyebrow. 'This nicely parked object here your van?'

'Sure is, and this here's Maggie Lennon who parked it. Or tried to park it!' Zollie turns to me grinning broadly. 'Maggie, honey, looks like you flew in from above, how'd you get it at that angle? Maggie here is Irish, Nate, and she cain't drive for shit.'

Zollie roars with laughter at his own wit. Nate looks at the four of us and I smile at him. He obviously expects me to say something.

'I'm sorry,' I say. 'I'm afraid I've only been driving for two weeks and that bloody thing is as big as a Chieftain tank.'

Nate smiles back. 'That bloody thing,' he repeats, smiling that dazzling smile at me. I try not to melt and roll under the van in ecstasy. 'I'm sure you're right, ma'am.'

He climbs out of the car, leaping over the door without opening it, and holds out his hand to me. He is tall, I notice, about six feet, maybe more. His hand feels dry and warm, his handshake firm. 'Nate Gilmore, Maggie, I'm pleased to meet you. I've heard your show. I love to listen to your voice, makes a change from all the good ole boys on the air here. I think we like the same music,' he adds.

I'm sure we do, I think. We must.

Zollie grins at him. 'Well, Nate, that's real nice of you, I'm real pleased to hear you say that. Maggie here is going to do a show for us from Hits for Less Records, and we need us some help here, so since you're on your feet why not give us a hand with all this? Get yourself a free Q92 T-shirt.'

He points to the stack of equipment, which has been left beside the van. While we've been chatting, Bilbo and Rick have loaded the sound system on to the trolley and are heading towards the record store.

Nate smiles, shrugs, and says, 'Hell, why not?' He lifts a box of giveaway albums and I take the coloured lights and Q92

sign and walk beside him into the mall. He has long, easy strides. I make quick little running movements to keep up, and I rattle away, turning on the charm full-blast, showing off I suppose.

Zollie comes up behind me, and whispers loudly, 'You got the hots for him, Maggie?'

I ignore Zollie and continue chatting to Nate, hoping he hasn't heard, while he helps us set up the equipment. He can't have had anything else on, at least he doesn't seem to be in a hurry to leave. With an exaggerated wink at me, Zollie suggests he stay while I do the show.

I am really nervous. I have only done one other outside broadcast in my life, in Daytona, but lack of experience doesn't seem to be a factor in anything to do with my new life. I am learning fast to busk things. Zollie and the guys help, so I just have to intro and outro records, read a few requests (mostly from the crowd in the store), and give away the latest Warren Zevon record, 'Excitable Boy'. During tracks I feast on Nate. He sure is easy on the eye. I am on a high, and even better, a completely natural one. I flirt with him, the people in the store and, of course, the listeners. I am flying.

The only thing that is really pissing me off is Rick, our new DJ. He is hanging out of me as if we are an item. I catch Nate looking at him a couple of times and I feel like screaming. I just know Nate is clocking Rick's pathetic attitude to me – he's fixated on me purely on account of my accent.

Rick is a weedy guy from Cleveland, Ohio. He's had a complete charisma bypass as far I as can see, and his personality on and off the air is exactly the same: shallow, loud and full of clichés. He is a nerd with a head that is a mine of Rock information. He knows everything from the fact that 'Dear Prudence' was written in India about Mia Farrow's sister, Prudence, to how many guitar strings Jimmy Page breaks in a year. He needs to get a life and obviously thinks Q92 is it. He is working for peanuts too. Zollie has convinced him that Q92 will be the start of an amazing career. He is a sad git! I should feel sorry for him. But no! Anyway here he is, smiling away at me like his big, ugly face had got stuck at 'beam' and handing me the music carts, laughing at every stupid thing I say, and calling me babe. I am not his babe! I have just spotted someone whose babe I really want to be, and here is ole shit features queering my pitch. I fervently hope Nate will stay till I come off the air so I can put him right, but of course he doesn't. Just about ten minutes before I play the last track he catches my eye, gives me a friendly wave, and leaves. Just like that. Gone, the most beautiful man I've ever seen. I am incandescent with rage at Rick. Nate didn't even wait to get his free Q92 T-shirt!

'Well,' Zollie pats me on the back after I come off the air. 'You were good, Maggie. Real good, you'll make you a DJ yet!'

Rick sidles up to me. 'Great show, honey! Great show, classy! Whoa yeah, real classy honey!'

'I'm not your honey!' I snap. His face falls.

'It's just a manner of speaking, Maggie.'

'I don't give a shit. Don't call me honey, okay?'

'Fine, fine. I didn't mean nothing by it.'

He starts to pick up the bits and pieces and slumps off looking dejected. I don't even feel guilty. What a stupid bastard. He has just about convinced Nate I was his, I can tell. Boy am I sore. I suddenly feel like bursting into tears. I am lonely. Underneath all the fluff and jollity, I am lonely. I am homesick, I miss my mammy, my daddy and my four sisters, and I have no friends here. No female friends. Maybellyne is maybe coming after Christmas, maybe not. I decide to go back to my apartment and call home and talk to my sister Sinead. It's bedtime in Belfast so she'll be home. I need a comforting chat, and we always tell each other everything. I walk towards the bloody Cruzer. The Porsche has gone. I am about to leave but Zollie has other ideas. He calls me back with a wide grin on his face.

'Maggie, we're all going over to this real nice Chinese restaurant on Hixson Pike for dinner, you fancy joining us?'

'Is that asshole going?' I point in Rick's general direction.

'I expect so.'

'Then I'm not. I can't stand him. He paws all over me. It makes me sick.'

Zollie eyes me up and down. 'You wouldn't be feeling sore about ole Nate leaving early, would you?'

'Don't be ridiculous! What gave you that idea? I don't know the guy from Adam. Anyway, he's probably married or has a girlfriend.'

'Nope, he ain't married. I know that for sure. His rich ole daddy would love that. The Gilmores own half the county. Somebody has to inherit it. Ole Nathan Gilmore the fourth would love for lil' Nate to settle down. And I know he don't have a girlfriend either, leastwise not at the moment. I believe there was someone, just before I moved to Florida. A girl he met at Ole Miss. She was a real good looker, I believe, a runner-up in the Miss America Contest. Everyone thought they'd marry.'

My heart sinks. Miss America. Obviously he prefers looks to brains.

Zollie laughs. 'What's up, Maggie? Cupid hit you raaght between the eyes?'

'No, I just thought he was good-looking and polite, which seems to be rare. I'm going home. I'll see you tomorrow.' I turn to go and Zollie calls after me.

'Well, Maggie, that's a real pity, 'cos I thought maybe you were in the mood for a little bit of lovin' and I've asked him to join us for dinner. He went on home to purdy himself up.'

I could hug Zollie then. Suddenly I am in brilliant form. 'In that case,' I say, trying to sound casual, 'I'll go home and change and I'll meet you there.'

'It's a deal! Now maybe you'd better have my car, and I'll take the Cruzer.'

I certainly agree to that. I don't want to arrive at the restaurant in a sweaty heap.

We go to Ho Lo's Chinese restaurant. I am in a state of high anticipation. I have spent the previous hour deciding which items in my paltry wardrobe look the best. Zollie tells me I look 'Like a fox', so it must have been worth it. Nate arrives looking like a movie star, and throughout the meal he chats mostly to me. I ignore Rick, which isn't hard. He is still wounded by the remarks I made to him earlier. The food is lovely and the beer is cold. At least I think it is. I waft through the whole evening delirious with happiness. Love is the drug, no doubt about it. Finally it's time to go. I stand up to say goodbye and Nate helps me on with my coat. I can barely get my arms in the sleeves I am so thrilled. He offers to walk me to Zollie's car. I try not to catch Zollie's eye but I can see he is watching everything with a large grin on his face.

When we part in the car park, Nate kisses my hand with

an exaggerated flourish and tells me how much he's enjoyed the evening. He doesn't suggest taking me home, but I figure it is because we each have a car, and when I am tucked inside the car he asks for my phone number and suggests we might meet for lunch the next day. I tell him I will see him tomorrow and drive home in a state of undiluted bliss.

8

When I get home I immediately phone Sharla, then Maybellyne for intensive post mortems. They are thrilled for me and say they can't wait to meet him. In the morning I finally phone home and talk to my mammy – all the girls are out. She tells me to be careful, especially when I tell her he is rich.

Later Nate arrives to pick me up in his Porsche (his Porsche!) and drives me out to his house on Chickamauga Lake for lunch. I try my best to act blasé about being in a Porsche but I am giddy with delight. Nate's house is one of the most amazing I've ever been in. It is very modern and has wooden floors throughout, all covered in exquisite Turkish carpets. The living room has a high ceiling and is made of wood and stone. We sit on one of two huge settees with a glass coffee table as large as a double bed, scattered with coasters, in front of us. Nate vanishes momentarily and comes back with two ice-cold beers in frosted mugs. He eases himself on to the sofa beside me and starts to nuzzle my neck. Every hair on my body stands to attention. I think I am about to swoon.

'Where are your parents?' I ask.

He looks at me, a smile hovers about his lips. 'Why? Don't you want to be alone with me?'

'No,' I stutter, 'eh, I mean yes, of course, but what if they come in?'

'Well, I guess I would just say that they hadn't been invited to dinner. This is my house,' he continues. 'My parents have a big old family home on Lookout.'

'You mean *you* own this?'

He nods, smiling. 'Yep, I sure do.'

'All by yourself?'

'Yes ma'am. All by maself.' He lapses into the Nilsson tune on the last few words. I have to laugh.

'Wasn't it expensive?'

'Yep, but my Granddaddy died two years ago and left me some money, so I decided to invest in a place of my own.'

I am thunderstruck. No one at home would believe this, a man of twenty-four owning a real grown-up house. We finish our beers and he leads me into the kitchen. It is incredible, all ceramic tiles and old pine. I feel like I am in a Hollywood movie. This is a feeling I will get repeatedly during the day. He has a long piece of meat marinating: he has decided to barbecue a filet mignon, a *whole* one.

'I can use it for sandwiches next few days,' he explains.

There is a gas barbecue on his outside deck which over-looks the lake, and there is also a hot tub. I sit contentedly enjoying the view while he 'fixes' Sunday lunch. He serves the steak with baked potatoes, a green salad and an absolutely gorgeous Californian wine. It is the first time I have tasted good Californian wine, mostly we buy the jug stuff.

We smoke a joint before we eat. I am flying, and horny as hell. Horny is my new word. Sharla has introduced me to it. In Ireland we say randy, but that is a boy's name here. After lunch, we snuggle up on one of the big sofas, and listen to James Taylor's *Sweet Baby James*. I realise I am behaving like something out of a *Playboy* spread. I pose and pout and rearrange myself provocatively. I do everything but rip my clothes off and jump him. Nothing! He cuddles me a bit, nibbles my ear, and strokes my hair a bit and we talk, and talk, and talk! We swap life stories. Then about eight o'clock, he says, 'Well, Miz Maggie Lennon, I guess you need your beauty sleep.' I look expectantly at the bedroom door. Not too obviously though. But he misses the cue. 'I better drive you home.'

My jaw drops but I try to act normal. It is too soon anyway. What has gotten into me? I am behaving like a slut. At home I would have died if a guy had expected me to sleep with him on a first date. We part with an arrangement to go to a movie during the week. I tell myself to calm down, take things slowly, stop smoking pot, my God! The things I want to do when I am stoned.

Maybellyne and Sharla are both reassuring on the phone once again. I call Sharla first. After all, she is a girl with experience. She takes me step by step through the day.

'Had you shaved under your arms, Maggie?'

'He didn't see under my bloody arms!'

'Never mind, honey, all it is, he doesn't want a quick screw, Maggie. He would only do that to a girl he didn't respect. He must be in love with you. He must be regarding you as a potential wife.' Sharla is adamant.

An hour later as I obsess to Maybellyne, she agrees with this pronouncement. 'If he looks like you say he does and he's rich as well, *and* kind, don't you be rushing things. You know, honey, you've been away from home a while now, and you don't know too many people yet. You go easy. You just want someone to love. Take it slowly.'

She is right actually. They both are. Nate is the first guy I've fallen for. Jay had just kind of slid into touch, rescuing me from the dreaded curse of virginity. I am quite sure Maureen and Patricia have gone home to tell everyone I was leading a life of sin. I have had a card from my mother to say she has enrolled me in some kind of perpetual novena to the Blessed Virgin. Perhaps she is trying to tell me something. I have always felt a certain affinity with the Blessed Virgin Mary, or 'Our Lady' as we all call her in Ireland. We have the same initials – BVM. My full name is Brigid Veronica Margaret Lennon. That drove me mad when I was at school. My mother has always sworn that it wasn't deliberate. She had wanted Brigid, and then added the Margaret on the insistence of her mother, Veronica, who felt my Daddy's mother, Margaret, would feel annoyed that she wasn't featuring. Daddy hates the name Brigid and began to call me Maggie, thank God. Mammy needn't have bothered calling me after the two grannies, but she didn't dream she would have three more girls. She could have gone back several generations of grannies and still not run out of names.

I float into work the next day. I need to collect my car from the body shop. Rick offers to take me.

'Well,' he says, leering at me, 'did you have a nice weekend with Pretty Boy?'

I ignore the jibe. I can be magnanimous to him now, though he still makes my toes curl. Zollie has made him Music

Director, which really pisses me off. Up to this point it was a non-job. But it sounds good. Unless I move fast he will get to go to all the record conventions, talk to the trades every week, and when the record promotion men come to town they will take *him* out to lunch. What a bummer! I like that expression.

Al had done the job in Daytona, and I had watched him. Al had the whole thing sewn up. He was a real lurker. Always on the make. He landed a huge job in Tampa after WA1A folded and is down there now making a packet. That's why he hasn't joined us in Tennessee. Al had really intrigued me in Florida. He did a morning shift and then spent the rest of the day on the phone. He seemed to be able to get all the free albums he wanted. He spent large parts of his day being chatted up by the record companies and they sent all the freebies to him, along with all the promotional stuff, T-shirts, baseball caps, and other goodies.

I want to be the Music Director. It is the only bloody job at the station worth having. Normally the Program Director gets all the kudos, but Zollie already calls himself Program Director. That is the main job. He is supposed to consider what the new releases are each week, listen to them, then add the ones he thinks are good. Call the stores, find out what people are buying, and report all this to the trade magazines. This is all too much bother for Zollie. He needs a slave to do all the shit work. Calling the trades alone takes up an entire morning, mostly on 'terminal hold'. Trouble is, not all the trades want to hear from you, unless you show up in the Arbitron. That is my first real brush with ratings. Ratings are everything. No ratings no nothing, and if you report to all the top trades, then you get lots of goodies. Since Q92 is a new station we don't report to anyone. Not yet.

Yes, I definitely have my eye on Rick's job. I am working my way up to it. I have been working for Zollie longer than he has, and apart from his encylopaedic knowledge, he is fairly useless. For starters Bilbo hates him, and Bilbo likes everyone. Anyway, we have a rock encyclopaedia and it has a better personality.

My chance comes out of the blue. Rick and Zollie have a knock down, drag out row about money, and as quickly as he arrives, Rick is out. Within two days he is on the air at the competition. It seems like he had already been talking to Dream 103 and had accepted a job from them. The row was only a pretext.

After a bit of wrangling, Zollie agrees to me taking over as Music Director. He will have to pay someone else to do it otherwise. This is my chance and I go for it with a vengeance. I call all the trades and turn on the charm, with the accent. I nearly make myself sick. I give them the low-down on the station, talking it up a storm, and two of them eventually say we can report weekly. They are two of the less prestigious trades, but all stations and record companies buy them anyway, and any publicity is good. At least now we get the name about, and it means the record companies will take an interest in us. I establish a contact at two of the main record stores and set about finding out what Chattanooga likes to listen to. Then I have a stroke of luck. Well, that's an understatement really. I add a record that no one else is playing. I don't think this is a big deal, but I don't quite understand the rules yet, you see.

Sinead has sent it to me from home. She loves it, and naturally when she heard I was back on the air as a DJ she wrote and asked me if I played it. I wrote back saying I'd never heard of it, so she sent it to me. It's different from all the other stuff the girls have sent, less punky, so I put it on the air on a heavy rotation, which means it gets played every two hours. People start to request it. We generally ignore requests as it's too much like hard work. Besides, people are so predictable. If you play a record a lot they begin to think it's their favourite. Over exposure is what it's called. If a record is played every couple of hours, chances are people will think it's because they have asked for it, even if it's on the playlist anyway.

The record I add to the playlist is called 'Dogs in the Moonlight' and it's by a singer I have never heard of called Jimmy Farrell. It has been number one in the charts in Britain for ages. This in itself is an achievement, because it is 1977 and the Brits are mainly into punk and all that shit. This song isn't cursing the Queen and there isn't one swear word in it. It's just a brilliant love song. Americans are so different, they are still enthralled with the Eagles, Fleetwood Mac and the soft West Coast sound, with the odd stadium bands like Supertramp and REO Speedwagon thrown in. Oh, and they love the Bee Gees.

'Dogs in the Moonlight' is special though, and it genuinely gets requested a lot more than anything else we are playing. It has a madly wonderful sax solo and I love it. So does Nate. It becomes 'our song' and he tries to buy it, but it isn't available. Not in Chattanooga. Not anywhere. This worries me. I phone in my second weekly report to *Golden Ears*, one of the two trades we report to. '"Dogs in the Moonlight" is my most requested single and it isn't stocked in town,' I tell them.

'Come again?'

'"Dogs in the Moonlight".'

'Never heard of it. What label's it on?'

'Shine Records.'

'Nope.' The person on the other end of the phone pauses. 'Hang on, I'll let you talk to the boss.'

Abe Goodman, 'the boss' (his favourite line, I am to find out, is that he was called 'the boss' way before Springsteen), is fascinated by my news, and also that I'd added a record not yet released. Apparently it is not the done thing. But he is also interested in me. I can tell that at once. He likes my accent and the fact I am a woman. There are very few women in the business.

'I suppose I should call Shine Records and tell them to send stock,' I suggest, trying to sound more knowledgeable than I am.

'Hang on, I'll give you the VP of promotion's direct line, you tell him I'm featuring it on the "Soaring to the Top" section this week. And,' he adds, in that way only Americans can without sounding like eejits, 'I like you, Maggie. You call me direct each week, don't talk to anyone else. This is my number. Okay, baby?'

I am delighted. I even let it pass that he called me baby. I don't know then that Abe Goodman is one of the 'heavyweights' in the music business, I am just pleased that I won't have to wait on terminal hold for a researcher to take my weekly report next time, and fight with Zollie about the phone bills. So I do what he says and I call Rolly Young at Shine. It takes me a while to explain about the record, and even longer to explain myself. He isn't too friendly. *He* certainly doesn't say 'I like you, Maggie'. He more or less wants to know who the hell I am, how I got his direct number, and why I am wasting his time talking about a record he's never heard of. He seems to have a major problem with the fact that I am in a 'small market' (not LA or New York), don't report to *R&R*, *Gavin*, *Billboard* or various other prestigious trades. A bit up himself, I think. I don't get too far. I let it go. He does give me the name of his local (Atlanta) promotion guy and suggests I call him. I do, he is not there, but he calls me back and mentions other records I should be on – they all make it sound like a drug – and says he will come to see me in the New Year. His name is Tom.

The following week I again report 'Dogs in the Moonlight' as our top song to Abe at *Golden Ears*. I speak to him personally and tell him that when I mentioned his name Rolly Young didn't seem remotely impressed, didn't seem to believe someone like me would know Abe, oh, and that he's mad at Abe for giving out his phone number. It is like lighting a touch paper!

'Leave it to me, babe, just don't miss next week's *Golden Ears*.'

As Abe hangs up I can hear the snarl in his voice as he orders his assistant to 'Get me Rolly Young now!'.

I don't think about it much as I am still totally involved in the Seduction of Nate.

Nate Gilmore is wooing me like a real Southern gentleman. He takes me to dinner, twice, at the most expensive restaurant in town, and we have long, sensual moonlight cuddles at his place on the lake. Yes, cuddles! Much to my chagrin, that was as far as we'd gone. Jaysus, am I becoming a sex fiend or what? I ask myself. Less than a year ago I was struggling to stop at cuddles. Well, a bit of a poke and grope, too, I suppose, but I certainly didn't want to bonk the bejasus out of every man I met. Losing my virginity has turned my head. I am mistaking lust for love. I am mad for it. I am almost beginning to think of masturbation. I've never tried it, it hasn't really occurred to me, don't ask me why. Sharla has been on to it for years. Maybe it's the hot weather in America, or the fact of wearing so few clothes. Anyhow, the way Sharla explains it to me, masturbation could wear you out. It sounds like I'd need a waterbed for it too, to get the motion right. There is no point in trying it if I am going to end up disappointing myself.

The brilliant thing is, though, that Nate has invited me for Christmas, and maybe the Christmas spirit will turn him on. Sharla has invited me as well, but she will understand if I want to spend it with Nate. Besides, with only a day off, going to visit Sharla will mean my spending most of the holiday driving. The Gilmore Christmas is to be staged in his parents' house. They live in a huge house on Lookout Mountain. Like I said, they are SUPER RICH. The day after Nate invites me, I tell Zollie.

'Nate has invited me to spend Christmas Day at his parents' house,' I say, trying to sound casual. Zollie is disappointed. He looks at me pityingly.

'Spend Christmas with old Nathan Gilmore and his old tight-ass wife Bitsy? Maggie, you cannot be serious! Momma's already knitting you a Christmas stocking. She'll be real, real sorry to hear that you aren't coming to us. My brother and his wife and my nephews are coming from Arkansas.'

'But Zollie, I had no idea. You didn't say.' I love Annie Mae and I know in my heart I would be more comfortable there, but Christmas without Nate? 'I'm sorry. I've told him yes – you didn't ask me.'

'Well hell, Maggie, I just thought you'd know you were invited. You didn't think I'd let you spend Christmas on your own, miles from your momma and poppa?'

I would have preferred to be back in Belfast, sitting in a smoke-filled bar with my sisters and our friends, even with the iron security gates, but at least here I won't be allowed to be alone. People are so friendly. I decide I'll wait and see about Nate, see if he mentions it again. Zollie wants me to work right up until Christmas Day anyway. A lot can happen before then. A lot does.

9

We are going to launch the station to the public with the giveaway to beat all giveaways. We are running a competition, SKI ALABAMA. This is some deal Zollie has struck with Lee, Bilbo's old wheeler-dealer brother. We are giving away fifty free weekends in Alabama at the new ski resort, Alpine South, which is located just south of Birmingham off the Interstate. All people have to do to win is call the station when they hear sleigh bells ring. Corny but effective. Most of them think it is a joke and I don't blame them. Here we are, mid-December, yet the weather is nowhere near freezing in Tennessee, and Alabama is further south again. Besides, who the hell would want to go to Alabama except a Lynyrd Skynyrd fan? 'Sweet Home Alabama' is one of our top three requests, and I always follow it with Neil Young's 'Southern Man' just to be balanced, though I expect only the real fans notice. You can play Lynyrd Skynyrd all day in the South, people never tire of it, especially now, after the tragic deaths of Ronnie Van Zant and Steve and Cassie Gaines. Then, unexpectedly, it snows. Snows and snows and snows. Seven inches fall overnight and the town grinds to a halt. The nearest snowplough is in Chicago, people haven't a notion how to cope and cars are stuck on the highway. Next morning I am terrified driving to work. There are cars skidding everywhere, lots of 'fender benders'. Half the population stay off work, just stay in all day and listen to the radio. The request line lights up like crazy and the competition phones go mad. In one day we give away all forty-eight remaining SKI ALABAMA weekends. They are all up for grabs but no one at the station wants one, and the old Christian lady who is called Miz Zillah Ruth Knightly has already won the first one. I am worried about her because, according to Zollie, she really is seventy-six, and her proposed companion is her eighty-one-year-old sister, Miz Beulah May Knightly. He has called out to visit her, hoping maybe she would change her mind on account of the insurance liability and accept a gift voucher for Mamie's Modes, but she is heart set on it. She is crocheting a ski sweater and a matching bobble hat in lime green.

The resort is due to open over the New Year. I have never been skiing, it seems so exotic. Sharla has suggested that we have a weekend skiing in Gatlinburg sometime, which allegedly becomes a ski resort in winter. Gatlinburg is in the Smoky Mountains and is possibly one of the tackiest places I have ever been in my life. I was there with Sharla and two of her friends while I was staying in Johnson City. It is unspeakable, a cross between Lourdes and Hollywood, set to a country music soundtrack.

Nate is horrified when I tell him I might be going to Gatlinburg to ski. He tells me that if I want to try skiing, the Gilmores have a lodge in Aspen and he usually manages a

97

couple of trips between now and Easter. He'd love me to come with him. A ski lodge in Aspen! Well, I suppose it fits in with everything else. I mean, I still find it hard to get used to a twenty-four-year-old guy who owns his own house, let alone one the size of Nate's.

Even Zollie, who is thirty-seven, can't afford one half that size, or any size for that matter. He is renting an apartment in the same building as me and is looking at property, but he is limited financially, he told me, because he is paying alimony to Sherilee the witch. She still drives him crazy calling him collect from Florida just to tell him what a bastard he is. It happens every time she has drink taken, or is smashed on dope. But I am not too concerned about Zollie's house problems, I fully expect him to come in one day and announce he has traded one out. I tell this to Nate. He has some funny opinions of Zollie. You can tell they are from such different backgrounds and despite money being the great equaliser, the snobbery is still there. It isn't obvious on the surface, you can't even go by the accent like at home, it takes some scraping away to figure out social mores in the Southern states, but I am learning fast. Old money is definitely better than new, but being nouveau is better than not being 'reech' at all. The Gilmores are most definitely old money. They own half the town; their money came originally from steel and then from property. Nate is Nathan Gilmore the fifth! Zollie says least-ways they are not Yanks, that is the only thing they have in their favour.

Nate likes Zollie, but I can also tell he thinks Zollie is crazy. I agree, but I don't tell him. I still have loyalty to Zollie. When I tell Nate about the SKI ALABAMA contest he laughs so hard he cries, says it is the most insane thing he's ever heard. But that was before the snow started. It is still snowing steadily and now there is so much snow that even Nate begins to think it might work. We all hope he is right. This is the giveaway that will establish us.

Christmas week I have a mild distraction in the form of Tom, the local Shine guy, who drives up from Atlanta to take me out to lunch. According to Tom, I am 'happening' because of 'Dogs in the Moonlight', and should capitalise on this by going to a radio and record convention in LA in the new year. I mention this to Zollie, but he is not keen on the idea. For starters, you have to pay your own fare and registration money. We are in a bit of a pickle – it would be one way to raise the profile of the station, but beyond our budget. The idea is dropped, maybe the next one, there are loads of them apparently. I don't mind, but I am sufficiently intrigued.

Meanwhile, Christmas approaches relentlessly. Nothing in my life has ever prepared me for Christmas in America. For a start it is actually going to be a white one. I have discovered that weather forecasts in America are accurate. I can't understand this. I have never taken weather forecasts as anything but a hopeful estimation of what weather should be like. No matter what was predicted at home it usually rained. Here they say things like: 'Today's high will be ninety-six degrees with some precipitation at seven o clock,' and it is right. Maybe the government have discovered how to control the weather. They can certainly make the sun shine more often. So, when they say the snow is expected to stay for Christmas, well, we all go out and buy fur gloves and toboggans. Actually Zollie trades us out the toboggans and the fur gloves. We spend the Sunday before Christmas sledging up and down the golf course and then Nate takes me home to his place for hot punch, and in front of a big log fire we finally do it.

He is so gentle and sweet. I can't get used to it. I have

99

nothing to compare him with except Jay, the surfer, who was sort of eager and puppy-like. Not that I have direct experience of puppies, but Jay was sort of vigorous. He bounced around a lot and whooped and yelled things like 'Help me, baby!', and, 'I'm on the Stairway to Heaven now!' (He loved Led Zeppelin.) This was usually followed by a loud scream of delight. He always satisfied himself, and if I got any pleasure out of it, well, that was grand, he was delighted and encouraged me to whoop as well, which I have to say I don't do instinctively. But I had loved making love to Jay. He made it feel so natural and basic. He had been a good one to deflower me as it were.

Nate is different. He is intent on satisfying me, which I find very touching, but I also find it harder to come. He is a slow, deliberate lover. I am longing for him, but he kisses me for about two hours before we get undressed. I am wet, soaked with desire. In Florida, Jay and I never had much on, so getting naked took seconds. Maybe, I think after the first time with Nate, I'll have another chat with Sharla about the masturbation lark. Somehow, for all his tenderness and attention to detail, Nate leaves me vaguely dissatisfied. No, make that totally dissatisfied. I wasn't even sure if we had done it or not. I couldn't feel much, although he very definitely has a big penis. I have a good look at it, touch it even. That is when we are having the foreplay bit. It seems to diminish rapidly after penetration. Not a promising start, but I know things can only get better. He seems to be interested in me as a person, not just for sex, and that is the important thing. The sex will improve. I have read that in a book, and at last, the deed is done. We are officially in love. After we finish he seems so happy I don't say anything, that's when he asks me again if I would like to have Christmas dinner with his family.

I accept at once. I call Annie Mae and explain the situation. She says of course she understands and I am right to accept: 'But honey you make sure and be here for dinner next day. And,' she adds, 'don't go opening your heart too much to that Gilmore boy. Those Gilmores are trouble.' I put this down to a sort of mild jealousy, a bit out of character for Annie Mae, but understandable. The Gilmores do own half the town after all, and that doesn't usually spell popularity.

I am more than happy to go to Annie Mae for Boxing Day. I will have no chance to feel homesick, being invited out two days in a row. Boxing Day is usually a very lazy one at home, spent in front of the television. They don't call it Boxing Day here, just the day after Christmas, the day the sales start. We have lots of sales advertising lined up at the station, and now I am not going to see Sharla, Zollie has me working that afternoon doing a live shift. The plan is that I will finish work at three and then Zollie will pick me up and take me to Nickajack. Annie Mae will doubtless have a grand feast laid on and I will spend the night there. I am looking forward to it. No effort for me, and best of all, no driving. I don't fancy driving there in this snow. No way.

Meantime, I need a dress for Christmas day, something a step up from Mamie's Modes, and I also need to go see 'Herman the Hair man', as Zollie calls him. I am starting to say need. Everybody needs everything in America. I think they are afraid to say want, in case it looks as if they actually need it. I call in to Mamie's Modes anyway – there is still a lot of trade-out left, no one can use it up. They are thrilled to see me and rush to make me coffee and show me the array of Christmas clothes. There is Mamie and two assistants, Jolene and Luanne, who all have big hair, bright smiles and are incredibly friendly. They think I am a celebrity and are

101

permanently tuned to Q92. The clothes for Christmas are, not surprisingly, red and green, or green and red. Many of the sweaters feature fancy embroidery, mostly of Santa, or reindeers or baubles. A feeling of despair creeps over me. How will I get out without buying anything? I give in and model a few numbers for them but feel totally absurd in all of them. Just as I have run out of excuses for not taking a bright red dress with green stripes and large leg-of-mutton sleeves, which they assure me 'Looks darlin' on you honey, jest' darlin',' I notice a few plain sweaters sitting on the counter. There is one which is pale grey cashmere, and one of plain red wool. I pull the grey out and take it to try on. It fits perfectly and feels wonderful. Reluctantly they allow me to buy it, although I have to take a silk red and green scarf which I promise I will drape round my neck to cheer it up. They insist on wrapping it for Christmas, even though I tell them it is a waste of gift paper. 'Nonsense, honey, you are worth it,' Mamie says. 'You're our little Christmas star.' I wish them all Merry Christmas, promise to play some requests for them tomorrow, and make my escape.

10

I don't know how we make it up to Christmas. The town is chaotic. The station is insane. Every five minutes it seems Zollie is rushing in with copy and I have to cut yet another commercial. I am almost starting to speak in tongues to change the sound of my voice. He really needs another DJ, a fresh voice. I am on the air virtually every commercial break, and add to this the fact that he has programmed in everything Bob Seger has ever recorded, which means virtually every second song is a Bob Seger song, means the station sounds demented. He is doing this purely to impress Sue Lynne who has a thing about the Silver Bullet Band, and Zollie wants to screw her. He sort of sees himself as the embodiment of a silver bullet, he tells me. 'Lean, mean, fast and precious. A killer!' It is so bloody Freudian and I think he actually means it. What a joke.

Sue Lynne has some sort of a boyfriend though. His name is Clarence Lee Dunne and he hangs about the station a bit when Zollie isn't around. He is a total moron, dresses from head to toe in polyester, and wears an aftershave that smells like cheap carpet freshener. He has little piggy eyes, pointy, sharp little teeth like a pterodactyl, a wispy little goatee beard, and a huge Afro, which adds about eight inches to his height. Just as well, he is only about five feet tall. He hasn't really got a body, just a sort of bone structure with loose wrapping over it, leaving no room for any internal organs. The opposite applies with his large head, for he obviously has no brain.

He really gets on my nerves. He thinks he is witty, makes constant funny remarks about my accent, and leers at me. I plan to poison him. Well I don't, but it would be a good idea if someone did. Zollie has met him a few times and loathes him. I feed his loathing. I enjoy saying horrible things about Clarence Lee Dunne. Clarence Le Dumb is one of the things we call him. Not too imaginative, I admit, but it works in an insidious way. Clarence Lee works in the nearby nuclear power plant that dominates the landscape not far from the station. This is a truly terrifying thought, both the fact that it is there and that Clarence is employed by them. We get lots of calls for requests from the workers, most of whom sound not right in the head. The radioactive stuff must be corroding their brains even as they are on the phone to us. They wear wellies, or gumboots as Americans call them, full, I'm sure, of radioactive water. I think if I ever form a rock group that would be a good name for it. Radioactive Wellies.

In the meantime, Clarence Lee and his like stand between us all and the total end of mankind as we know it. What a thought! It is one of the things I worry about when I am homesick in the middle of the night. Clarence Lee makes me feel that Ireland is the only viable alternative. Sue Lynne appears to love him. She pats him a lot. This is a very American thing,

I feel, patting. Their routine goes something like this. Clarence Lee sits there looking like the insignificant slime bag he is. Sue Lynne then addresses everyone, usually Bilbo, and me, 'Isn't he just adorable?' she'll say, patting his Afro. We say nothing and try not to choke. 'He's so darlin',' she says, and then she pats his knee. Clarence Lee just sits there with a shit-eatin' grin on his excuse for a face and replies, 'Hey baby, you're giving me active love'. At this point I gag and leave, Bilbo turns bright red, coughs and starts tidying the LPs. The funny thing is, she never does this in Zollie's presence, she is too sly — sleekit, we would call her at home. She needs the fix of Zollie's devotion so she downplays the relationship to him, two-faced cow that she is, and Zollie lives in hope, set to the soundtrack of Bob Seger's 'Stranger in Town' and 'Night Moves'.

On Christmas Eve, Sue Lynne and Clarence Lee almost ruin my Christmas. Sue Lynne is working late, we all are. Zollie had done a trawl for lots of last-minute advertising and had come up with a ton of commercials for me to cut. I am furious — my voice is already wall to wall on the stupid station, advertising everything from white wall tyres to a protein drink that tastes like roast turkey and makes you lose twenty pounds by being in the same room as it, or something like that! The ad starts with the immortal line 'Why not drink your Christmas Dinner?'.

Clarence Lee comes in to pick Sue Lynne up. The very look of him makes me want to spit. 'Ah'm here for my little baby doll,' he says. 'Ah'm going to buy her the biggest, bestest ole Christmas gift in the world.'

Sue Lynne comes simpering out of the office and straight into his spindly arms. Seeing them there together, I feel a wave of revulsion. I want to be back at home going out for a drink with the gang. I want to be with my lovely close family. What on earth am I doing here?

Yesterday I got a card from Maureen. She is getting engaged to Dermot Brady – one of 'our' gang from university. They have been going out since fresher's day, and her absence this summer made him realise what a treasure she was. I am happy for them. She says in her card that no one at home knows yet, but she thought she'd tell me since I was far away. I feel a stab when I read the words. They are getting married next summer when she has been teaching a year. Well, I suppose I wouldn't want that either. Why am I such a malcontent? Mammy was nearly crying last week when I said I definitely won't be home for Christmas. 'I wish we had the money to send you a ticket,' she said. 'It won't be the same without you.'

I am in lousy form. I look over at Clarence and Sue Lynne. Is this what Christmas in America is going to be, full of idiots and numbskulls? Nate Gilmore might be my 'boyfriend', but I feel appallingly alone. I can't wait to get out of the station and go home to feel sorry for myself in peace.

It is really late by the time I get all the commercials cut and finally leave. Bilbo is spending the night at the station and then driving down to Alabama in the morning. We swap presents. I kiss him and thank him, but I am not remotely full of Christmas spirit. Snow or no snow, I just want to get home and crawl into bed. Nate is coming to get me after church tomorrow. I have decided I will go to mass as it is hard to think of Christmas without any sort of religious aspect to it, and my apartment is near a Catholic church – ironically it's about the only place I can walk to.

I wish Bilbo a Merry Christmas, leave the station and walk out into the night. The cold air virtually takes my breath away.

106

The light is glinting off the branches of the trees, which are coated in a thin film of ice, and if I wasn't in such lousy form I might think it beautiful. It is freezing cold. I scrape the ice from the windshield and wait for about ten minutes running the engine until the car seems warm enough to sit in. I am fearful of the drive home. This will be a challenge for me.

I drive as carefully as I can, but I am simply petrified of the ice. It has barely been any time since I passed my driving test and I've never experienced anything like this, even as a passenger. It seems that any pressure at all on the brakes sends the car into a waltz. I slither along as far behind the driver in front as possible. There isn't a whole lot of traffic on the road up to the Interstate, but everyone is driving like me, very gingerly. My armpits are beginning to smell like Bilbo's. Brake lights flash on and off. The temperature has dropped dramatically and the snow has frozen. It sits by the roadside in stiff meringue-like peaks, and occasional flurries drift in the headlights. It may well look like a winter wonderland, but driving in it is the scariest thing I've ever done. It is an almost unearthly quiet, like someone has turned down the sound. I turn the radio off to concentrate – there are only so many times one can listen to John Lennon singing 'So this is Christmas' anyway. The windshield wipers thrum, swishing the snowflakes from side to side and I concentrate hard on my driving.

Just as I am indicating to get on to the highway, a car comes racing up behind me flashing its lights and dazzling me in the process. I brake instinctively and hear a sort of shush and crinkling sound, and then BANG! My car is spinning round and nothing I do seems to stop it. I am in some crazy ice waltz in the glare of oncoming traffic. I hold on to the steering wheel. My mouth is open, I think I am screaming, then there is another loud bang, then a thud. Then silence. The car has stopped. I can taste blood on my lips. At least I'm not dead. Paralysed? I wiggle my toes. I can feel them. Is that a good sign? I move my hand up towards my face and press it into it. It comes away covered in blood.

Just then the car door is wrenched open and there stands Sue Lynne with the ghastly Clarence Lee behind her, peering intently at me. Jesus! I am dead and in hell already!

'Maggie? Are you all right? Honey, I am so sorry, but Clarence was just trying to be cute, and beep hi to you. I guess he didn't realise it was so icy.' (She actually pronounces it assy.)

I leap in a rage from the car. Thoughts of paralysis vanish at once. I want to choke him. I am screaming abuse. He backs away with a look of terror on his face and as he does I notice another car on the left-hand side of the road. A tall, well-built man wearing a cowboy hat gets out and walks towards us.

'I've seen it all and I've radioed on my CB to the police. They'll be right along. I hope y'all weren't drinking?' He looks directly at Clarence who shakes his crazy Afro at him. I notice it has a layer of snow on it. ''Cos that sure was some mighty stupid driving, buddy.' He turns to me. 'Are you all right, young lady?'

'I'm not sure. I feel a bit faint,' I say, and I do, suddenly. I am also shaking quite violently, not just with rage at Clarence.

'Well, I guess the paramedics will be along as well. Hey, why don't you get back in the car, it's freezin' out. Hold on, I have an emergency sign.'

He goes over to his car and pulls out a triangle on a sort of easel, and props it by the roadside. It glows in the snow and the cars silently curve out to pass us, making sweeping

tracks as they do. A few stop to offer help, but Buford, that's
how he's introduced himself, thanks them graciously and says
everything has been taken care of. He comes back over, and
hands me a cup of something hot.

'Ma'am,' he says, 'I just bought this coffee and I haven't
started to drink it, waiting for it to cool a bit. Maybe you
should have it.'

I do think for a moment of throwing it at Clarence, but I
get into the car and sip it gratefully. It hasn't cooled. Clarence
and Sue Lynne shuffle uneasily outside in the snow. Clarence
rubs his slimy hands together and clears his throat from time
to time. I wish they would get in their own car, but they
seem rooted to mine. The snow is piling on top of Clarence's
hair and he looks absurd.

'Listen, Maggie, it was jest a kinda joke that backfired on
me. I swear I didn't mean no harm. Look on the braaght saad,
Maggie, leastways nobody done got kilt.'

'Done got kilt,' I mimic. Not yet you stupid moron, I think.
Some bloody joke.

By the time the police come and take statements I have
calmed down. Buford takes control and everything is sorted.
I have only a small cut on my lip, no other injuries. Buford
lends me a clean, white real hanky and I press it against my
lip until the blood stops. Somehow the police manage to get
a call to the station and Zollie comes for me. He has called
his momma and told her that he is taking me home with
him, so Annie Mae will have a bed ready. Zollie is unusually
solicitous for a change.

'Why Maggie, baby, you pore ole thing,' he says when he
arrives, whereupon I burst into tears. 'Hey, baby, don't fret.
Momma is just thrilled to have you stay over.'

'I have to go to mass tomorrow, it's Christmas.'

'I'll take you, I ain't ever bin to mass, that'd be fun.'

'I have to call my mammy and daddy tonight.' I am regressing to pet names.

'You can call 'em from my place.'

'But Nate, he's picking me up tomorrow.'

'That's fine. What time?'

'About one.'

'Ain't a problem, Maggie. We'll have you there.'

Clarence Lee and Sue Lynne are dispatched home. Unfortunately they don't go directly to jail. I get into Zollie's car and wait while the good samaritan, whose full name is Buford Dewayne McConnell, nickname 'Big Boy' (yes, I think it is weird too, but this is Tennessee), has a long chat with Zollie and I hear Zollie promise to call him and keep him up to date on my progress. Then he wishes me a Merry Christmas and leaves. Zollie and I drive off in the snow, passing the tow truck with its eerily revolving red light, on its way to get my car just a mile or so down the road.

'Well, Maggie,' said Zollie, as he fires up a joint. 'You need a lil' toke to help you relax. This has been a pretty damm dramatic Christmas Eve now, hasn't it?' He sounds delighted, as if he'd staged the whole thing for my entertainment. He takes a deep draw off the joint and hands it to me. 'You know who your good samaritan was, Maggie?'

I shake my head.

'He's a country and western singer from round here. Used to be big, real big.' Zollie starts to sing (My God he has an awful voice) 'Let your love pour down on me like maple syrup.'

'Oh? I've never heard of him?' The dope has kicked in and I feel more relaxed.

'Nice guy. "Maple Syrup" was a huge hit. Yep, humongous

hit, sold millions.' Zollie pronounces it *miiyons*, drawing the word out with a satisfied sigh. 'I guess he's still living on the proceeds.'

We have reached Annie Mae's by now. The snow is unlike any I've ever seen at home. Outside the town it is thick, white, and soft. Huge drifts of it blanket everything. The Americans do everything on a grander scale, weather included. We crunch our way through into a warm glowing house, which smells of Christmas: spicy and comforting. A bath is ready for me, with hot, fluffy towels piled beside it and a clean cotton nightie several sizes too big. About a half an hour later I am in bed, exhausted. And a minute after that, fast asleep.

11

'Merry Christmas, honey,' Annie Mae's big friendly face smiles down on me as I open my eyes. It is nearly ten o'clock, and there is a strong smell of bacon permeating the house. I shake myself fully awake. My first Christmas away from home. I push any feelings of that out of my mind for I am among friends. The house is warm and snug and, best of all, there are presents at the bottom of the bed. I push them with my toes.

'Looks like Santy came while you slept.'

'Oh Annie Mae, yours are all in my apartment. I was going to bring them tomorrow.'

'Honey, don't fuss. We just wanted you to have something to wake up to.'

She watches, beaming, while I rip them open. There is a gold chain with a Tennessee River pearl from Zollie, and another little box with instructions to open much later, alone. Intriguing. And absolutely the most perfect patchwork quilt from Annie Mae, which she's made herself. I can't believe my luck. And finally, all Springsteen's LPs that Zollie has somehow lurked from Columbia records. I am so chuffed.

'Well, Maggie, you're in the good ole U S of A for Christmas! What's it feel like?'

'Not bad at all,' I say, and it doesn't. Zollie is as good as his word and takes me to mass. He even goes to communion, which I let pass – the Foleys must have been Catholic at some stage – and then he takes me home. I will see him tomorrow.

Nate picks me up at one-thirty exactly. He listens sympathetically as I describe my ordeal of the previous evening. I guess Zollie has told him some of it on the phone already. He seems somewhat uncomfortable when I burst into tears, and pats me on the back limply. I would prefer a bear hug, but I am a bit over-emotional, realising perhaps for the first time what a really rotten experience it had been and what a dumbass jerk Clarence Lee really is. God knows how long my car will be out of action. What if Buford, whatever his name is, hadn't happened along in time and seen it all? I'd probably still be at the side of the Interstate, frozen to death. I stop crying and dry my eyes, I am being self-indulgent, and suggest we exchange presents. Nate kisses me, smiles, and tells me it is a Gilmore family tradition to exchange presents just before dinner, after they have had their eggnog, whatever that is. I have got him expensive cufflinks from a jeweller's shop at the Chattanooga Choo Choo that Zollie had traded me instead of my Christmas bonus, and I have got his mother a present, a 'hostess' gift. I am not too keen on handing them over in front of an audience, but if it's a tradition then I guess I'll have to live with it.

We leave in the Porsche and set off for Lookout

Mountain. Am I presentable enough? I am wearing black velvet trousers, a cream silk blouse, and my grey cashmere cardigan, my last-minute 'find' from Mamie's. Boring but tasteful. But that's what I am aiming for today. Zollie had pushed a small vial of coke into my palm as he left my apartment. 'Last part of your present, Maggie, you might need this honey,' he said meaningfully. I am puzzled. I had figured that the mystery present was coke. What is this? I am too dumbstruck to argue. It is in my handbag – it feels radioactive to me.

Ochs highway goes right up Lookout Mountain, and about halfway up we turn into a long, winding gravel driveway and stop outside a largish, two-storey brick house. A wide veranda wraps the house and the front porch is supported by columns. It is an old home, obviously built some time in the last century, but then you could never be sure in America as they have this knack of building a house in a month that looks like it has been there for ever. Tasteful white Christmas lights twinkle on two of the large fir trees nearest the front porch, the snow sitting heavily on their branches, and the front door is decorated with a Christmas wreath, a muted green arrangement with a large red bow.

Nate rings the doorbell. That surprises me. Doesn't he have a key? A black woman answers so quickly that you would think she had been standing behind the door. That surprises me too. Do people still have black servants? Even in the South? It is, after all, the last week of 1977. Nate positively whoops with delight when he sees her.

'Hey, Miss Cora, how are you doin'?' Big as she is, he picks her up and swings her round. She seems chuffed to bits, and is chuckling but she pretends to slap him away. He ducks. 'Hey, Cora, Merry Christmas, you look just pretty as a picture.'

'Why, Mr Nate, you behave now, yo heah me? Yo ole flirt you.' After she has smoothed herself down she hugs him warmly. She looks to me like a different coloured version of Annie Mae. 'Now,' she says, turning to me and eyeing me up and down, 'you must be little Maggie, why honey, you are just a little doll.' She grins at me, a wide ear-splitting grin. 'Here, give me your coat and y'all go into the library and get yourselves by that big old fire, get yoursels warmed up.'

She scuttles off with my coat while I stand in the large hall with its high ceiling and minstrel gallery, looking at several portraits of rather severe, older versions of Nate. Although it didn't appear overwhelmingly large from the outside, it is deceptive. The house is enormous inside. This is another building trick perfected by Americans. In Belfast, we specialise in small outsides and minuscule insides. We both do as Cora tells us and go into the long, gracious, and exquisitely appointed drawing room. It looks like a scene from *House & Garden*.

I gaze around the room. It is furnished with four large, comfortable sofas in muted tones of honey and cream, occasional cushions in tapestries of reds, blues, and ochre, and polished mahogany end tables with large, gleaming ceramic lamps with Chinese patterns. They look very expensive. It is all absolutely tasteful, nothing in the room jars. It doesn't exactly say money, it whispers it softly with total confidence. The walls are covered in paintings, the one above the fireplace is a Wyeth print I am fairly sure. It features a solitary barn at the end of a wide field with a figure of a boy in the distance.

'Is that a Wyeth?' I am pleased with myself for spotting it.

'Hell, Maggie, I guess it is. I know we have two or three by him, my daddy likes art. He collects American painters. He has a couple of Hoppers as well.'

'You mean it's real?'

115

'Hell yes, it's worth a lot of dollars I think.'

He says this as if it was the most matter of fact thing in the world to have a real painting. I think of our house with the block mounts of Van Gogh's *The Yellow Chair* and *Starry Night*, Turner's *The Fighting Téméraire* and the picture of the Sacred Heart with the eternal lamp below. God, I could just imagine bringing Nate home to meet the folks and see our art collection. I reappraise the Chinese lamps. I ease away from them in case they fall on me and break. It is the sort of thing that happens to me.

The most beautiful Christmas tree I have ever seen is placed exactly centre in front of the French windows. I walk over to inspect it. It is perfect. Each ornament seems to have been placed on exactly the right branch, and they are all pointing in the right direction. Little stripy candy canes, angels, trumpets, drums, rocking horses, all in shades of red, green and gold hang from the branches. There is no sign of the vulgar gold tinsel I am used to. The fairy lights are shaped like candles, and although they are electric, they look real. There is one placed exactly at the end of each branch, and another halfway up, they must have used a measuring tape. It is a real tree too, the heady smell of pine hit me the minute I entered the room. The little flames on each candle twinkle at me but my eye is drawn to the top of the tree where it is crowned with a large, confident star. It isn't even crooked like ours at home always is. Our tree at home is usually bought a few days before Christmas and bedecked with the remains of the ornaments that haven't been broken the previous year, plus a few new cheap ones if anyone has bothered to buy some. Unlike this masterpiece, the ornaments on the Lennon tree persist in turning the wrong way, and all our attempts to make them face out end in either another breakage or a dent in

116

the ornament. But tacky or not, each Christmas we have such fun putting it up, with all five of us girls giggling like idiots and mammy fretting about whether the lights will work again this year. We always seem to have to get a new set or go out at the last minute for spare bulbs. We usually fill in all the bare bits of the tree with horrible tacky tinsel, and the crap ornaments we had all made in school every year. My mother, for reasons best known to herself, has always kept these faded bits of coloured paper with glitter stuck to them. They are wild looking.

'Well,' I say to Nate, 'I see your mum hasn't kept your school ornaments.'

'She hasn't kept my what?'

I explain about the school ornaments. Nate thinks it sweet. He obviously hasn't seen them, plus rich people can like all the tacky shit they want and people think they're starting a new trend.

'The tree. It's so beautiful!'

Nate smiles indulgently at me. 'Yes, baby, it is real pretty isn't it? But not the prettiest thing in the house, that's you.'

'Who decorated it?' I ask. 'It must have taken ages.'

'Oh, my mother has someone come in and do it. Bitsy, well she takes Christmas real serious. Least it's coloured this year. Last year she had it done all white, and I think she had it blue one year. Daddy didn't like it, so we're back to colour. It's more traditional. There's a smaller one in the dining room.' He indicates an open door.

I am dying to get a good look around before the horde arrives, as it were, so I go in. Yet another spacious room, several more paintings, of course – one of the Hoppers is in here, a Rauschenberg, and another version of Nate on one of the walls. A long mahogany table almost the length of the

117

room is laid to perfection. Twelve places are set, the distances between place settings precise. Three crystal glasses in ascending size sparkle at each place, and each beautifully starched, white linen napkin is embroidered with a discreet little Christmas tree on the corner. An impressive row of silver cutlery gleams. I am glad the nuns have drummed into us the 'work from the outside in' rule. And then, the only touch of frivolity, an enormous cracker placed at each setting. Shit! I am starting to feel just a bit unsettled now. Who will be coming, and when?

Not one member of the Gilmore clan has shown up yet. Where the hell is everyone? I want to get this over with. After all, I am the 'object on view' today and Zollie hasn't exactly made me feel relaxed about meeting this lot.

'Isn't there anyone at home?' I venture. 'The place is so quiet.'

'No, baby, they all went to church. They should be back any time soon.'

Cora bustles back in. 'Let me get y'all something to drink. Y'all go cosy up by the fire in the library, get yoursels warm. It's real cold out.'

She returns in minutes with two eggnogs sprinkled with nutmeg, and we take them and settle luxuriously into a large comfy sofa beside the huge log fire. The logs are about six feet long and the fireplace is enormous. I snuggle up to Nate and let him stroke my hair and nuzzle my ears. He begins to fill me in on just who I will be meeting: three sisters, all older than him, two husbands, and three grandbabies, his grandmother Gilmore, known as Mimi, and her sister, his aunt Belle. Quite a clan. I hope I'll fit in, and not find it too intimidating. I'd have preferred Nate to myself for Christmas though. He is truly gorgeous. I snuggle closer to him, I feel cosy and in love. No one I know at home has a house like this, it is so perfect. There is something very seductive about the comfort and ease of this vast wealth. I could get used to this much luxury in no time at all. I wish the Lennon clan could see me now.

There is a crunch of tyres in the snow outside. They are back. We hear the front door open so we untangle ourselves, get up and walk into the hall. Bitsy, Nate's mother, is first in the door. She has bright blue, glittering eyes, perfectly coiffed frosted-mink coloured hair and a wide, tense painted smile. She has smooth, well made up skin, but I can't quite decide on her age – she is oddly expressionless, sort of young-old looking, no wrinkles at all. In fact a few wrinkles might loosen her up. She is tall and exceedingly thin. I know she and Nate's father have just returned from St Lucia, and she is tanned to perfection. I notice the diamond dazzlers on her fingers, it would be hard not to, and two the size of snowballs in her ears, quite masking her earlobes. Nathan Five, or Faave as the family calls him, pushes me forward with the alarming sentence 'Mama, I know y'all have been dying to get a look at Maggie, well here she is.' I think it a rather gauche introduction from such a cool guy, but Bitsy pauses and again smiles her wide, tense smile. I stand there being inspected while she shrugs off her coat to a waiting pair of hands (Cora's), and smoothes the front of her navy wool dress, which is hanging perfectly on her coat hanger body. There is not one single crease in it, and I wonder briefly if she has travelled in the car standing up. I am never to discover how she did this. She is the only person I ever met who can sit in *linen* and not crease it. Maybe the car has a built-in steamer, or she has.

We remain standing in the hall as she eyes me up and

down, air kisses somewhere about a foot above my left shoulder and, touching my cardigan, says semi-approvingly, 'Cashmere'. The 'eer' lingers. I find it a constant source of fascination, this ability some Southern women have that allows them to drawl the last breath of a word out, making it sound sexy or disapproving or whatever they happen to feel at the time. Bitsy obviously approves of the cash*meeer*.

'Why, how do you do, Maggie?' she exclaims. 'We are so privileged to have you join us for dinnah. Nathan has told us so much about you.' She then turns abruptly from me, hugs her only son, and plants a bright red kiss on his cheek. She strokes his sweater. 'I just love blue on you, honey,' she says approvingly. 'Doesn't it suit him, Maggie? He looks adorable. You need a hayer cut though,' she adds. 'You look like a hippie.'

She glides into the library and we follow, as other members of the family enter from outside, kicking snow from their shoes and making little squeaks at being back indoors. Bitsy had had no snow clinging to her shoes of course. Maybe she walks an inch above the ground as well, she is light enough. I am familiar with her story, thanks to Zollie. Bitsy Lee Shames is a former Miss Tennessee, who married Nathan Gilmore IV for his money, and to her eternal regret had fallen deeply in love with him. Every fibre of her being suggests this patent adoration. I soon come to realise that it makes everyone else in the room feel slightly superfluous and uncomfortable, and Nathan, her husband, perpetually irritated. It is hard being in their company. Her eyes rarely leave him, yet she manages with little furtive darting movements to take in every little detail of everything else going on around her while still gazing adoringly into his bored face. From the moment I first meet her I only see about three expressions on her face, and two of these are undying adoration for Nathan and for Nate. I guess the other is indifference.

Once Bitsy has checked that the room is up to scratch she then excuses herself profusely while she checks on 'the progress of our dinnah'. Nathan, who has been standing behind her smiling quietly, visibly relaxes and shakes hands warmly with me. No air kisses for him. I have obviously read the word patrician before, but rarely use it. Nathan Gilmore the fourth is the embodiment of it, and Nate is a clone. This is what he'll look like in thirty years, I think, still handsome as hell. Perhaps it is the familiarity of his looks, but I am instantly relaxed in his presence.

'Well ma'am,' he says with a broad smile on his face. 'I believe you are Irish?'

'Yes, from Northern Ireland.'

'My family originate from there.'

'Oh, do they? Gilmore is quite a common name in Northern Ireland. My cousin is married to someone called Gilmore.'

'Is that right? Well, maybe we are kin. We might have some relations in common.' He gestures towards my glass of egg nog. 'Nate, take that away.'

Nate obediently takes it from me. I had been struggling with it anyway.

'Now,' Nathan says, steering me to the seat by the fire, 'let's get you a real drink. I sure as hell need one after listening to that lil' creepin' Jesus rant on about charity at Christmas for ovah an hour.' He pauses. 'I know all he wants is more of my money. I say charity begins at home, right, Maggie? Now, what's your poison?'

Nate interrupts. 'Maggie just drinks wine or beer, Daddy.'

'Wine? Beer? Nonsense, Nate, she'll have plenty of wine

121

with dinner. Let's get her a real drink. Now, Miss Maggie, what about some Jack Daniels with ice? Or a bourbon?'

I nod. Either. He pours me a Jack Daniels. It looks roughly about a half-pint. I sip it. It is smoky, sharp, like whisky. I am not sure if I like the taste.

'Good,' he says 'now you come with me.' He guides me gently out the door. 'I'd like to introduce you to all my girls, and my little grandbabies.'

None of them have yet appeared in the library though I had heard people go upstairs, no doubt to ready themselves. Just as well, one at a time introductions are fine by me. Nate's three sisters, the Gilmore girls, Beth Anne, Eveline, and Priscilla, are really friendly too. Priscilla in particular, who is just two years older than Nate, treats me like her new best friend, promises me we'll meet without Nate and do 'girlie things', whatever they are. I agree of course. I would have agreed to most things after the Jack Daniels Nathan Four has poured me. I gulp it in record time and am flying.

Jeb and Cameron, the two husbands, are polite, rich, Southern boys. I have met a few of them before now. These two are clean-shaven, tall, dark-haired, with symmetrical features and, of course, the obligatory even white teeth. One of them is maybe a little bit tubbier than the other, but on first meeting, they are confusingly alike. Maybe they have a template for Gilmore husbands. They are wearing button-down shirts under smart patterned sweaters with little alligator logos, chinos, and loafers. They laugh respectfully at Nathan Four's jokes and flirt mildly with Bitsy before drinks, and more pronouncedly after a few. She appears to thrive on this and twinkles shamelessly to the 'boyahs' – she pronounces it as if it had three syllables.

122

The children are cute too, three little girls and a boy. Christopher joins the grown-ups for dinner for the first time. He is seven. The girls are paraded in a haze of expensive red and green velvet outfits with various appliquéd Christmas motifs, and after various cooing noises have been made they are whisked off by Cora to get dinner in the kitchen. Cora seems to fall into the role of nanny pretty quickly. I wonder, does she live here permanently? She'd need to. She doesn't stop throughout dinner. There doesn't appear to be any other help, though there might well be two dozen slaves tied up in the kitchen for all I know.

Before dinner we have the present giving and they give me wonderfully generous presents: suede driving gloves, a silk scarf, which actually matches my cash*meeer* sweater, a leather-bound diary and, best of all, Nate gives me a watch. I don't have one so I am really pleased. It is a nice one too, and looks real gold, with a snakeskin strap and a little blue stone in the winder. He tells me he just loves his cuff links, and the Waterford rosebud vase I have brought for his mother seems to meet with her approval. Finally we all assemble and go into dinner. I am seated beside Nathan and Mimi.

The meal is just splendid, and of course the drink continues its job on me as well. It is flowing freely and, fuelled by it, I have my predictable bout of verbal diarrhoea. A captive audience listen enthralled as I answer all their misconceived questions about Northern Ireland. The entire family are agog with the idea that I have escaped from the 'War' in Ireland and are delighted I can have a peaceful Christmas courtesy of them, so it would be churlish of me to dissuade them of this fact. After all, what harm is it doing? It makes them feel like the March family, taking in poor war orphans

123

for Christmas. During dinner they all listen, apparently fascinated, as I tell them all about my family, and with amusement when I tell them about my job. A visit to the loo and a little pop of Zollie's 'present' gives me a boost of false energy. Dinner passes in a whirl of food and drink and general goodwill. I finally begin to relax. Zollie has put the fear of God into me, but they all seem determined to put me at ease. Nate is at his charming best. His granny and Aunt Belle are two classy Southern ladies straight out of Eudora Welty who seem impressed by the fact I have 'foah sistahs'. 'There were faave of us girls too and it is such fun to grow up like that,' Mimi confides in me. I feel we have bonded. She leaves me in no doubt that as long as I stand by Nate I'll be fine with her. She gazes at him fondly.

'Nate here is the dearest boy imaginable, any gal is lucky to have him, and why, he just loves his old Mimi.'

'We all do, Mimi, we just love you to bits,' Priscilla nods enthusiastically.

'Why, I do believe he needs a waafe, and to settle down soon, he's too pretty by fah foh a man,' Aunt Belle chirps.

Mimi snaps at Belle instantly. 'He's not pretty, Belle, he's plain handsome, entirely different thing.'

Nate, half hearing from his part of the table, calls to me, 'Don't you heed them, Maggie, whatever they're saying.'

'We are merely remarking that Maggie here would make you a real darling wife.' Belle is not to be silenced. Bitsy raises her eyebrow but says nothing. I change the subject.

It is well after midnight when Nate and I leave and drive back to the lake. We do some more coke, listen to music and fall into bed. Life is good. Nate is adorable. I am in love and happy. I finally open Zollie's surprise present. It is two Quaaludes with a note saying 'Just in case y'all want

124

to sleep'. We each take one. I am still a bit bowled over by the extent of my drug taking, but the Quaalude does its job. I am soon sleepy. I have survived my first Christmas away from home.

12

I go into work grudgingly the next day. Christmas is over fast in America – in Ireland by this time they are just getting the feel for it. They take the 'Twelve Days' seriously there. The station has a worn out, after-Christmas feel to it. The decorations already look jaded and tired. Bilbo isn't in the best of form. His brief excursion to Alabama has left him deflated. His mom was in mourning for Elvis and was in black from head to toe, and all the Christmas wreaths were tied with black ribbons. Since Elvis's death in August she has been behaving strangely, and has been in consultation with a medium to help her connect with 'The King' even though, Bilbo tells me with a look of despair, she doesn't really believe Elvis is dead. I find this intriguing. Mamie from Mamie's Modes doesn't think Elvis is dead either.

Apparently Bilbo's mum spent most of Christmas day playing 'Crying in the Chapel'. Bilbo shows me his Christmas present from her. It is a perfectly ghastly white polyester jump suit with gold braid trim, similar to Elvis's Las Vegas costume. It has the name 'Bill' monogrammed on the pockets. He hates the name Bill more than he hates the costume. I guess Bill makes him feel ordinary – Bilbo is his alter ego, his more exotic self. He says his weaselly brother, Lee, had been there too, and he got one with 'Lee' on it, but he didn't seem to care. His mind is on other things. Bilbo says he is full of delight that the SKI ALABAMA venture is going so well.

Sue Lynne is back at work too, at her desk with her head down. She has the grace to look shamefaced when she asks how my Christmas has been, a look that quickly turns to a scowl when I show her my watch. One thing that cheers me up is the fact that Tom from Shine Records has been on the phone about 'Dogs in the Moonlight', which is number one and looks like it is going to go platinum. Tom is absolutely delighted. He tells me Rolly Young sounds like the cat that got the cream. There is also a message from two of the trades asking for interviews with me. I am chuffed to bits. 'Mull of Kintyre' is number one in Ireland, my sister Sinead told me when I talked to them all on Christmas morning. She has sent me a copy for Christmas. It is the fastest-selling single of all time, though not in America. They hate it. Zollie hates it, but it is, after all, Paul McCartney and Wings, so he only protests mildly when I add it to the playlist. I play it a couple of times and am surprised to get a few calls from irate listeners complaining about the bagpipes.

Bilbo takes a call from some eejit of a guy who claims the sound of the bagpipes has sent his dog 'right clean into some sort of fit'. Allegedly it is foaming at the mouth. Bilbo worries all morning after taking the call, but Zollie's hunch is that the dog had probably eaten the guy's dope and he is looking for an excuse to sue the station if the dog dies. So Zollie calls him back and tells him the station's lawyer and a photographer would be along to take statements from witnesses. We will play the record at two o'clock sharp, directly after the news, especially for the dog, and observe the dog's behaviour at close range. He doesn't suggest the guy change stations because he never wants to lose a listener. Anyway, the guy suddenly changes his tune. Says it doesn't matter, go right ahead and play the record as much as we like, on second thoughts he hates the crazy goddamm mutt anyway. Maybe if it foams at the mouth again he can get the thing put down for free. Zollie is pleased his ploy worked. He promises to send the guy a free Q92 T-shirt. He confides in me that he thinks the guy has actually invented the dog, there was no tell-tale barking in the background, for example, but the call indicates an unhealthy attitude towards the song so we cut down the rotation of 'Mull of Kintyre' and eventually take it off the playlist.

I have talked of going to Aspen with Nate towards the end of March even though it will have to be unpaid leave – I haven't exactly worked long enough to get a holiday – and before I met Nate I was vaguely thinking at the back of my mind that when I did, I would be going home to Ireland. Little fits of homesickness have been hitting me a bit when I least expect them, and the idea of spending New Year as well as Christmas in Tennessee is a bit much. I won't even have Nate's loving embrace since he is spending New Year in Aspen with some college friends. It had been arranged long before we met. He hasn't invited me, which hurts my feelings a bit even though I know I can't go. I hate the idea of being away from him for a week. I hope he'll be faithful to me and several times am on the point of asking him that when I manage to bite my tongue. I feel instinctively that Nate wouldn't like me to be clingy.

Sharla has said she might come down to visit me from school, but that is dependent on her current squeeze. He is coming on hot and cold and she is keen on him and doesn't want to just abandon him, not till she has him firmly in her grasp. I understand this, after all I had forgone the pleasure of Christmas with her for love of Nate, so I can hardly complain. The prospect of dinner with Annie Mae and Zollie is cheering and I have decided to accept their invitation to spend the night, so I am going to drive with Zollie. I have no car anyway, since it is still in the body shop, and this morning I had to come in with Nate. Zollie is going to run us past our apartment block so I can pick up my presents for them.

'Well, Maggie, don't you just love Christmas in America?' Zollie is grinning widely as he steers the Cruzer up the I-24. I don't answer at first as I am tired and hungry and just a wee bit sad. I still can't believe we had to work today. I want to be at home in Ireland tucking into the big box of Quality Street we get from our Auntie Martha every year, and fighting with my sisters for stealing all the purple melty caramel ones with the nut inside. We always just sit around the house on Boxing Day watching naff things on TV, eating leftovers and opening any unclaimed presents.

'I miss home,' I say, 'it's weird being away at Christmas.'

'My home is your home, Maggie, my momma is just thrilled we're having a homesick lil' Irish girl to eat with us, she has been cooking up a storm.' I can't help smiling at his enthusiasm. 'And you can bet your ass you'll have you a better time than at ole Nathan and Bitsy Gilmore's.' He pauses. 'How was that? Y'all like my presents?'

'Yes,' I say wishing I had a little pop now to brighten me up actually. I hope they like my presents. They are in my bag. There are to be four of us for dinner as Bilbo is joining us.

Zollie's brother Sam and his family have gone back to Arkansas already.

We make it safely through the snow and I notice several of the houses on the way have the most fantastical Christmas decorations: huge, lavish light displays, more like something you'd expect to see in a department store than on a normal house. Each house seems to be vying with the next one for displaying the most lights. I can't make up my mind whether it is ghastly or jolly, or jolly ghastly. Annie Mae has outdoor lights on the trees and the house is sort of edged in fairy lights, which makes it seem very welcoming. The minute we go in the door she is clucking round me and hugging me, taking my coat and telling me to cosy right up to the fire. Zollie hugs and kisses her and she pretends to swat him off. The house is snug and warm and smelling blissfully of food. Zollie 'fixes' us both a drink, and Annie Mae doesn't drink liquor so she is having ginger cordial, 'On account of his pappy, lord rest him, being just a touch too fond of it'. She nods towards Zollie and exits to the kitchen again. Seconds later she bustles back in.

'Here you go, Maggie,' she says, 'take those cold boots off and get your feet into these.'

She hands me a toasty pair of knitted socks and I oblige. I am starting to thaw and I suddenly feel at home. I am happy. We will eat dinner as soon as Bilbo arrives, if he can tear himself away from the station. Annie Mae scolds Zollie when Bilbo doesn't appear by six-thirty.

'You work that poor boy too hard; he needs to get him a life.'

Zollie protests. 'He loves to work, Momma.'

'Yes, but he needs to eat as well.'

Zollie rolls his eyes at me; we both know that this is not

130

one of Bilbo's problems. Annie Mae is also fretting that I am not warm enough on account of Jimmy Carter asking everyone to keep their thermostats at sixty-eight degrees. She offers me an Afghan, which I discover is a crocheted woollen blanket. I don't need it. It is stifling in this little house.

Finally Bilbo arrives, puffing and panting. Annie Mae claps her hands in delight, he has brought her two large poinsettias. She already has four, but obviously more is better. Bilbo refuses a drink, he is just ready for dinner, and now that he's here we move quickly into the dining room to begin the feast. The table is dominated by a simply enormous ham. It is criss-crossed with honey and cloves, and there is also a plate of sliced turkey from yesterday, sweet potato puffs, which I have never tasted before, and endless vegetables and muffins. We heap our plates and begin. I think at first that we are going to have iced tea with it, but that is just for Annie Mae and Bilbo, Zollie has come prepared. He has brought some Cabernet Sauvignon for us.

'Here you go, Maggie, this is real fine Californian wine,' and he pours me an enormous glass. I know that there will be pie so I try to go easy, but the boys seem to be competing to see who can pile in the most. We have crackers and hats and our napkins are rolled in little knitted Santas, and I have brought my camera so I can take some photos to send home. I didn't dare do that yesterday, somehow I don't think the Gilmores would have liked it. When I feel as if my stomach will burst from eating, we sit by the fire and swap presents. I have bought Zollie some Celtic design cufflinks from an Irish shop in Atlanta, but for Annie Mae I have an Aran sweater knitted and sent by my Aunt Martha. She is thrilled with it and thankfully it fits her.

Zollie insists on calling Maybellyne and singing 'Maybellyne

131

why can't you be good', and we have a great chat – she has lost more weight and counting the days with the pounds. Then Annie Mae and Zollie extract every single detail about yesterday out of me and I tell all, wondering at the end of it if Nate is the guy for me, but he'll do for now. By the time I curl up in the little guest room under the patchwork quilt I feel I have had a real Christmas.

Over the next few days, I have to contend with SKI ALABAMA. Our first major giveaway is coming up fast. Work on the resort is almost complete and the first lot of prize-winners are due to go the weekend after next, the first after New Year. We have agreed before Christmas that Bilbo will organise the weekend. After all, slimy Lee is his brother, and surely family loyalty will ensure the whole thing isn't a fuck up. Zollie has been banging on to Bilbo about it non-stop.

'This has got to work, Buddy!' Zollie declares as we have our coffee back at the station. 'Our reputation will be made on this giveaway. You better believe it.'

Bilbo shifts uneasily and assures Zollie that he will do his very best. I feel sorry for Bilbo, the prize-winners are becoming a pain in the ass, calling a few times a day to check about accommodation, ski passes, meals and even what the weather will be like. But sorry as I feel for Bilbo, I still wish I hadn't agreed to go along for the weekend. It is a moronic idea, one of my worst decisions. It is all because I have acquired a new ski suit. Bilbo and I were in the studio cutting yet another commercial for a local ski shop when Zollie comes in looking excited and waving a large bag with the legend 'Southern Skiers' on the side.

'Maggie, honey, you have got yourself the ski outfit of a lifetime. It is real real classy and drop dead sexy. I was just in the door of the store and I spotted it and thought it would be real perfect on you. Here it is, all two hundred dollars' worth.'

He pulls open the bag and takes out a grey, red, and black ski suit. Right enough it is really gorgeous, but I don't exactly need it just yet. I have decided I am not going to Alabama. However, I appraise the suit. It is my size.

'Try it on, Maggie, you'll look real good in it, I promise you.'

'If I take it will I still get paid this week?' Trade-outs are a curse when they come instead of wages, and they are a favourite ploy of Zollie's when the cash dries up, which it does, frequently. Zollie does his totally aghast look.

'Maggie, honey, why you know I wouldn't do that to you.'

Yeah right, I think, but I take the suit from him, go into the loo and squeeze into it. It feels good.

'Hell, honey, that looks real purdy on you,' Zollie says as I emerge from the bathroom. Bilbo nods enthusiastically.

'How much is it?' I am not exactly well off.

'Well, it costs two hundred, but to you, Maggie, just half that. Special discount – the owner just loves your voice in the ad, says you sound real sexy. I told him you were Swiss.' Zollie beams, delighted with himself.

'Swiss? Swiss? Why on earth did you do that?'

'Well, think about it, Maggie, I told him that on account of the Swiss being so into skiing and used to snow, I told him we try to find the right nationality for every spot we cut. He really likes that attention to detail. Says that's why he is going to keep running commercials with us.'

'Great! I expect you'll want me to yodel in the next one!'

Zollie cackles loudly. 'Maybe, Maggie, maybe so. I'll suggest that. Now are you having the suit or aren't you?'

'I don't know. It's still a lot of money.'

'Well then,' says Zollie, 'maybe Sue Lynne would like to have it.'

At this point, emboldened by the fact that the spotlight has moved on to her, Sue Lynne begins to simper at Zollie. I haven't exactly been too friendly to her since the Christmas Eve crash, and she hasn't been doing her usual 'available slut' acting around Zollie – she is trying to stay in with me in case I sue Clarence, which I intend to do if his insurance doesn't pay for a new car for me. She forgets herself for a minute though, momentarily blinded by her own vanity.

'Why, I do believe those are my colours,' she says, smiling sickeningly at Zollie. 'And maybe closer to ma siaaze,' she simpers again. 'The red would pick out the haaalaaghts in ma hayer.'

'How can *you* afford it?' I snap, wanting to smack her hard in the mouth.

'Well,' she drawls, 'I do have some Christmas money from ma daddy. Maybe you can go get you a cheaper one in the sales, Maggie.'

She smiles at me, a trifle too triumphantly I think. Suddenly I want it. 'No, forget it. I'll just take it,' I say. 'I am going to Aspen later this year and I'll need one then, possibly two.'

'Way to go, Maggie. You get you two suits. Get you three even. You're gonna be a skiing mother. This here is the first of many. Yes ma'am!'

Zollie cackles again loudly. Yes, he is fired up, he loves these sorts of scenes. He thrives on them. Poor Bilbo, on the other hand, has slunk off to stand at the door and fan himself in case his nerves get the better of him and he needs a spray of deodorant. Sue Lynne scowls and goes back to her filing, and

I suddenly have a ski suit and only the vaguest prospects of a ski trip ahead.

I like the idea of owning a ski suit – I feel it adds a new dimension to my personality, and it gives me access to a hobby I have only dreamed of having. I like the feeling more than that of being a car owner – that is commonplace. All Americans own cars, not all Americans ski. I have joined the elite. Or so I think at the time. Before I am properly initiated in Aspen, there is the prospect of a weekend's skiing in the alpine state of Alabama.

About an hour after I get the suit Bilbo asks me plaintively, 'Maggie, honey, why don't you come to Alabama? I'd sure appreciate it, and you have you a ski suit now. Lee will rent you some skis, free of charge, and I would sure appreciate your company. Please? Pretty Please?'

I give in and agree to go. Bilbo is touchingly thrilled. Perhaps I do need a break from Nate as I have seen him every day since Christmas. I am besotted with him and I could look at him all day long. He is so handsome, such good fun and so perfect that part of me is constantly afraid he'll evaporate, disappear, and all those letters home to my sisters about the perfect man with money and movie star good looks will turn into some ephemera I have conjured up to stave off my homesickness, for the truth is that when I am with him I have few thoughts of home. I am in a perpetual state of arousal. On the other hand, when I am alone I have time to dwell on the distance between here and Belfast. And it can be painful. My mother was so upset about my missing Christmas and the girls said it wasn't the same without me. Daddy only said, gruffly, 'I don't know what in God's name you're doing out there playing records anyway, when you could be building up your teaching pension,' which, translated, means he misses me too. I am torn. Politically things are at a stalemate at home, and drab grey Irish winters hold no appeal.

Tennessee looks wonderful right now. The snow is lying white and cool on the ground, the trees laden with it, the stalactite-like icicles hanging from the side of the mountain roads are set off to perfection by a bright blue sky and crisp cold air. No, I have little need for the relentless damp cold of a Belfast winter.

13

The SKI ALABAMA weekend has run into a spot of bother. First of all the long range weather forecast predicts a thaw. It comes through on the machine we use to get our news. I break the bad tidings to Bilbo and he gets on the phone to Lee straight away. I am in the habit of reading news head-lines and weather at the top of the hour – we aren't quite flush enough to get a network news bulletin or, like some of the competition have, our own dedicated newsreader. About a half minute after I have finished the news, Zollie is on the phone. He sounds quite deranged. I tell him to hang on and line up 'Hey Jude', which I know will give me seven and a half minutes to try to talk him down.

'What's wrong, Zollie?'

'What's wrong? What's WRONG? Godammit, Maggie, did you *hear* that weather report?'

'Of course I did, I just read it.'

'Precisely, and you should not have done that. No ma'am,

Maggie, you should NOT HAVE DONE THAT TODAY OF ALL DAYS!'

'Why on earth not? It's accurate. It came down the wire.'

'Because, Maggie, that is dangerous information, we don't need to give it out over the aayer when our prize-winners are listening.'

'But Lee told us he had a contingency plan, a snow machine.'

'Yep, he did, but when it snowed, he decided not to get it.'

'Not to get it?'

'Precisely, Maggie. You heard me right.'

'But how can he run a ski resort in Alabama without one? It hardly ever snows this far south.' I know this because all I have heard since it snowed before Christmas is that it never snows this far south and that the last ice storm they had was legendary.

'Well, they cost a lot, and use a lot of water, and he figured since there was so much snow he'd be better putting the money into the Alpine Lodge until it was a going concern.' Zollie pauses.

'He's crazy!'

Zollie sounds sheepish. 'It was my idea, Maggie, I thought the lodge could be a bit smarter, more Swiss-like, it looked real tacky before. Oh hell, Maggie. Listen here, forgit that last report, just read last week's weather report on the next bulletin and let me talk to Bilbo.'

Poor Bilbo, he has been listening to my half of the conversation anyway and is a sickly green colour. I hand him the phone and rummage till I find last week's weather. It predicts further freezing and more snow. Oh well, at least the competition winners will be happy, even if all the other listeners end up totally confused. I certainly am. Do all radio stations

138

in America do things like this? I couldn't imagine the BBC behaving this way.

Despite all our hopes and wishes to the contrary, the weather forecast as usual proves correct. By the end of the week the thaw has begun. The stalactites slowly turn to puddles, patches of wet appear in all the fields of snow, and the roads are clear. There is little doubt that one hundred miles further south in Alabama it's a similar story. We are about to cut our losses and offer alternative prizes (which Zollie is frantically trying to trade) when Bilbo comes in and tells us that Lee has hired two snow machines and that Alpine Peaks is thickly carpeted with the false snow. We are saved. Hallelujah!

The dreaded Saturday morning arrives, unfortunately. As planned, Nate leaves for Aspen. The weather for Colorado predicts several feet of snow. They are going to have blizzards and snowstorms, mounds of the stuff. We are predicted a high of forty-seven degrees. It isn't fair.

Nate flies out on the Gilmore jet on Friday afternoon. We have spent the night before in a torrent of passion and I am hoping the glow will last all week. He tells me several times he loves me and promises to call. I have managed to go the whole week without uttering one clingy word and am proud of myself. The next morning, Bilbo, Zollie and I drive to SKI ALABAMA, followed by forty-eight prize-winners. We are two short because Miz Zillah Knightly and her eighty-one-year-old sister Beulah have finally seen the wisdom of Zollie's advice (not to mention the obvious change in the weather), and have settled after all for a complete new wardrobe from Mamie's Modes and a new hairstyle from Herman. They are deliriously happy, and lucky! We have left Sue Lynne and a weekend guy called Bonzo in charge of the station. I think Zollie traded him out from central casting, but apparently he's a great engineer. It is a two-hour drive. Zollie is in manic form, elated one minute and extolling the virtues of snow machines, and down in the dumps the next predicting all kinds of horrors in store for us if the weekend is a disaster and, to quote him, 'we lose our goddamm asses'. Every few minutes he quizzes Bilbo about Lee.

'Well, Bilbo, you think your brother can pull it off? Or is he gonna make us look like fools! Can we trust him?'

'Gee, Zollie, I don't rightly know. He's done real good up until now, don't forgit his ass is on the line as well.'

This is hard talk indeed from poor old Bilbo. He is obviously under severe stress. He is getting redder and redder and tugging at his underarms. My heart goes out to him.

'Leave him alone, Zollie, it was all your bloody idea.'

'I'm telling you, Maggie, we'll be looking for another licence if this fails.'

'It'll be fine. Sure, hasn't he two stupid snow machines?'

'I hope they ain't *stupid* machines, Maggie, they got a lot of snow to produce.'

He is certainly right there, the sun is burning my arm through the window as he speaks. We are zooming down the I-24. The temperature outside the American National Bank had read forty-four degrees as we left Chattanooga. Zollie saw it, but at the time he didn't say a word. Bilbo and I had exchanged looks of desperation.

The ski lodge is hard to miss. Lee has fifty-foot-high posters every ten yards from the Interstate exit to the location. All of them show snow-laden slopes with happy skiers and depictions of mountains roughly on the scale of the Himalayas. SKI ALABAMA, they proclaim in large letters and several exclamation marks!!!!!!!!!!!!!!! Spend your days on the slopes!!!!!!!!!!!!!!!!!!!!!!! AND your après ski moments at

ALPINE PEAKS!!!!!!!!!!!!!!!!!!!!!!! Alabama's answer to the SWISS ALPES!!!!!!!!!!!!!!!!!!!!!!!!!!!!!! No, I haven't made it up, it is spelled that way.

The lodge itself looks fine, suitably faux Swiss, apart from the inflatable fifty-foot-high Santa and sleigh anchored precariously on the top. Though there isn't a peak in sight, I wonder briefly does Alabama even have any mountains. Still I don't suppose he could call it Alpine Humps, doesn't have quite the same ring to it.

It is eleven when we check in. I am already in my ski suit and feeling uncomfortably warm. The prize-winners too are mostly checked in and there is an orientation talk at noon followed by a free eggnog promotion. Lee meets us at the door with the reassuring words that the machines are operating at full throttle and the slopes are looking good. We relax somewhat, trying not to remember that tomorrow's high is predicted at 48 degrees.

We fix our grins, helped by a small toke to settle our nerves, and get ready to meet the 'fifty luckiest listeners in the whole of Tennessee' (well, forty-eight as I have already explained, but we haven't corrected the ad). Ten minutes later we enter the fray. The lobby is a riot of would-be skiers, and Lee is dashing to and fro like a little tornado handing out eggnogs. He is wearing a pair of lederhosen and a pointed hat, and he looks utterly preposterous. He seems unaware of this, and indeed maybe I am just a sour bitch because some of the prize-winners tell him he looks real cute, like a proper Swiss gentleman. He has tried to get Bilbo to don lederhosen too, but Bilbo has his principles and refuses. There are four waitresses charging about in short little Swiss maid outfits of red and green, smiling brightly and telling everyone they all are real, real happy to welcome everyone to Alpine Peaks. All have their hair braided, and they look like cocktail waitresses from a mildly seedy nightclub as they hand out the drinks. Sue Lynne would fit in perfectly. After tasting one of the proffered eggnogs, which are being served from a large glass bowl in the lobby, Zollie vanishes, only to reappear minutes later with a huge flagon of liquor which he proceeds to empty into the bowl. Bilbo looks at me and rolls his eyes. The fun is just beginning.

It is time to hit the slopes. I have never skied, therefore I see nothing too unusual about the ski lift that consists of a cable with little t-bars which you either grab with your hand or hook your ski pole on to. You are then dragged up a slope covered in snow, rather slushy snow, and patchy, but snow nonetheless. There are no cable cars and no chair lifts. A procession of people line up in their gear to get to the top of the only hill. Most of them have never skied before either and that is fortunate. Many of them are wearing denim and sweaters, and several people have discarded their jackets since by now the sun is shining brightly and the drink has kicked in.

Bilbo, dressed in denims and a bright yellow ski jacket with matching bobble hat, is taking tickets at the bottom. A guy in a dirty white jump suit with *De Wayne* woven above the left hand pocket is hooking people on to the t-bar as it passes at about forty miles an hour. Every second person misses it and is hurled to the side, but De Wayne ignores them and concentrates on catching the next hook by hand. I am not taking any chances. I place my poles firmly under my left arm and lunge for it, grab it, and I am yanked so hard I think my arm has been dislocated. I have no feeling in my right hand, just a numb tingling sensation but, clinging on like grim death, I make it to the top and am promptly flung sideways on to my arse. I right myself and take a deep breath.

There are two signs, *Beginners – Green runs only*, and *Experienced skiers – Black runs only*. This is all very well, but the second arrow points the same way as the first. It is like something out of *Alice Through the Looking Glass*.

I launch myself downhill gingerly. Skiers are passing me at varying speeds, most of them totally out of control. Some of them are roaring loud Rebel Yells. I reach the bottom in one piece in time to see a guy fly past me at about ninety and go splat! He zooms straight past the bales of hay at the bottom (the crash barrier) and falls into a pool of melted snow. From the pandemonium going on about me it's evident he isn't the first to do this.

Total chaos reigns for the entire afternoon. As the sun warms things up relentlessly, Lee cranks up the snow machines, and at one point a virtual avalanche of machine snow is shooting over the heads of the skiers on top of the hill. Some alpine peak this is, it is really a humpy field as far as I can make out. Several of the skiers have serious co-ordination problems due to the alcohol content of the complimentary eggnog. Most of them belong to the 'last to the bottom is stinking' school of skiing, and even though the number of hay bales at the bottom have been increased, several people still land splat in the mud, or go headlong into the 'Swiss Souvenir' stand which is to the left of the crash barrier. The best buy of the day is a cuckoo clock with SKI ALABAMA painted on it and a rebel flag decal above the door where the bird comes out. This appealing touch is Zollie's idea. Unfortunately I told him it was a traditional Swiss souvenir, but they are selling like crazy.

De Wayne is covered in mud from head to foot but he doesn't seem to mind, he is grinning broadly and still hooking people absentmindedly onto the ski lift. He is probably on some class of drug that anaesthetises him. Luckily there are no broken limbs – another by-product of the alcohol level no doubt. There is one dubious moment when one of the skiers, overcome by the exuberance of the experience, hurls his ski pole in the air as he hits the hay bales. He really should consider a career as a javelin thrower, because it sails over the roof of the motel and bursts the fifty-foot blow-up Santa and sleigh on the top. The loud bang causes yet more pandemonium on the 'slope', but fortunately several people take it as a signal that the day's skiing has come to an end. The light is starting to go anyway, and people peel off looking like a pack of hippos after a mud bath, to prepare for the 'Ski Hoedown with guest Yodellers'.

I prepare myself for the barrage of complaints. Surprisingly we only have one or two, and these Zollie and Lee deal with skilfully. Free albums are promised and a good meal, and allegedly after the Swiss yodellers (from Birmingham, Alabama), there is to be a well-known country and western singer making a surprise visit. I hear Willie Nelson mentioned. Even I like Willie. We finish quite an appetising supper of hamburgers with Swiss cheese and Swiss fries and settle down for the entertainment.

The yodellers are execrable, and they look truly comical in their lederhosen and alpine hats, but they get a standing ovation; I think perhaps Americans have a highly developed sense of irony after all. I start to relax and am looking forward to the mystery guest. Zollie has refused to tell Bilbo and me who it is. Suddenly, I hear the immortal line 'Let your love pour down on me like maple syrup'. It is my good samaritan, Buford, aka Big Boy McConnell. The crowd go through the roof. Gosh, I think, he must be popular.

Buford McConnell isn't bad actually. He puts on a tight

show. We all feel enormously grateful to him, because he certainly saves our bacon. Although Q92 is strictly 'Balls to the wall rock 'n' roll' and NOT country and western, many of our listeners can't shake the old c&w out of their blood, and they respond to it with yells and whoops and hollers. The room rocks. Buford makes a good attempt at what we call crossover. He's brought a couple of the session musicians with him and they are dynamite. It is great fun – we have a little bit of polypharmacology to brighten us up even more though. Zollie seems temporarily to have forgotten his 'only organic' pledge, but I figure we need it, we are emotional wrecks.

Buford does a few Van Morrison covers and sings the blues as well, and he even does a tribute to The King, and finishes with a rather impressive rendition of 'Your Cheatin' Heart'. The audience love it and I even find myself singing along. The beer and liquor is flying, everyone seems to be wearing Q92 T-shirts and Zollie is working the room giving out mugs with the station's logo on and chatting up the crowd as only he can do.

It seems Buford had been in Muscle Shoals, Alabama, cutting a new record, and Zollie had found that out and booked him (after the doomed weather forecast). They've kept in touch since my Christmas Eve fiasco. He's rung once or twice to enquire about my health, which I think is thoughtful of him. Buford joins us after his set and I am instructed by Zollie to be 'real nice' to him because he has saved our asses. I oblige. I am so sweet I nearly make myself sick. Maple syrup has nothing on me. I am, I hope, sexless, nun-like, pure, and virginal, because although Buford Big Boy seems a decent enough sort, he is not remotely my type on account of the large gut, wispy beard, and general good ole boy demeanour, not to mention the series of crowns, one of them gold. Plus he is old, at least thirty-five, and looks it. And also I have my lovely, lovely Nate, skiing down real snow fifteen hundred miles away, and hopefully thinking of me. But I am very nice to Buford. I am a good-mannered girl, and besides, Zollie has pushed a lot of coke up my nose. This helps. I am even nice to Lee the ferret.

Sadly, Buford seems *very* interested in me, and I haven't the energy for a sparring match. At about eleven, despite the fact that Zollie's eyebrows are through the roof and his smile is fixed and rigid, I excuse myself and go to my room, where I lock the door very firmly and try to sleep. I can't sleep. At one-thirty I am still twitching. I call Bilbo in his room. I am scared now. I will never do drugs again. God is punishing me. God says NO. He must be from Ulster. Bilbo surprises me by suggesting further drug abuse, namely that I should immediately take one of the famous Quaaludes, so beloved and abused by Vance and Chance Prince, and my Christmas surprise from Zollie. Apparently it is a legal sleeping pill. He drops one by my room. Soon my limbs stop twitching and I fall asleep with a smile upon my face and dream blissfully of Nate. Not for long. At about three a.m. my phone rings. It is Zollie, who is obviously still laying out the white lines. He has Buford with him in his room, two down from mine, and a selection of musicians. They are in party mode. The background din is deafening.

'Goddammit, Maggie, you party pooper, whut the hell you doin' in bed?'

I groan, 'Zollie, please go away. I am fast asleep.'

'Well, we have lots of stuff to wake you baby.'

'No,' I say, 'let me take a rain check.'

Zollie starts. 'Maggie, goddammit, here I am with one of the finest—'

'Please, Zollie, I've got my period. I feel awful.'

That shuts him up immediately. Bilbo has told me that Sherilee the witch was a monster when she had her period. She used to beat Zollie with kitchen utensils of enormous proportions and several times had tried to run them both off the road to their deaths. One time she filled all the pockets of his three best suits with scrambled eggs. You only have to mention 'monthly' and Zollie starts to quake. The gambit works.

'You get you some beauty sleep, Maggie. Buford and I will join you for breakfast.'

Oh goody, I am reprieved. I snuggle up and drift away back to my dreams of pretty boy. I am so horny. I think I have several erotic dreams, before I get back to sleep. Perhaps I am getting the hang of the masturbation thing. Personally, I blame the Quaalude.

14

It takes me a couple of days to recover from the Alabama caper, but we are back at work on Monday morning, cutting commercials and spinning discs. I don't hear from Nate at all while he is in Colorado. I don't really expect to until about halfway through the week, then I find my heart stopping every time the phone rings, and a little pulse of expectation rising in me, until it is confirmed that IT WAS NOT NATE. By Thursday I am starting to feel wounded, gouged, ripped apart. I run though several excuses for his lack of contact in my head; there is no phone at the lodge; there are no phone booths in Aspen; there is a time difference of one, two hours?

He has rung home when I am at work.

He has rung work when I am at home.

He has met someone else.

He has someone there.

He has fallen down a crevasse.

He has forgotten I exist.

He doesn't love me any more.

Finally I phone his parents' house. Bitsy picks up the phone.

'Hello, Mrs Gilmore,' I stammer, 'it's Maggie.'

'Maggie? Ah'm sorry?'

'Yes, you know, Maggie, the Irish girl, I'm a friend of Nate's, I had Christmas dinner with you . . .' I trail off.

'Why of course, Maggie, how are you doin'?'

'Oh fine . . . Eh, I just wondered if there was a phone at your home in Aspen?'

'A phone in Aspen?' She echoes me.

'Yes, you see Nate has called me and I wasn't there', this could be true. *It is true,* 'so I thought I'd call him back, but I don't have the number.'

'The numbah?' Long pause.

Is there an echo in my head? 'Yes, the number of the phone in Aspen, if there is one?'

'Why, yes, I believe there is a phone. Howevah, I am not sure I recall the numbah off hand.' Longer pause. 'But,' she brightens, 'I am quite sure he will call you back if it is important.'

I am not important, I think bitterly. Not enough. 'Well thanks, I'm sorry to bother you, thanks again for Christmas.'

Another long pause. Is she still alive? 'Oh, well yes, we did enjoy meeting you so much at Christmas.'

'Yes, thank you very much. I had a wonderful time.'

'I am so glad.'

The conversation is finished. I hang up. I feel worse. I call Sharla for a long dissection of the possible reasons Nate hasn't called. My heart is sore. I want him. I want to see him. I want to hear his voice. I want to touch him. Oh God! I am obsessed. Nothing else breaks through. I have a calendar from Alpine Peaks, an eight by ten copy of an awful photo of Lee, and I stare at it fixedly while Sharla tries to reassure me. He will be back on Sunday night, I think. Only three days to go. How will I survive?

At work I am a zombie. Bilbo empathises. Cups of coffee appear, BLTs at lunchtime (Zollie has arranged a trade-out at Delroy's Diner, a nearby restaurant, and this is the only edible thing they do. Everything else is 'Fried or Smothered', including Delroy himself.) I feel smothered too. My heart has taken over my body, my whole being is receding. Every chance I get I play a love song. Paul Simon, Neil Young, James Taylor, slow Beatles. Zollie doesn't like this pining version of Maggie.

'Goddammit, Maggie, you still got your period? You oughta see someone.'

'I am fine,' I lie.

'Fine? You call this fine? You cain't hear yourself. Playing all that goddamm *dirge music*. You are dismal, honey, real dismal. I'd sure hate to see you in a badass mood if this is you being fine.'

'I just haven't been sleeping well. The bed is too hard.'

'Oh, you need me to trade you out a soft one?' Zollie pauses and eyes me up and down. I feel my soul is visible. There is a window in my heart. 'You wouldn't be lovesick, would you?'

'I don't know what you're talking about.'

'When does Nate get back?'

I try to sound vague, 'Saturday, I think.'

'Has he bin callin' you, honey?'

'He's only away a week,' I snap. 'Hardly any need for him to call!'

'But honey, your lil' heart is lonely, right?' Zollie breaks into song. 'I'm so lonesome I could cry.' Oddly enough the

150

words seem appropriate. Maybe country and western singers have a point.

I call Maybellyne in Florida that night and she has news for me. She has lost 50 pounds and has bought a truck. She is moving to Tennessee next week! I am overjoyed. I have really missed her. She listens patiently as I bore her to death about Nate, and go over the myriad possible reasons why he hasn't called me. She tells me men don't think about such things, so don't attach as much importance to it, but deep down I know this is significant, something is up. He mustn't love me. I replay all the moments of our last night in my head frame by frame to poor Maybellyne. She listens calmly, allows me to pour out my demented rantings. Eventually she excuses herself and hangs up. I go to bed and toss and turn. I am wretched. At eleven-thirty the phone rings. I grab it eagerly. It is Buford McConnell. I am not even gracious. 'How did you get my number?' I snarl. He apologises for calling so late. Then I instantly feel sorry I was rude and am now toe curlingly nice to him. I guess he has had a drink or two. He has rung for a chat and suggests we might have a meal some-time. I say maybe, just as friends of course. He tells me he knows I have a boyfriend and I am glad he knows I do. I sure as hell don't. I hang up and finally fall asleep.

I go into work the next Monday feeling ragged. However, one moment of sheer insanity that lifts me out of the gloom is the visit to the station of Miz Zillah and Miz Beulah. They have availed themselves of both the trade-outs in lieu of the ski trip. Zollie has picked them up in the 'Big Black Box' and promised them a tour of Q92. I am on the air when they arrive and I don't know whether to laugh or cry when they come in. In both cases their aging, wispy hair has been coaxed by Herman into Stevie Nicks perms, a sort of ripped out wool look. Miz Beulah, the elder of the two, though they look like twins, is wearing a hot pink trouser suit with sequined beading on the jacket. She has a fluffy lemon scarf tied round her neck which she tells me she had knitted for the ski trip. Miz Zillah is wearing a similar number in a lurid shade of tangerine, and perched on her head, atop the Stevie Nicks perm, is her lime green bobble hat.

'Don't we just look like the last of peatime!' Miz Zillah exclaims. It sounds about right, whatever it means. I think they look like opal fruits, but they are so sweet and so pleased to be at the station, they never stop smiling. It is hard not to smile back. They are both totally smitten with Zollie and have been across the way with him for smothered chicken in Delroy's Diner. I am introduced to them and they assure me they never miss my show. They are in rhapsodies over Herman. He has treated them with niacin. I hope briefly that is all. They love their hairstyles.

'Whaa, we have bin given a whole new lease of laafe,' they tell me in unison. It's hard to feel down in the dumps all the time. I forget about Nate for at least an hour. When I get off air I drive by his house, even though it is miles out of the way. I am by now a gibbering wreck and I have lost weight. Part of me is thrilled to have such classy hip bones and to have my jeans so loose, but the sane part of me knows I am moronic. I can't help it, I am a woman possessed.

The Porsche is outside. He is back. I feel faint. Should I go in? Maybe there is another woman with him. I drive out to Nickajack, to Annie Mae. She opens the door to a sobbing wretch. I blurt it all out to her. She listens without comment. Then she hugs me, goes into the kitchen and brings me some hot chocolate. I can barely swallow.

'Honey, you look like a lil' wisp, you need to eat some.

Now can I fix you dinner? I'd sure like the company,' she says. I nod, but I'm not very hungry.

A feast is laid out nonetheless, and I do my best. My appetite picks up. It is hard to resist Annie Mae's home cooking. Despite her pleas for me to spend the night, I drive home. As I go into the flat the phone is ringing. I have just missed the call, and though I wait, it doesn't ring again. Once more I go to bed with a heavy heart. I am wrung out. I don't call Sharla or Maybellyne. I still have a Quaalude that Bilbo has given me so I take it. It is only nine o'clock. I take the phone off the hook in case Sharla calls. In minutes, I am fast asleep, a numb, dreamless sleep.

Nate has been back for a week now and still no word. I have phoned his number and hung up several times. While it rings I rehearse the speech I am going to make when he picks up. The 'Well, I know it was all a bit fast and intense and maybe you're scared, but is that any reason to quit cold turkey?' speech. But the few times he picks up the phone my voice dies in my throat. I am constricted by a large lump of emotion, and I know that if I speak I will dislodge it and everything will pour out: the hurt, the pain, and worse, the tears. I didn't think I could cry this much, but I am a walking bundle of damp tissue.

Even Zollie starts to get sympathetic. 'You're hurtin', Maggie, ain't you?' he asks me one day after I have finished my show. I had tried like mad to sound 'up' but I expect he can see through it. 'Maggie, I told you, honey, those Gilmores are trouble. He is acting like a grade A asshole. Forget him and get yourself a nice boy. Rich people are spoiled and mean.'

I have no appetite, and I have begun to enjoy the little pop of coke Zollie gives me before I go on the air. It gives me a sort of false courage. It numbs my sinuses and numbs my brain. I am disquieted underneath, but I keep excusing myself to myself. It's just for now, till I get over Nate.

Then, unexpectedly, I meet him on my way to work. I stop by Hits For Less Records and there he is, in the flesh, in an aisle beside the 'B' records, 'B' for Beatles that is, although in his case it should be 'B' for Bastard. He looks tanned. He looks like he has eaten my heart and is feeding on it. I feel sick. We stare at each other. I recover first.

'Hello, how are you? Did you have a good ski trip?'

'Maggie, I was going to call you, I'm sorry, things have been kinda crazy since I got back, I guess I left things—'

I interrupt. 'It's okay, I was just surprised not to hear. If you don't want to go out with me that's fine, but I always thought we could at least have stayed friends . . .' I trail off. I am trembling, and I don't want to look weak in front of him. I want to kill him and hug him simultaneously.

'Could we maybe have coffee?' He indicates towards the mall.

'Yes, but not now. I'm on the air in thirty minutes.'

'Of course, well I guess I'll call you this evening. You home?'

'I'm not sure. You can always get me at the station.'

'I did call the station yesterday.'

'Oh?' I must sound sceptical.

'Yes, I talked to the girl, what's her name? Sue Lynne?'

The girl! The *bitch*! I feel like killing her. I will check as soon as I get there. We both start to leave.

'Sure, well I'll call you then, it's good to see you. I'll be in touch.'

Is it my imagination or does he look more miserable than I feel? In the parking lot I see the Porsche. I feel like ramming it as I drive past. I have gone over every possible reason for his lack of communication and exhausted every theory, and now I am mad as well as hurt and shamed. I go to work. Zollie isn't there. Sue Lynne is. I am a mad seething lunatic. Taking a deep breath I ask her as calmly as I can manage, 'Did Nate call looking for me yesterday?'

'What, I believe he did, you was gone.'

'Were gone!' I snap at her. 'Were gone.'

'Yes, you were.'

'Why didn't you give me the message?'

'I figured he'd git you at home?' She looks at me, sudden realisation flooding her stupid face. 'Wha Maggie, is everythin' okay?'

'Yes. Everything is fine, just fine.'

'Are you sure? I hope he's treatin' you good.' She manages to suggest she means exactly the opposite.

I go into the studio. Now the silly bitch knows something is up. A wave of tiredness washes over me. I go on air and I put on some upbeat stuff. Some Bee Gees, 'Staying Alive', but it's too impossibly cheerful. I play 'Running on Empty' by Jackson Browne. It fits my mood better. Maybe I will meet Jackson Browne and run off with him.

In our last late-night chat, Sharla diagnosed Nate as a commitment phobic. It's a new term in one of her textbooks. 'Hell, honey, he probably is scared just how much he cares, I guess he missed you so much it frightened him.' Yes, it is an interesting but completely unconsoling philosophy. He loves me so much he can't bear to be in touch, or spend time with me. Fucking great! Nate doesn't call that night, though I have been on the phone to both Sharla and Maybellyne for an awfully long time, so perhaps he has. I toy with the idea of calling him, but decide against it. I put some music on and write letters home. Then suddenly I can't wait until they get the letters so I phone them. I speak to all of my sisters in turn, and then Mammy comes on the phone and I am talking to her about the station and basically how wonderful everything is when she says, 'What's up? Are you missing us?'

She sounds so concerned that I burst into tears and tell her all about Nate.

'Look, love, no man is worth all that, anyway it sounds as if you're a wee bit out of your depth. All that money couldn't be good for anyone. Why don't you come home? You know your daddy and I were talking about you last night. He has a wee insurance policy which will pay out when he's fifty. That's next month. We'll send you the fare.'

'No, Mammy, honestly, don't worry. I promise I'll have enough saved to come home soon. Really, I'm okay.'

'It's far from okay you sound to me.'

'I am, I feel better now I've talked to you.'

'Sinead is thinking of coming out to see you.'

'When?'

'Soon I think, maybe over Easter, during her holidays.' Sinead has just started teaching. 'She has almost two weeks then, and sure, maybe you'll get home in the summer.'

I suddenly feel a lift of optimism, but then I remember that's when I was supposed to be going skiing. Well, there's not much chance of that happening now. There's only thirteen months between myself and Sinead so we are close.

'That's great news, Mammy, I can help her with her ticket and she doesn't need any money while she's here.'

'Well look after yourself, pet. I'll get your Auntie Martha to light a candle for you.'

My Auntie Martha's candles always work. She is a master candle lighter. On Tuesdays her house looks like Lourdes (Tuesday is St Martha's day). Several times she has had incidents with the candles and once nearly burned her house down. She also lights candles in churches all over Belfast. Touch of pyromania, I think, but of course I don't say this to my mother. I hang up feeling cheerier. Nate can go to hell. I don't need him. I soothe myself to sleep with this mantra. It doesn't work.

15

Next day Buford calls yet again and I agree to meet him for a beer; a reward, I suppose, for his persistence. He takes me to a trendy new restaurant/bar in the centre of town and offers to buy me dinner. I have no appetite, but I have a beer. We have an amiable time. I don't let him know that I am single again. I can barely let myself know. I talk too much, but he seems to like it.

'You are some woman,' he tells me as he gazes admiringly at me. I am unmoved by his obvious admiration. Why do we only want admiration from those we admire? He tells me he has been married three times. He is thirty-five but looks ancient. His face has a lived-in look to it, it looks as if someone has chewed it. I notice a few of the people in the bar looking over at him. I guess he is famous in a sort of way. I am unimpressed. He tells me that he lives mostly in Nashville, but is originally from near Chattanooga and that he is thinking of moving back here – to escape a few ex-wives, he jokes.

'Just like Zollie,' I say laughing; I don't mention the Colombian mafia. It would seem excessive. Anyhow, Zollie *is* more frightened of Sherilee the witch.

I promise him we will have a few beers again soon. He is kind and sweet, and I expect it can't do any harm and anyway, secretly in one half of my frazzled brain I am still fantasising about the great reunion with Nate, even though in the other half I am getting on with life alone. I reason that I may as well not get a proper boyfriend yet, just in case Nate and I get back together, but I am not admitting this out loud to myself, or to anyone. Well, maybe to Sharla. The one cheering thing is that Maybellyne is back, and she *has* lost weight, rather a lot in fact. Admittedly she still classifies as fat, but she is so cuddly and it is so good to see her. She is still on her special diet – all liquids, absolutely ghastly milkshake things which expand in your stomach and fill you up. We are all banned from bringing fries and burgers to the station, and Zollie hasn't included her in the Burger Barn trade-out. He does ask me, I think in all seriousness, if we should get her on the toot, on account of it being an appetite suppressant, but I have always been a bit coy about drug-taking in front of her, and I tell him he should be too. In fact, I am determined to stop. It seems to make me do all kinds of things I don't normally. I have not yet worked out if this is a good or bad thing.

Zollie has traded us out a meal at the upmarket restaurant Bistro. We are all going, Bilbo, Sue Lynne, and me, to celebrate Maybellyne's return. The one thing she can eat is a steak, one a week. She can have a steak and salad with no dressing, and she will have one glass of champagne since it is liquid. She can now fit in the Cruzer, which is handy, though she can't drive because her arms are too fat, or maybe her legs. I don't like to question her too closely about this.

The mood is up and there are no drugs on board. Then, disaster for me, Nate is in the restaurant with his sister Priscilla. I nod frigidly and go to our table, but Zollie goes into overdrive and stops to greet Nate like a long lost brother. Nate looks over at me in a funny way and I think I might cry, except Maybellyne is holding my hand tightly under the table and talking me down. I hardly taste the food, then finally before we order dessert I go to the bathroom. Priscilla follows.

'I have tried to call you,' she says, 'but your phone is constantly busy and I guess I haven't been persistent enough.'

'That's okay, it's nice to see you.' I feel like crying.

'Maggie, I know it's not my business, but Nate seems real unhappy to me. I don't know what has gone on between you but he has talked about you all evening, won't you come and say hello?'

'I don't think so.'

'Please, for me? I know he cares for you.'

'If he cares for me he would have called me when he got back from Aspen.'

'Oh?'

'Yes. Look, Priscilla, I appreciate your trying to help, but I didn't break up the relationship, Nate did.'

She looks embarrassed. 'I'm sorry for butting in. I thought y'all had just had a row.'

I go back to the table and as I sit down I catch Nate's eye. He looks miserable. I feel miserable. Zollie leaps up as soon as Priscilla comes back from the ladies.

'Hey, if y'all are done eatin',' he says to the Gilmores, 'why don't you join us?'

My protests are drowned out by the shuffling of chairs to make room, and within minutes Nate is beside me, despite Sue Lynne having moved to make a space beside her.

'We are gathered here,' Zollie declares solemnly to the assembled group, 'to welcome to Tennessee our wonderful Maybellyne all the way from the Sunshine State.' He gestures to the waiter. 'I think we need us some champagne, ain't that right Bilbo?'

Nate interrupts quickly. 'Let me get it, Zollie, I insist.'

A list is produced, Nate looks at it. Zollie relaxes and sits back smiling.

'Maggie here tells us she had her some very fine French champagne in Atlanta, what was it, Maggie? Don Periyawn?' He deliberately mispronounces both words. I nod dumbly.

Nate looks again at the list and grins. He knows what Zollie is up to, but he seems happy to go along with it. Priscilla nods her approval.

'Well,' Nate says to the waiter, 'looks like we'll have some of that. I think you'd better chill a second bottle. Lucky we are in about the only restaurant in town that serves it.'

Zollie beams, satisfied, I can read his mind: the Gilmores can afford it. Everyone relaxes after that and between the seven of us we have three bottles. The awkwardness between Nate and me evaporates with the bubbles in the champagne. He is a very charming and handsome man and Sue Lynne is practically salivating over him from the other side of the table. I find myself telling amusing stories about Ireland, and by the time we leave I have almost forgotten Nate is no longer my boyfriend, he has been so attentive all night.

I remember he isn't as soon as I arrive back at my apartment. The drink is dying in me and I feel desolate. I still want him, there is no getting away from it. I call Sharla. Her line

is busy so I call Maybellyne for her 'view'. She tries her best.

'Anyone can see he still loves you, honey, why don't you wait, see if he calls.' She sounds tired, and why not? She has had one small filet mignon, one glass of champagne and nothing else all day and it is now almost midnight. I find a Quaalude and go to bed.

I am dreaming, someone is calling my name, I am floating. I hear a noise, a loud crack and I wake up, startled. My chest is tight with fear, I am being burgled. Christ! I sit up in bed, fumble for the phone, but can't remember the American number for 999. I find the phone and call Bilbo as I know he has gone back into the station after the meal, he virtually lives there. I am deranged.

'Bilbo, oh Bilbo, oh God Bilbo! I am being burgled. He's out there now. Please, what will I do?'

'Call nine-one-one, Maggie, and keep your bedroom door locked. Just calm down now, I'll be right over.'

There's no lock on the bedroom door so I pull over a heavyish chair and wedge it against the handle. I dial 911, give my address and wait. I am terrified. People have guns here. The effects of the Quaalude are long gone and now I am wide awake, trembling. But very soon, almost immediately in fact, I hear the wah-wah sound, the police are here. The doorbell rings. A deep voice growls 'Police'.

I leave the bedroom, go to the front door and open it, very slowly, keeping the chain on. I should explain, my apartment is on the first floor, though Americans call it the second floor. The front door opens on to a veranda. A very large policeman is standing outside on the veranda.

'Ma'am, I believe you called us, you have a problem?'

'Yes, I heard someone at my door. I think they were trying to break in. You got here very quickly.'

'Yes ma'am, we sure did. Lucky we were just nearby at the 7-Eleven. I believe Officer Goodrich has apprehended someone down below in the parking lot.'

I look over the railings and down to the car park where another policeman is talking to someone in a car, which looks like a Porsche – it *is* a Porsche. Oh God, no, it can't be. It is freezing outside. I have no dressing gown so I throw a coat over my nightie and run down leaving the policeman standing at the door. It is Nate and he is showing his driving licence to the other policeman.

'Nate? Oh Nate! I thought you were a burglar.'

The policeman looks at me suspiciously. 'You know this guy?'

'Yes, yes, he's my boy—' I trail off, uncertain.

'Her boyfriend, officer,' Nate finishes for me. He lifts an eyebrow and looks at me quizzically.

The ice-water that has been coursing through my veins for almost a month starts to thaw. Suddenly I am fizzling with joy, just about to burst. Bilbo drives up then, and gets out of his truck, a sweating heap of worry, his face anxious.

'Hey, Maggie, you okay? Hey Nate, she call you too?'

The other policeman has come down. They are starting to realise it's all been a waste of their time. They are annoyed at first and then the radio crackles and I hear Officer Goodrich say, 'Yessir, yessir, I sure will.' He comes over and mutters to the other guy, and suddenly they start acting real sweet to us and saying we should go indoors as it was fixing to freeze.

'Next time, Mr Gilmore, you be sure and call the lady first.'

They drive off and I notice I am shivering. We all go in, but Bilbo refuses my offer of tea, coffee, drink of juice, anything. He needs to get back to the station. He leaves and Nate and I are alone. I can't think of anything to say.

'I sure am lucky the police knew who my daddy is. I figured I was gonna need him to post some bail bonds.'

'I'm sorry,' I say.

'No, Maggie, I'm sorry, I have behaved like an asshole.
I've missed you. I owe you an apology. I guess I just couldn't
cope, after Aspen I just left things . . .' He trails off. He
puts his arm around me and pulls me to him. 'Mmm,
Maggie, you are freezin', why don't we get you back into
bed.'

'Yes, but . . .'

'It's okay, I'll just sit and talk to you.'

I want him though. I just want him. I know I'm not doing
a good job of hiding it.

'How about I warm you up?' he says.

'We should talk first,' I say, shaking my head.

'Why don't we talk afterwards?'

His blue eyes regard me with what looks to me like love.
I nod. 'Okay then.'

He gets in beside me and I inhale his smell. I have certainly missed that. He always smells of fresh laundry and love,
and his skin is soft. I'd like to nuzzle the back of his neck
right now, but I lie there completely still, thawing out. He
snuggles up to me and murmurs, 'I couldn't settle down after
the restaurant, so I figured I'd drive over and burgle you. Oh
Maggie, I've missed you so much. I think I might have to
marry you.'

I say nothing but my heart is thumping and I am scared
and excited. I excuse it as the champagne talking. I think over
my weeks of hell. It doesn't matter now. He cups my face in
his hands and meets my gaze.

'Did you miss me even a little bit?'

'I missed you, just a bit.' I measure a little bit of space

between my index finger and thumb. 'I missed you this much,'
I tell him.

He laughs and pulls me back down on top of him. 'I don't
think I'm gonna let you outa my sight again, you hear?'

'Yes, I hear.' And that seems to be it.

16

I have a little niggle at the back of my head – am I letting
Nate off too lightly? He has told me that he had a bad case
of cold feet, he felt we were getting too serious too fast. Then,
about a week after his return from Aspen, he realised that
actually that was the way he wanted it, but he had let things
drift and felt afraid to call in case I told him to go away. He
seems sincere and we have spent every night together this
week in a state of intense passion. Our lovemaking is getting
better all the time. I bounce into work every morning and
Zollie can't believe my good mood.

'Looks like you're really getting yourself loved up, Maggie.'

I smile and say nothing. Sue Lynne scowls behind my back.
Her scowls are penetrating things. I loathe her. Clarence Lee's
insurance has paid up for my car, and she is madder than hell
because, as she whinges to Bilbo about every five minutes (when
she knows I can hear), his premium will rocket. Good, I think,
serves him right, the stupid bastard could have killed me.

On Sunday we have family lunch at the Gilmores again. They are so nice to me, and seem only delighted that Nate and I are together, not that anyone but Priscilla knew we weren't. This time it's just Mimi, Aunt Belle, Nathan, Bitsy and Priscilla. Nate is all over me and they are tickled when I describe SKI ALABAMA. They insist I must go to Aspen at Easter. I say my sister might be coming then and they extend the invitation. 'We are taking the plane, of course, and there will be room.' Aspen, and by private jet too. I am dying to phone Sinead and tell her.

The next few weeks pass in a haze of music and love-making. I am happy. Nate asks me to marry him about a hundred times. Priscilla takes me to lunch and tells me the family just love me to bits. 'My daddy just adores you,' Priscilla says, 'and I can't think of a nicer sister-in-law.' I am bowled over, so on Valentines Day when Nate asks me for the thousandth time, I say yes. The next week Nathan takes us all out to the Mountain City Club, which is ultra posh, and they toast our future. I am both thrilled and scared.

The following week, Nate asks me to come to Atlanta with him for the weekend. He would like me to meet a jeweller friend of his father's who will fix us up with an engagement ring. There is a selection of family ones, and I am to pick one and have it altered to fit me. We have been through the family 'dinnah' again, and lunch at the country club, and although I will never get totally used to it all I promise myself I will try. Bitsy is emotional at losing her 'baby boy', but Nathan is gruff and tells her it might make a man of him and he is lucky to get such a pretty and intelligent girl, so she is complying. I like his Dad, there's no nonsense about him. Bitsy makes me nervous but Nathan has charm and strength. I can't help noticing he doesn't seem totally relaxed with Nate. I can tell he likes it when I am there.

We haven't set a date for the wedding and I am not in any rush, I'm still a bit freaked out that I've agreed to get married. Anyway, the Gilmores do so much travelling, what with the Kentucky Derby, the Masters at Augusta and God knows what else, we will be lucky if they can manage to come to the wedding at all.

In Atlanta we stay in the Gilmore apartment off West Paces Ferry Road. It is bigger than most houses and they have a live-in help there as well, also black and lovely. She is called Esther. She cooks us a huge breakfast that I can barely eat I am so worked up about the ring. Nate seems relaxed. He makes lots of jokes about choosing the most expensive. I haven't told my family yet, I am waiting till tonight when the ring is on my finger. Sharla and Maybellyne know, and I am spitefully imagining the look on Sue Lynne's face when I walk in on Monday. We go to Saks in Phipps Plaza first and Nate insists on buying me some new clothes. I try on various things and, unlike Mamie's Modes, most of the clothes look good, so I end up with four new outfits. I feel like Pollyanna. We pass Tiffany's where I linger outside looking at rings in the window. There are no prices on any of them, but we are not getting the ring there anyway. Part of me wishes we were: *Breakfast at Tiffany's* is one of my favourite movies.

We go to the offices of the Gilmores' family solicitors. Mr Jackson is the senior partner and he greets Nate as if he were the Messiah. He is waiting for Mr Loew who is the family jeweller? We have coffee from china cups and some awful biscuits, then Mr Loew arrives, apologising profusely for being five minutes late. The men beam at me and at Nate, they both seem to think it is a very good idea that Nate is getting married. Mr Jackson opens a safe and brings out seven rings on a tray. I have to pick one. They all look as if they are worth a fortune, but they don't look like anything I would ever wear. They seem the sort of thing the Queen would wear, or even worse the Queen Mother. Although nearly all the stones are huge, the settings are all twiddly and old-looking. I wish one would just fit me, then like Cinderella I could rush off with my prince. But it's not to be. I try them all on in order, and then try them on again. I take ages. Nate senses my discomfort and says, 'Shoot, Maggie, let's just go back to Tiffany's and get you something you'd like.'

This does not go down well with Mr Jackson. He smiles ingratiatingly at me. I notice he has a rubbery mouth. 'With respect, Mr Nate, your father would specifically like the young lady, Maggie that is, to choose one of your great-grandmother's rings. You are the only male, it's a tradition.'

What can I do? I finally settle on a square cut emerald with a diamond each side. It is enormous. It is so big it looks like a fake. Mr Loew gets a little measure thing and I poke my finger in it and he makes calculations. He says he will drop the ring by the apartment in the morning. I feel curiously flat. Mr Jackson produces a pair of earrings to match it.

'I haven't any holes in my ears.'

'I'm sure that's easily remedied.'

For a moment I expect a person to jump out of another door, hold me down and bore holes in my ears. We say our goodbyes and leave. Everyone is smiling but me. When we get to the car Nate turns to me.

'Let's go back to Tiffany's. You can have two engagement rings. I want to buy you one myself.'

I am suddenly happy again. I just love him for

understanding, but I can't believe I am marrying someone this rich. It is terrifying. I pick a heart-shaped diamond in a very plain setting. It fits me perfectly, which means I was meant to have it. I can't stop looking at my finger.

After lunch, two engagement rings richer, we phone my parents. It is Saturday night; all the girls are out except my sister Maeve, who is a cheeky wee shite. I tell her Nate and I are engaged.

'I thought Sinead said he left you.'

'Well, he came back and we're getting married.'

'Can I be a bridesmaid?'

'Maybe, if you're nice. Can you get Mammy for me?'

My mother comes on the phone. She always sounds hesitant.

'Is everything all right?'

'I'm engaged, Mammy, to Nate.'

'Oh Maggie love, how could you get engaged to someone we've never met? I think you've lost the run of yourself entirely. You should come home. You could get a job teaching. I hear they're looking for people.'

'Mammy, Nate wants to talk to Daddy.'

We had agreed Nate would formally ask for my hand. I had tried to dissuade him, but he was adamant it is the Southern way. I am in a state of trepidation, Daddy hates talking on the phone. I wait till he comes to the phone.

'Well?' he says, 'what's wrong?'

'There's nothing wrong, Daddy, I've just got engaged to Nate, and he'd like to talk to you, I think he wants to ask your permission.'

'Sure, what's the point of that if you're already engaged?'

I hand the phone to Nate. I listen while Nate speaks to my father. He calls him Sir and although I only hear one side

170

I can tell that Daddy is actually being nice. Nate is saying things like 'Yessir', and 'I sure will', and finally he hands the phone back to me. It's my mother again. Mammy is rushing me off the phone; she's started to worry about the bill. I tell her it's okay, but I can't exactly say he's a millionaire in front of him so I give in and promise to write. I put down the phone.

'Well,' Nate says, 'looks like we're going to Ireland for the honeymoon.'

About a week after I am officially Nate's fiancée, Buford McConnell calls and asks me to dinner. Bolstered by my flashy engagement ring, I feel there is no harm in going. I call Nate and tell him I am having lunch with my Good Samaritan. He seems 'cool' (his word) with it. I meet Buford in town at the beer and burger place. When I walk in I see him sitting in the corner by a window with his hat on the table and his lank hair tied back in a meagre little ponytail. I think of Nate's thick chestnut hair and feel sorry for Buford. I go over and his face lights up when he sees me. I show him my ring and he congratulates me, but without enthusiasm. During the meal he seems quite dejected that I am engaged.

'How I wish I had met you sooner,' he tells me, 'and then nobody, not even rich old Nate Gilmore, would have gotten their hands on you.'

I laugh it off, but I can tell he is serious, I swear to God his eyes are moist. I tell him I am flattered and that I'm not really that big a catch. He almost chokes on his reply.

'You are a truly wonderful person, Maggie, a warm, lovely, exceptional human being.'

To my utter horror, he sings a line of the song 'You light up my life'. I hate that song so much, it makes me puke. It's

171

puerile shite. I have banned it from the playlist. Sue Lynne loves it, of course. I check quickly to see if anyone is watching. If they are, they have turned away quickly. I am trying not to laugh because he is making me feel quite hysterical and I can tell he means every word, or thinks he does.

'If ever things' – he says thangs – 'don't work out between y'all and Nate, I will marry you, Maggie. I would be real proud to spend my life bah your side.'

Oh shit, I think, please don't let him break into song again. I thank him profusely, but I tell him things are perfect right now, just perfect. Nate and I are in love. I reckon next time I see Buford I will at least smoke a joint first or get some kind of pill from Zollie. You would need to be on some form of drugs to be with him. He is hard to take straight. I am touched by his devotion though, and his seemingly true desire, despite his thwarted hopes, to remain friends with me. I can always use another friend; after all, I am a poor little Irish girl far from home.

It is going to be awkward going to Ireland and getting back into America unless I am already married. Something to do with the fact I will need a visa and I have overstayed on my J1. I am alarmed, but Nate seems thrilled. He is using this for a reason to get married sooner rather than later. I am unsure if I want to rush things. As long as I don't go home in the meantime it'll be okay. But it has been so long since I saw them all. After several phone calls home it is agreed my sister Sinead will definitely come here for a visit. She can give the family seal of approval. I would prefer Mammy to come, I miss her, and honestly she would be more fun than Sinead who is a bit on the serious side, but Mammy won't hear of it. She thinks it will be a great thing for Sinead. So Sinead will come in two weeks. I am paying half her fare, but I can only do this because since I have been going out with Nate I don't seem to spend any money. I have my car payment and my rent and utilities and that's it. I have been saving a bit and Nate wants me to move in and give up my apartment, but I don't want to do that, not yet. I am not there very much but I like having a place of my own. I have always shared a bedroom and here I have a whole flat to myself. I am expanding my record collection and I have even begun to get back catalogues of all my favourite groups and singers, everything from Atlanta Rhythm Section to ZZ Top. I love it. I have put them in special crates in alphabetical order and I get a real kick out of owning them. The record companies give me lots of giveaways since Abe Goodman gives me so much press and I have broken a few more records 'wide open'. They send me records early and ask for my opinion, and when I add the song it gets splashed over the trades. I have become a 'flavour', as Tom from Shine tells me, mainly 'cos I 'give good phone'.

Maureen and Patricia have both sent engagement cards and seem genuinely delighted I am to marry a millionaire. I expect our ones have told the entire neighbourhood. They are all just dying to meet him. Everyone would like to marry a millionaire, wouldn't they? The only thing about Sinead's visit that I don't like is that she is bound and determined that she doesn't want to spend one of the weeks in Aspen. She doesn't like the idea of skiing. I can't go off and leave her, but Nate promises me we have forever to ski and it will give me a chance to spend time with her. I feel somewhat cheated, but I suppose he is right. So Nate goes off to Aspen, he'll be back next week. I don't feel as threatened by his departure this time. There's Sinead's coming, plus I have my insurance policy in the form of my ring, well my two rings.

The night before Sinead arrives I go to an ELO concert

in Atlanta. It is a record do and the record company pay for the hotel, but Nate offers me the use of the Paces Ferry apartment. I am reluctant to stay there without him, but he insists, so I do. I can't understand why this annoys me a little, but it does. The concert is great, absolutely spectacular. The ELO rise up 'Out of the Blue' in a large trippy spaceship and the audience at the Omni goes berserk. Bob, another Shine record promotion man, had taken me and a few other radio people to dinner beforehand. We had partaken liberally of various polypharmacological substances. At one stage during the concert I think Jeff Lynne is levitating, or maybe it's me. Concerts are so much better in this altered state. Bob and a few radio hangers-on drop me off at the apartment, well the limo does. Bob is impressed with the location, he is dying to come in and have a snoop around, but I have calmed down now and Esther would be nosy, so I say I have to get to bed because my sister is arriving from Ireland tomorrow and I am meeting her at Atlanta airport. He immediately suggests he organise a limo for her. I think this is a brilliant idea. She will be impressed, I bet. We don't have limos in Belfast, except for funerals and weddings.

When I get back to the apartment at one a.m. the phone is ringing. It is Nate calling from Colorado to check I am back safely. I am still somewhat stoned so we have a very smoochy conversation. I am horny and wish he was here. Being horny is drug-related, I think. Next time I'm away I won't smoke any dope unless Nate is with me. Well I mightn't.

Next morning Esther makes me breakfast, about six dozen pancakes and bacon and eggs. I nearly get ill finishing it. We chat while I eat. She says she is so happy Nate is getting married, and to such a sweet girl. I don't feel too sweet, but I smile anyway.

174

'His Daddy was just real worried about him not finding the right gal.'

I am not sure why, he is not exactly over the hill. I'm sure people would be queuing up to marry him. Maybe they just want him to have a family, although I don't want kids just yet.

Esther tells me all about herself, she has had a sad life. Her only son has died from something called 'smilin' mighty Jesus', and her abusive husband has left her. Later, on the phone Nate tells me her son died from spinal meningitis. I suppose it sounds the same the way Esther says it and smilin' mighty Jesus is a happier sort of death, I think.

The Gilmores treat her real good, she tells me, although she implies rather than says that Bitsy can be difficult at times. That doesn't surprise me, although she hasn't been difficult to me. I do find myself puzzled from time to time at how quickly Bitsy and the whole family have accepted me. I am not rich and you would think they'd be looking for an heiress for Nate, but they don't need the money. I suppose I am a blank canvas of sorts. I don't fit the white trash definition, and no one here will ever find out too much about my family background. Maybe they've told all their friends I am Irish aristocracy, or arse-a-crockery as my Auntie Martha says. I dismiss the thought at once and concentrate on the next twenty-four hours. I want everything to go well for Sinead. Perhaps I am being too cynical? Maybe they just want Nate to be happy. I hope he will be. I do love him.

Sinead is arriving at lunchtime. Bob and I will pick her up in the limo and take her to a launch party for a new album from a hot group called Acid Drops, and then afterwards I will drive her to Tennessee. I can't believe she is arriving, it seems just yesterday since we discussed her trip. I am apprehensive. It is nearly a year since I last saw her, although she's been great at writing. Bob wants to pick me up in the limo, but I decide that I'd rather Esther didn't know all that was going on as she asks such a lot of questions, so I pack up the car, thank her profusely, and leave.

As I drive into town, my brain is teeming. I sort of assess what has happened to me since I last saw Sinead. A lot, really. I am driving my own car for a start, I have my own apartment, I am on the air, I am Music Director and, of course, I am Nate's fiancée. Fuck! It's scary. Bob Seger's 'Still the Same' is playing on the radio. Am I still the same?

I park my car at the hotel where the launch is to take place. Bob arrives in the limo to pick me up. He is smoking a joint and he is buzzing. He offers me some. I refuse; I have a drive to Tennessee ahead of me, not to mention picking up Sinead who misses nothing. Bob also has some toot, so he offers me that as well. I haven't had any for ages. I think what the hell and do a few lines. I am ready for Sinead. Bob is lying back in the limo, legs splayed. He is totally off his face and he is singing 'Born to Run'.

The limo drops us at the terminal and we go in and race to the gate. I am in turmoil, I hope Sinead will like it all. Does it matter? How could she not? Then suddenly she is here, looking ridiculously non-American and ill at ease in too warm clothes. I rush towards her. She is exhausted, hence exhausting; she was always a grumpy kid when she was tired. She is full of complaints about how long the flight was, how big the airport is, and how long she had to wait at immigration. I listen and smile and hug her, I can see through this, she is feeling overwhelmed. She suddenly collects herself and grabs my hand and oohs over my ring.

'God, Maggie, it's huge. It must have cost a fortune. It's gorgeous.'

We get her case. I introduce her to Bob, who has been waiting for me to get my hellos over, and we go outside to wait for the limo to pick us up. It is circling.

'Who on earth is he?' Sinead asks me when Bob is flagging it down.

'He's a friend, he works for a record company.'

'Where's Nate?'

'In Colorado, skiing. I told you. He'll be back on Friday. I thought you might like to meet Acid Drops, they're a really good group, from New York, a bit like Talking Heads.'

'Who are Talking Heads?' Sinead sounds puzzled.

'An American group, they're hot.'

'What do you mean, they're hot?'

'Never mind, I'll explain later.'

'Do you play The Clash?' she asks. 'The Jam? The Stranglers?'

'No, we don't play punk much. It's more a rock 'n' roll station.'

'Well, they don't exactly sing ballads.'

'The music is different here.'

'Not all of it.'

'I know, but punk just hasn't caught on, I suppose people like to be happy all the time, or romantically sad. They don't like to hear about anarchy and stuff. It's all love or broken hearts and flowers.'

Sinead has brought me the new Clash LP. 'I can't believe,' she says with some contempt, 'that you could be a DJ and not play The Clash. I can't wait to hear this radio station.'

Yes, she sounds as if she can't wait. The limo arrives and we get in. Despite herself, Sinead is impressed.

'Gosh,' she says, 'I've often wondered what these were like

inside.' She sinks back gratefully into the seat and then I realise what a bad idea it is to bring her to this do. Poor thing, she looks wrecked.

'You're tired, maybe we should just head home.'

'No way José,' Bob says. He takes out his little travelling coke kit. 'Why don't y'all just do a few lines.'

He proceeds to lay some out on a small mirror. I look towards the driver, but he has his eyes very firmly on the road. He's probably inured to this sort of thing anyway. Sinead follows my eye.

'Don't you think it's a bit rude to keep the window closed? He might think we're talking about him.'

'Hell no,' Bob says, 'he's probably sick of listening to all the bullshit.'

Sinead is staring now at the cocaine. Bob has pulled a little tray out of the seat and has his mirror placed there. Sinead seems mesmerised.

'What *is* this?' she asks Bob archly.

'It's toot.'

'Is that a drug?'

'Yes, it sure is.'

'Is it not illegal?'

'I guess.'

Sinead turns to me. 'I hope you haven't been doing any of this, Maggie,' she says.

I shrug. 'Occasionally,' I say. 'Everybody does.'

'Well, I don't want to try it. I'd be frightened something would happen to me. I mean,' she continues, with a stern expression on her face, 'are you not afraid you might jump out of the car when you're on it?'

Bob rolls his eyes at this, but says nothing, and then snorts two lines hastily as we curve round a corner. He doesn't offer

178

me any and we change the subject. He is trying to persuade us to spend the night in Atlanta and go to the concert at the Fox, but I can see that Sinead is not in the mood so when we get to the hotel I say I will pop in for a short time and then Sinead and I will head off. Bob offers us a room in case Sinead wants a shower. I guess it was a bad idea trying to impress Sinead. I have been here too long and have forgotten that people at home are normal. I have grown too used to crazies.

Sinead showers and we go in to meet the group, but maybe because it's a daytime bash, it doesn't seem any fun, although the drummer latches on to Sinead and spends most of the time telling her how the rivalry between the two lead singers depresses him and how he's the only true talent in the group. She tells me this later, adding that the lead singer had asked her if she wanted to 'suck a stick'.

'What did you tell him?' I ask, feeling slightly panicky.

'I said *certainly not*,' and she looks at me with her eyebrow raised. 'I suppose that's another drug.'

I say nothing. The explanation would upset her. I'm just bloody glad he was so out of it that he was slurring his words, though Sinead wouldn't have heard of dicks anyway; everyone in Ireland has willies.

'That drummer,' she says, once we are on the road, 'he's very friendly, but he was obviously getting a cold, his nose was running and his eyes were red.'

I decide not to explain that either, it will only make her paranoid. I change the subject. Sinead loves my car, and she likes what I am wearing, jeans and a silk shirt. We fall into our old, comfortable, easy chat. I tell her all about going to the lawyer's office and getting the 'family' ring, and all the little details about Nate that it is hard to fit in on the brief phone calls or even the rambling letters. She asks endless questions and gives me all the craic from home. My other sisters are dead jealous that they didn't get to come with her, so Sinead is already worrying about what she will buy them and if her money will last.

'Look, you don't need money. You can spend all you've brought on presents.'

'How can I? I can't stay with you for two weeks and let you pay for everything.'

'Sinead, you *can*, Nate is a millionaire; he won't let me pay for anything.'

'I hope that's not why you're marrying him.' Finally, on the home straight, she falls asleep. I turn the station to a classical one and drive carefully. I feel protective of my big sister. I can't wait for her to meet Nate.

We arrive at my apartment and find about ten buckets full of flowers outside the door and a large piece of cardboard with 'Welcome Sinead'. At first I think Nate must have lost it, but the note says *Please call Zollie at the station.* I might have known it was something to do with him. It turns out Zollie has fixed a trade-out with a florist who is moving premises. There is some mix-up and they got three times their daily delivery so Zollie took all the flowers in lieu of advertising. I try to explain this to Sinead, I'm not sure I make much sense, but she is touched at the welcome, overwhelmed in fact. We bring them indoors and arrange them as best we can. I have only one vase, so we have to leave most of them in the buckets. When we finish the place looks like a funeral parlour.

Next day, after a good night's sleep and a meal at home, the 'grand tour' begins. Everyone is so hospitable and friendly to her. She meets and adores Annie Mae, and thinks Zollie is a hoot. Bilbo and Maybellyne are both given the seal of approval and she even makes valiant attempts with Sue Lynne. I decide a visit to Herman's Hair Haven is a must, so we drive off to Racoon Mountain. She leaves with streaks, or 'sun-kissed highlights' as Herman prefers. She suits it. She passes on the perm, even though she likes mine. All the Lennon girls have straight hair. When we were small my mother spent hours coaxing our hair into ringlets. Every Saturday night we were all lined up for bed with foam curlers in, only for the precious ringlets to fall out on the way back from mass if it rained, which it did, a lot.

Sharla comes down for Sinead's first weekend. Sinead takes to Sharla immediately, of course, everyone does, although she has some trouble understanding Sharla's east Tennessee twang as I once did. I increasingly feel like a tour guide, though everyone pitches in, and she has a selection of drivers and guides.

On the Saturday, Nate comes back. We are a bit awkward with each other at first, but Sinead appears to adore him. On Sunday he gives a party for her and invites the 'gang' and Priscilla. After some persuasion she has her first 'go' in a hot tub. We forgo the obligatory joint in her honour, and we are all wearing swimsuits, of course. I hope fervently that she is generally having a ball. I am exhausted with all the goings on. Back at work on Monday I come off my shift to find Zollie waiting.

'You know, Maggie, I sure do like Miss Shin-aid, but don't you think she needs to lighten up just a little itty bitty?'

'What do you mean?'

'Well, she's so serious, and she's just on holiday from a god-damm war zone, don't you think she needs to have her some fun?'

'She is having fun.' But unfortunately I do see his point. I am in manic entertainer mode and she has remained throughout somewhat unrelaxed. 'Listen, Zollie, I've been doing my best to entertain her considering I *am* on the air every day,' I explode at him.

'Hell, Maggie, just think about it. All she's done since she got here is eaten her some food, and visited some dumbass tourist things. She hasn't had any FUN. I am talking *real* fun, some *sex'n'drugs'n'rock'n'roll*.' He has started to say it as one word. He is losing it.

'She doesn't do drugs.'

'Hell, she needs to, Maggie, believe me, honey. She is one tense young girl. How old is she?'

'Twenty-three.'

'Is that all? She acts like she is thirty.'

'That's not true,' I protest, but he does have a point. 'I guess she is pretty straight. I never did drugs till I moved here. People aren't drug fiends in Ireland.'

'Hell, they oughta try some, it might cheer 'em up, then they wouldn't need to bomb the fuck outa each other.'

Zollie isn't too informed about the Irish question. He seems to think it's a bit like the Wild West. I guess he has a point. He pauses mid-rant and beams at me. I can almost see the light going on in his head.

'What now?' I say crossly.

'Never mind, you leave this to me.'

Next day, Zollie asks Nate, Sinead, myself, Bilbo and Priscilla out to the Steak House. Poor Maybellyne refuses. She's doing so well with her diet she can't place herself in an occasion of sin. She thinks the steak fries there are 'to die for'. Although I sympathise, I wish she could come. She has been wonderful at showing Sinead round while I am on air, and Sinead seems to have really hit it off with her, and why wouldn't she? She has made Maybellyne promise that when she reaches her target weight she will start saving for a trip to Ireland. Maybellyne has always wanted to go there. Her great great grandparents were from Wexford. She has confided in me her touching but surreal notion of Ireland, one where the South is green and pleasant, full of leprechauns, pots of gold and cosy pubs teeming with fiddlers and happy people drinking Guinness. But, on the other hand, the bit where I hail from, the top right hand corner of the country, she believes to be teeming with murderers, bombers and bigots. Actually, she might have a point there. She often asks me things like why we don't all escape 'down South'. She is worried I might go back and come to a bad end. I think I'm managing that here, actually.

Zollie says he will pick us up in the Cruzer so that we can relax and drink more. Priscilla is pleased to be included. She is my new best friend and is trying to assimilate me into the family. I can tell by the smell of the van that Zollie has had a joint, and as soon as we're on the road he cranks up the radio, lights another, and offers it to Nate and me. I still can't really smoke, and I feel self-conscious in front of Sinead, but I take a puff and Nate does too. Sinead refuses, though the smell is so strong she must be getting stoned anyway. Suddenly there is a loud bang like a gunshot. Everyone screams, except Zollie who starts to cackle like a madman. He has burst a large balloon filled with nitrous oxide, laughing gas. He has been to the dentist today – he probably traded it out, or robbed it. Within minutes we are all shaking and laughing uncontrollably. I am crying with laughter and feeling very out of control. Sinead is a bit dazed but is cackling away. I think I am about to burst a blood vessel. Nate is bright red and crying. None of us are in any condition to get mad at Zollie. He stops the car for what seems like an age and allows us to laugh it off, and fortunately it wears off quite quickly.

Finally our laughter subsides and we calm down. We are all somewhat confused. I am weak from laughing. I feel as if I have been tickled mercilessly, this is all I can compare it to, and I need to go to the bathroom soon, very soon. I may have wet the seat. I am glad it is not my car.

'What time is it?' I ask, thinking of Priscilla waiting at the restaurant.

Zollie pauses dramatically and grins at me. 'Early summer, baby, early summer.'

It is a demented thing for him to have done but it has certainly lightened Sinead up, probably killed off millions of her brain cells in the process. I expect her to be furious and start giving out to us all, but she doesn't say a word, just sits there smiling like an idiot, and when we get to the Steak House she is the liveliest I have seen her in years. It would not be an understatement to say she has fun, even if she does flirt with Nate all evening.

The rest of Sinead's visit just flies past. We are getting to know each other again. As far as possible she is having a good time. She thinks Nate is wonderful and she is just as gobsmacked as I am with all the trappings of wealth. We have been up to the big house, since Priscilla insisted on cooking dinner for us one night, and Sinead can't believe the paintings. She writes down all the names and titles. She finds a Kandinsky on the upstairs landing and is thrilled by it. I wish Nathan had been here for her, he would have loved to natter on about his art collection. Before they went on holiday he had just bought another Rothko, but it hasn't been hung yet.

Before Sinead is due to leave we decide to have dinner

alone and talk about the wedding. It looks like Nate and I will get married in September, mainly because I would like us to go home for Christmas. It'll mean an awful lot of planning, but I'll have plenty of help. Priscilla has a sort of job in the family business – it isn't too demanding and she seems to have appointed herself as the wedding organiser. I am pleased, I can't be doing with lists and all that shit. She and Sinead have had loads of chats about it this past week. I hope I'm allowed to voice my opinion, or at least pick the dress, or maybe the lawyer has a load of old wedding dresses in another closet.

A few days later I help Sinead to pack. Her case is awful, so Zollie has got her a new one from Lenny's Luggage – I had to cut the commercial. She is delighted; it's a Samsonite, red plastic, and huge, just as well since she seems to have bought a present for everyone in Ireland. We talk a lot about Nate while she is packing. Sinead thinks it is a flaw in me that I am so impressed by looks. I can't help it though. She says she can't understand why I think it is so important that Nate is handsome, as long as he is a nice person. But I get pleasure from looking at him. He's tall, that makes me feel secure – I am small, or short, as they say here. I love the limpid blue of his eyes, and the whiteness of his teeth, and the way he dimples on one of his cheeks when he laughs. I don't think there's anything wrong with that. Sinead can marry some ugly bastard if she wants, I am certainly not going to. Sinead looks at me earnestly.

'You do love Nate, don't you, Maggie?'

'Of course, why are you asking?'

'No reason, just that you both seem very unpassionate.'

'Unpassionate? I'm not sure if that's a word.'

185

'You know what I mean, you're sort of calm when you're with him.'

'Isn't that good? That's how you know you want to marry someone.'

'Really?' She sounds unconvinced. I am not sure I like this conversation. I do want to marry Nate. I think back to the painful time without him, I think about the nuzzly bit at the back of his neck, I think of kissing him. He is such a good kisser. He has a melty mouth.

'I couldn't imagine life without him.'

'Good, Maggie, I hope he'll make you a good husband.' She pauses. 'Are you going to have babies?'

'Of course, but not till I'm about thirty.'

'Oh?'

'What do you mean, oh?'

'Just something Priscilla said about her daddy hoping you two will start a family right away,' and she adds, 'are you leaving work?'

'Why would I leave work?'

'Well, you'll hardly need the money.'

'It's got nothing to do with money, I love my job, it's great fun, and I get to travel.' I tell her about all the rock concerts I've been to, and about the record conventions I will be going to. She appears unimpressed.

'Won't Nate be jealous of you going off to things like that?'

'How do you know what they're like?'

'I don't, but that launch party, I mean I know I was jet-lagged, but apart from Dave the drummer, they all seemed so . . .' She searches for the word, 'sordid.'

My heart sinks at her answer, but what did I expect? I thought they were fun, and the bloody party was dull compared to some rock parties. She hadn't liked Bob, probably

186

because of the cocaine. She thought he was relentlessly repulsive.

'Well, I am not quitting my job, and that's it.'

'You should talk to Nate about it.'

'Maybe I will.'

I don't like this conversation. We finish our dinner and talk about home. Safer territory. Much safer.

17

I am utterly lost after Sinead leaves, and have a bad bout of homesickness. Nate tries to cheer me up by taking me to Atlanta for the weekend, where we have lots of stoned sex, which is consoling. We are getting good at it, the sex, yes we are definitely improving. I have discovered that you can sort of train men up to do what you enjoy by making the right sounds, sort of reinforcement grunts, and then next time you work on another bit. The cumulative effect is great fun.

Miz Beulah has crocheted me a bright pink bobble hat. It looks like a tea cosy. I wear it on the air and thank her. There is no way in hell I would wear it out, I'd get sectioned. She and Miz Zillah listen to my show every day, and have really got into Bob Seger, and a new group called Tom Petty and the Heartbreakers. Every Friday they come out to Delroy's Diner and have the smothered chicken, which they declare is as good as their own. Bilbo usually joins them and then they have the weekly tour of the station. Herman is still doing their hair. I expect he'll have them on the weed next, nothing surprises me any more.

Out of the blue, the Goodman Report call and ask me to appear on one of the women programmers panels at a record convention in Seattle as someone has dropped out. They are obviously desperate for people – there aren't too many of us women DJs. It is one of the smaller meetings. They will pay my fare and I will be there from Friday until Sunday night. I am unsure about going, but it would be good to see what these things are like, and for me to get to meet some of the record people I talk to several times a week. I have met the local guys at some of the rock concerts in Atlanta, but I speak to people from all over the country, and of course I have never been to Seattle. I ask Nate what he thinks and to my surprise he says I should go. He had been thinking of snatching another weekend's skiing, the last of the season, and there won't be much snow on the lower slopes so he is going to powder ski by helicopter. It sounds very impressive. He will be back Monday, same as me, so I call Goodman and agree. It's exciting.

Sue Lynne informs me that Buford has dropped by the station to leave some tickets for his next show. He gave her two. She thinks he is wonderful, so does ghastly Clarence Lee. They never miss a show. I hope we are not sitting beside them.

'I just love his voice,' she tells me with a sycophantic grin on her face. 'And my Lord! Have you heard his Elvis Tribute? It makes me cry my heart out.'

If you have one, I think, but I smile anyway and thank her for taking them for me. I have promised Buford we will go to hear him next time he is in town. I genuinely liked his show at the ski weekend in Alabama, even allowing for the gratitude we all felt at him saving our asses, but it isn't really my type of music.

While I'm away, Zollie is to split my shift with Steve, our new morning man. I leave for Seattle on the Thursday morning. It is quite far away and I have to change planes in Atlanta. I finally get there and check in, feeling somewhat awkward. It shouldn't be too intimidating as this is not one of the big ones, and I am only here because I am on a panel.

Record conventions are sheer babble. The noise level rarely drops, especially in the lobby. I am issued with my badge and I put it on, *Maggie Lennon Q92*, and I blithely launch myself into the middle of the sea of faces. There are lots of thin smiling people who appear to know each other really well, though I suspect they really don't. I watch as people exclaim, hug each other in an unrealistic, over the top way, and give high fives and repeatedly ask each other 'Whenjageddin? Whennyaleavin?'

Several people look pointedly at my badge and ask me 'Which Q92?' I say 'Chattanooga, Tennessee,' and they say things like 'Not with that accent', or they mimic my voice. They are relentlessly friendly. Several of them seem to have heard of me. I guess Abe's tip sheet has quite a following. I wander about saying hello here and there, and before long I feel as if I have heard of all of them as well. They like my accent, they like that I'm a woman, but they seem confident and forward so it takes me a while to relax.

Rolly Young is here briefly. He looks like I expected a record guy to look – golden and confident. I run into him in the CBS suite and he acknowledges me with, 'Hey, the single is nearly platinum, way to go, babe!'

I am unsure what this means but I smile anyway.

'I'll be in touch. Before LA.'

Before LA? What's happening in LA? But he's gone before I can ask. Then there are meetings, and various forums on Arbitron ratings and demographics, which is all about finding out precisely who listens to your station so you can boost your ratings and make more money. Me, I think it should all be about the music.

I am sitting in one of these meetings, watching a panel of big-name jocks talk about their station and how they came to dominate the market, wondering vaguely if indeed it might all be, as we would put it in Belfast, a load of wank, when I hear the woman next to me mutter under her breath, 'Assholes, every last one of them'.

I turn around and she grins at me. I notice her teeth are very white. She has thick, black curly hair, freckles, and she wears little round granny glasses which make her blue eyes look huge. She is trim. She wears a T-shirt which says *Who do I fuck to get off this label?*. She grins at me again.

'Hey! I'm Lindy Konnig, I work for . . .' She mentions a well known VP of promotion. I introduce myself.

'Wow! I've heard of you, you broke "Dogs in the Moonlight" right under Rolly's nose job, didn't you? Boy, did you make him look like a dumb piece of shit.' She shrieks with laughter.

'I did? How?'

'You mean you don't know?'

'No, I don't. I thought it helped him. They told me last week it looks set to go platinum.' I toss the words out like I've always known what they meant. Lindy looks at me and laughs.

'You wanna get a sandwich?'

'Yes, I'd like that.'

We go to the lobby restaurant and order, and before I have finished lunch I have made a new friend and had my first real lesson on the business of rock 'n' roll from Lindy. I learn a lot. And she picks up the check. She insists.

'Always let the record person pick up the check.' She waves an American Express card at me. 'But never act grateful, it's a killer.'

I am grateful to Lindy though. I feel I know a bit more about what is 'coming down'. She is a New Yorker, a sharp, funny Jewish woman with a wicked sense of humour and a visible contempt for most of the men present. Rolly Young seems to feature high on her hit parade of assholes. I expect she is good at her job. We talk a lot about music and she says she will call me each week and send me stuff. She likes the idea that I listen to the songs before I add them and only add what I like. I am surprised that this is not the norm. Apparently some Music or Program Directors add what certain promotion men or 'Indies' tell them. She is amused when I describe Zollie and Bilbo and the station, and promises she will come in some time soon. She is so easy to talk to I tell her all about Nate. She is impressed but asks me my age. I tell her twenty-two and she says 'I guess that's okay for a first marriage.' I must look stricken because she immediately laughs and says 'Just kiddin', he sounds amazing.'

Seattle is a wonderful city; there is an amazing energy about it. Although we are mainly confined to the conference hotel, we do leave on the Saturday night to visit a wonderful fish restaurant. Bob has come and tries to 'hit on' me, twice, but in a sort of nice, affectionate way. I have just picked this expression up from Lindy. It means he fancies me. I am not interested though, well if I am even a little bit, I am not supposed to be, so I'm not. If I talk to a man for too long Lindy walks up and asks them if they have seen my *second best* engagement ring and sings 'Who wants to be a millionaire?'.

I quite enjoy the attention from the men, though I know it is because of my accent mainly.

The Women in Radio and Records panel is the last one on Saturday, and I think I do okay. There are bigger names and bigger egos than mine, so on the strength of my accent I get away with a few interjections. I am glad when it is over. And then it's back to the station, and to Nate of course. He tells me the skiing was great and he certainly looks tanned and healthy. I feel awkward though, vulnerable, because he seems to be in a funny kind of mood again, and almost pulls his photos out of my hand when I look at them. I think there might be some girl in them, but it's mainly Nate and a buddy of his called Tommy on the slopes. But he cheers up quickly, and in a few days it appears we are back to our routine.

I am giving up my apartment and moving in with Nate. I won't do this until the end of July because I have paid the rent until then. I suppose it's practical, but I know I will feel sad leaving it. I have enjoyed my short bout of independence.

The wedding is going to be an awful lot of fuss, I can't really believe how much. We have decided on September 20th. It is settled that it will be at the Country Club, and not the Gilmore house. This, unfortunately, is because they are inviting half of America. This is my list:

Sinead, Aileen, Anna and Maeve – my four sisters
Mammy and Daddy
Sheila – my cousin from Canada who has loads of money and wants to come
Annie Mae, Zollie, Maybellyne, Bilbo and Sharla
Connie and Angelina – my two ex flatmates from Johnson City
Lindy

And that's it. We shall be outnumbered by the Gilmores' guests by about twenty to one. I am beginning to panic. We are now in the habit of having Sunday lunch on the mountain and Bitsy is on overdrive. She says I should have a wedding list, it is a list of things you would need to set up home. It makes no sense to me at all because Nate has everything that I could possibly want for a home in terms of 'things'. He has two TVs, food mixers, plates and salad bowls and endless towels and bed linen. But of course I agree, what else can I do?

Bitsy tells me where the 'lists' should be. One at Saks Fifth Avenue in Atlanta, and one at Millers in town. She twitters on endlessly about which pattern we will have on our dinner service, which silverware, and which crystal. Waterford is fine, she says, but Baccarat, which I thought was a card game until now, is better; not so tacky. Well thanks a lot, Bitsy. I'm sure I will never use crystal anyway. And here's the mental bit, I am having six bridesmaids. Jaysus! You'd think it was a royal wedding. I can't take it in. Six! I wanted just Sharla, but I got a strong hint from Nate that I should ask Priscilla as well. I am happy to have Priscilla, she is sweet to me, and she is pretty, but I think they just want her to be bridesmaid so she can catch the bouquet and increase her chances of being the next bride. Bitsy is in a perpetual panic that Priscilla hasn't found a man, though Priscilla seems to be in no rush.

'Maggie, I presume you would like to ask your sistahs.' This is Bitsy at lunch last Sunday.

'Well, it might be awkward . . . I mean them not being here and that.'

'Nonsense, you can't possibly leave all those pretty babies out, they can send ovah the measurements and we'll have the dresses made.'

Numbly I agree and hope fervently none of the girls gain

any weight at the last minute. I have to go to Atlanta again to get my dress and pick the material for the bridesmaids. My dress is to be bought, and Bitsy has a dressmaker there who can do alterations. Priscilla is to take me and we will stay at the apartment. Nate says I am to have whatever dress I want, he'll buy it, but I think it is unlucky to let the groom pay, isn't it? I have this insane recurring thought that I should send the whole thing up and get my dress traded-out from Mamie's Modes. I am sure they have some little number covered in sequins. Or maybe Miz Beulah can crochet me one, in acid lemon. But this is a passing insanity. Nonetheless, I am starting to feel queasy at the thought of it all. I wish we could just live together for a while first. If I hadn't screwed up my stupid visa all would be well – I know I definitely want to marry Nate, but it's all going too fast for me.

I try to remember what that theory from the Bible is about one moment changing your life, something about a mouse I think, or a leaf falling. It's something to do with fate. Well, it seems my fate is to be Mrs Nate Gilmore or, as I can be called here, Maggie Lennon Gilmore – I only know that because today Bitsy asks me if I want the towels monogrammed MLG in red or navy. I noticed Nathan roll his eyes and pour himself a large bourbon when she said this. I think he finds the whole thing as ridiculous as I do.

'Does your Daddy enjoy a drink, Maggie?'

'I think that is a distinct possibility,' I say, 'and not just one.'

Nathan laughs out loud, and his eyes crinkle like Nate's. 'I like you, Miz Maggie,' he says, 'Nate is a lucky man.'

Oh God, I hope he's right. Later I tell Nate that it all freaks me out.

'Baby, you can have the linen monogrammed with a marijuana leaf for all I care.'

I snuggle up to him, pleased he understands. 'I'd prefer that. At least it would be funny.'

'Just agree with her, baby, this is her project. It gives her something to do and keeps her from nagging Daddy.'

But wedding arrangements aside, I enjoy living here. Tennessee is beautiful in late spring. The trees are a froth of pink and white, a profusion of blossoms: magnolia, cherry and dogwood. Magnolia is my favourite; I have seen small ornamental magnolias at home in Ireland, but here they are full and blowsy, voluptuous, and the scent is intoxicating. Daffodils too seem to grow all over in Wordsworthian quantities. They call them jonquils here. The gardens in front of my apartment building are full of them, and Nate's parents' house is choked with them. They have a gardener who sees that the house is full of flowers, though Bitsy arranges them – she says it relaxes her. I expect it's the most energetic thing she does. I feel guilty that I haven't quite warmed to Bitsy, or she to me for that matter. I expect she would find it hard to be warm towards anyone who was going to take her only son from her. Maybe I am not trying hard enough, but she intimidates me, she makes me feel just that little bit too opportunistic, and that is wrong. But maybe she recognises something of herself in me, perhaps the fact that she wasn't exactly an heiress herself.

18

The station has settled down to a routine that is less manic than WA1A. Zollie is still trading-out like crazy, but he's selling some advertising too. I'm supposed to sell as well, but I've become complacent. I hate that bit of the job anyway, and I have slowly started to think of myself as rich by default. I can't help this, and underneath I feel uneasy about it. I wouldn't think of stopping working though, I love my job, it's great. I do the afternoon shift from twelve till three and am supposed to sell advertising in the afternoons when I come off air. I talk to the record companies and the trades in the mornings. We are heading into high summer now and I have lived in America almost a whole year. The skies here are blue and big and airy, not grey, heavy and sitting on my shoulders like they are at home. I tell myself this when I am feeling homesick. I have a theory that people are in good form all the time here because of the weather. Sunny skies must make for sunny personalities, because I do think that on the whole the people here couldn't be friendlier or nicer. It doesn't annoy me when people say 'Y'all come back', and 'Have a nice day', I don't care whether they mean it or not. And I love getting my groceries packed. Sinead couldn't believe that bit. She's used to bunging everything into a carrier bag while the person behind's groceries are hurled on top of yours at ninety miles an hour.

Zollie comes in at the middle of my shift and wants to know if I would like a fish tank as a belated engagement present. He has one traded out from Aquatic Attic. It isn't an attic – I know this, because I have been there to pick up fish food for him – it's a modern, plain old store in a small development of shops. I guess the owner thought the name sounded good, but you'd expect it to at least have a pointy roof. I have given up on names of all kinds here. They specialise in weird. The other thing I can't quite get used to is the habit of spelling everything literally, like Krispy Kreme and Dunkin' Donuts, so you'd think everyone illiterate morons. My father would go crazy, he hates things like that.

The aquarium, do I want one? Apparently fish are very calming, and Zollie says they are amazing to look at when you're out of your head. I've seen him just sitting there spaced out, staring at the fish going round and round or up and down, whatever little multicoloured fish do. Maybellyne thinks it's a cute idea, and I am tempted. My apartment is sparse so an aquarium would look good. Aquatic Attic is out near the lake. I call Nate before I leave the station but he isn't there. I am not seeing him tonight since we were together all weekend and I usually have Monday nights at home.

Leroy, the guy at the fish shop, is very laid-back, really into fish. I want to pick them for colour and prettiness, but he explains that I have to choose compatible ones in case they eat each other. I am to have twelve to start with in the aquarium, and I choose some plants as well. It is big, about five feet across, and it has a stand. He will deliver it for me because it won't fit in my car, and he will set it up, all part of the service. I am delighted with it. Afterwards I think I may as well just call in and say hi to Nate if he is home as I am just a five-minute drive away. People don't tend to drop in here, it's different from Ireland that way, mainly because it's such a drive everywhere.

Nate is home because the Porsche is in the driveway. I don't have keys to his house so I go round the back. I call his name; no answer. I walk in through the kitchen to the living room, and then I hear something upstairs. I go up quietly, I don't know what makes me do that, but I suddenly feel uneasy. I don't know what I expected to see, but I certainly wasn't prepared for the sight of Nate and another man in bed together in an embrace. I recognise him as the guy from the ski photos, Tommy. They are both naked, it is warm, and the covers are pushed aside. As I enter Nate wheels round towards the door. I stand there rooted to the spot, unable to avert my eyes. The look on Nate's face is one of pure horror. Tommy, on the other hand, looks almost triumphant. I feel sick, my head is spinning, I can't speak. Finally I manage to say 'I was at Aquatic Attic, picking out the fish,' and then I turn on my heel and leave.

I hear Nate calling after me, 'Maggie, oh please, Maggie.' He sounds as if he is in pain. I don't care. I am in torment. I want to die.

I drive like a madwoman. I pay no attention to traffic lights or speed, but somehow I make it home alive, and without a speeding ticket. Once I get into the apartment I run to the bathroom and throw up. I wipe my face and go into the kitchen and pour a glass of water. I sit down on the settee. I can't stop trembling. What I am going to do? I can't think straight. Who can I talk to about this? Nate is homosexual, he must be, but he makes love to me, and he has had other women. And Tommy, I didn't even know he was in town. I thought he lived in Aspen. He must be Nate's boyfriend. It doesn't make any sense. I don't know very many homosexuals, it's not something I know a lot about.

Sharla will know about it, won't she? I dial her number. She is out. It is six o'clock. It's lunchtime in Ireland. Should I call Sinead? I can't. There's no one. No one at all. I can't face Zollie. I suppose I should have a drink, but I don't keep drink in the apartment, I suppose I really don't entertain much. I don't need any mind-altering drugs, my mind is altered enough. I can't even cry, I try to but it feels like I am faking it. I sob and heave and go though the motions but no tears come out. I have frozen. I try to clear my thoughts. What did I see? Two men, naked, in bed, in the middle of the day. There couldn't be any other explanation. They had to be doing it, having sex. I refuse to call it making love.

The doorbell rings. Unthinkingly I go to answer it. Nate is standing on the doorstep and I take one look at him and start to cry. My mind is split, I need someone to hold me so much, but he is the person who has caused my pain. Nonetheless, he is all I have right now. I fall into his arms, and we both cry together as if our hearts have broken. Eventually I stop, I can hardly see out of my eyes, but the cry has helped. Nate excuses himself and goes to the car. He comes back with a bottle of whisky.

'Did you bring that specially?' I can feel the acid thoughts curdling inside me. Hate and love are so close.

'No, I didn't bring it specially. I just remembered it was in the car.'

He gets two glasses and pours us each a large tumbler full. I am reminded of his father pouring me the drink at Christmas. I wait for him to speak. I am afraid that all my thoughts are too jumbled up and whatever I say will be the worst thing to say.

'Maggie, I am sorry. I am so very sorry. I hate that you saw us, and I hate that I did this to you.'

'Why is he in town?'

'He came to see me.'

'How long have you been lovers?'

'We aren't lovers.'

'Yes you are, I saw you.' I sound like a child.

He tells his story slowly, as if to understand it himself. He and Tommy had gone to college together and had been friends since day one. They dated girls who were best friends and played football for the college team. There are photos of this all over the place, I have seen them. At New Year in Aspen they were in the hot tub smoking a joint after everyone else had gone to bed when Tommy reached for Nate and kissed him on the mouth. Nate responded and felt confused and ashamed afterwards, but he had been stoned and excused it to himself as drug-fuelled craziness. I don't ask him what 'responded' means, I am hoping it just means he kissed him back.

'And did it happen again?'

'Yes, the night before I was due to come home.'

'Is that why you didn't call me?'

Of course it was. He had been confused and scared by the whole business. By the time he had put some distance between himself and Tommy, when his head cleared, he realised the episodes with Tommy had been madness. He missed me, he truly loved me.

201

I am shivering as I listen to this. He tells his story in a humble, wanting to be forgiven way. He looks dejected and he sounds wretched, but I can't feel it in me to console him. Tommy had arrived in town today unexpectedly because Nate refused to see him when he had been powder skiing and hadn't returned any of his calls since.

'But the photos?'

'They were from last time.'

I don't know if he's telling me the truth, but I let him talk. He tells me Tommy is really messed up on drugs and is threatening to kill himself. When he arrived today he was totally distraught. Nate tried to talk him down but somehow they had ended up in bed. He shrugs helplessly. But Nate wasn't drunk or stoned or anything. He knew what he was doing. I can't begin to fathom it. Why bed? 'Couldn't you have just told him to go?'

'I should have, but he's my oldest friend and I feel guilty, and worse I feel ashamed, he keeps reminding me of the other times, and I am afraid to refuse him now. He has threatened to tell my daddy. It would kill my mother to hear I had been to bed with another man. Nathan would disinherit me.'

I am scared, really scared. My heart is pounding. What will happen now? All the stuff about the wedding. It is like a whirlwind, out of control, unstoppable. I am mentally thinking of all the things we will have to undo. Due to Bitsy's grim determination, there has been an engagement picture in *The Times*, and of course I have the two rings. There is little point in saying all of this because Nate knows it anyway, but I do: I say it all, over and over until I am exhausted, and to use a local phrase, all cried out.

'What are we going to do?'

'I love you, Maggie. I still want to marry you.'

'What about Tommy?'

'Tommy has gone.'

'For now.'

'No, I have told him I don't want to see him again.'

'Just say he does tell your parents? What if he does kill himself?' Nate doesn't say anything. He just looks abject. 'Oh Nate, you have been to bed with him,' this is the scary bit, actually saying that out loud, 'I'm not sure I can marry someone who likes men like that.'

'I don't like men like that. I promise you, Maggie. It was just Tommy. I have never been with another man, just him, and only those times.'

I am not sure I believe him. I want to. But it is hard. I have no frame of reference for this. I guess I haven't been around enough.

'Are you going to tell anyone?' Nate's face is contorted with anxiety.

'Is that all that is worrying you?'

'No . . .'

'I have to talk to someone.'

'I saw someone when I got back in January.'

'What do you mean, someone?'

'I guess you could call her a counsellor.'

'I'd rather talk to a friend.'

'Will you tell Sinead?'

'No, I won't. Does Priscilla know?'

'I couldn't tell her, no way.'

He wants to spend the night, but I can't cope with it. It is now nine o'clock and all I have had since lunchtime is a large whisky. Ridiculous as it seems, I am starving. We phone for a pizza. We eat, and then he leaves. I look after the car as he drives off and I feel profound sadness. I can't handle all this alone. I try Sharla's number again. I get her roommate and leave a message to call me urgently, and I go to bed and lie awake unable to still my racing brain. I am still awake when Sharla phones at midnight. Calmly, I tell her the whole story. I hear my voice coming out flat and expressionless, like I was talking about someone I didn't know.

'You poor baby, this is just awful, I just wish I was there to give you a hug.'

Then I start to cry again.

'Honey, I can't believe it. Have you given him back the ring, I mean rings?'

'No. It didn't seem the right moment.'

'I'll be down tomorrow. This isn't something to talk about on the phone.'

'Are you sure?'

'Yep, I'll see you about six.'

I try to sleep after that, but when I get into work the next morning about an hour after my usual time, I look and feel like a ghost. Sue Lynne gives me a pile of pink message slips. I don't feel like returning a single call. I get through the day somehow, though Zollie calls once and sings the first line of 'Maggie May'. He always does that when I sound dismal. It certainly doesn't make me laugh today. Nate calls me twice. I ask him to leave me alone for a few days. I am still wearing my ring, the Tiffany one. Sue Lynne would spot immediately if I took it off. Maybellyne expresses concern that I look so bad but I tell her I'm having a bad period. She understands this; she has a condition called pre-menstrual tension and takes things for it. She offers me a pill. I take it, maybe it'll work for pre-possibly-cancelled-wedding tension.

★   ★   ★

Sharla and I are sitting in the Steak House at a window table. I watch my reflection pretending to eat a steak. Sharla thinks a meal will help, but all the pieces seem to stick in my throat and taste like paper. I chew slowly till it feels like pulp. I am drinking beer though. I have gone over everything that happened yesterday about twenty times. She has listened patiently. Sharla thinks Nate must be homosexual and repressing it. She thinks that is the reason he wants to marry so fast, so he can be 'cured'.

'But of course you can't cure 'em, honey. Some guys are just like that. They like to get it on with other guys.'

'I expect it isn't too popular in the South.'

'Hell no, homosexuals are more unpopular than black people. I tell you, they scare the shit out of all those rednecks.'

'Sharla, what do they do?'

'What do they do? Honey, what do you mean what do they do?'

'I mean, how do they have sex?'

Sharla looks at me as if my head is cut. 'Honey, I am not rightly sure, but I guess they might . . . are you sure you want to hear this?'

'Yes. I am. I feel stupid that I don't know. I suppose I've never thought about it before.'

So she explains. I can't really take it in. Sharla says Nate may be bisexual, and like to have sex with both boys and girls.

'He says it was only Tommy.'

'Honey, get real, maybe it *was* only Tommy until now, but later on he might meet another guy he would like to get it on with.'

'He says he won't.'

'Are you going to call off the wedding?'

'I'm not sure. I suppose I am, except it frightens me, y'know, telling everyone.'

'Well, honey, take ma word for it, you oughta. Just say you marry him and it doesn't work out? Think about it, a divorce if all of y'all have babies will be a whole bunch scarier.'

I know she's right but I am feeling overwhelmed thinking of all the people who will have to be told the wedding isn't going to happen. It would be easier to go ahead with it. Sharla leans on both elbows and faces me, looking concerned. I shrug.

'Listen, you don't have to give anyone a reason, you can just say you changed your mind, decided you were too young, whatever,' she continues. She finishes her steak and baked potato, and starts to pick at mine. I sit as if in a trance and watch her. I still don't know what I am going to do.

I don't notice then when Buford McConnell comes up behind me and bellows, 'Well if it ain't the purtiest Irish girl in Tennessee.'

Sharla lifts an eyebrow and I introduce them. She has heard about him from me, of course, but they have never met.

'What is that fiancé of yours doing letting you out on the town like this?'

'Girls' night out,' Sharla tells him.

'Well then, I'll go leave you two in peace. Real nice to meet you, Sharla, maybe we can have lunch some time soon, Maggie?'

'Yes,' I hear myself say. 'I'd like that. Call me tomorrow.'

'He's nice really,' I tell Sharla, 'even if he looks like a redneck.'

'Hell, honey, I know rednecks can be nice. He has the hots for you though.'

'Pity he's not my type.'

'Yes, it is a pity, 'cos *then* you could . . .' Sharla strums an air guitar and sings in a mock country and western voice, 'let your love pour down on him like maple syrup.'

We both laugh, and for the first time I think that maybe I will survive the whole bloody mess.

It's hard to hold on to that thought the next day though. Sharla has gone back to Johnson City as she has a term paper to write, and I have an air shift to do. We talked last night till the early hours and I think I decided that I would call things off. But now I feel frightened again, as well as having a sore head from all the beer we drank. I don't want to shock the hell out of my family by telling them Nate is bisexual, because that's what Sharla and I have decided he is, or alternatively that he is queer and won't admit it. My father is always scathing, in that Irish homophobic way of his, about men who are 'light on their hooves'. He has accused both of my previous English boyfriends of this, mainly because they talked posh and he equates posh with effeminate. I can guess what his reaction to Nate would be and I was already worrying about my parents being intimidated by all the wealth. I am going to see Nate after work. It has occurred to me to call Priscilla, but I don't. I'm not sure just how close Nate and she are.

Before work this morning I went up to see Herman for a long-standing hair appointment and I felt such a fraud when he admired my ring. He has cut my hair and streaked it and restored my keratin with something that smelled of strawberries. He has bought two tiny dogs, little Yorkshire terriers called Rupert and Ringo. They are utterly ghastly. They sit on a blue fur pouch thing and yap all the time. They look like long-haired rats. Herman says he intends to 'quaff' them himself.

I start giggling hysterically. He nods approvingly. 'Good dope?'

I say yes, although I haven't had any. I don't want him to think I am laughing at him. He offers me a puff of his joint and for once I take it. I sit laughing non-stop while he does my hair. I laugh like a maniac. I am glad Herman thinks this is normal behaviour. He keeps saying things like 'Well, Maggie, you sure are in sunny form today,' and 'Boy you are one happy woman,' and finally when the tears are streaming down my face, he comes out with, 'That's right, laughter is the best medicine'.

It occurs to me that I might be losing my mind. This whole deal with Nate has pushed me over the edge. I haven't laughed this frantically since the time Zollie let the nitrous oxide out on Sinead. Herman gives me some shampoo samples and promises he will do my hair for free for the wedding. I hug him and leave, I am glad I didn't cancel the appointment, it sure makes a change from all the weeping and wailing.

I am wearing a really lovely blue silk shirt, which Nate bought me in Atlanta, and my new jeans and I have taken extra care over my eye make-up – I want to look good when I see Nate. I want him to know what he has thrown away. I have the other ring in my handbag. It probably would have fitted Tommy if it hadn't been altered for me. Tommy has long, thin fingers. I noticed them. He's not as pretty as Nate though. Sadly I can't think of anyone more beautiful right now. It is a disadvantage. I wish he repulsed me, but it's hard to hate someone on demand, at least when you're in love with them it is.

Nate seems sad, he compliments me on how I look and then almost starts to cry. I have said I will stay for dinner, but not for the night. He has the barbecue lit, and because I have told him I had steak last night he has bought some spare ribs, and silver queen corn, which he knows I love. I don't love it enough to make me happy though. I want it to be last week and erase everything.

I am glad spare ribs are nibbly things and no one checks how much of the actual meat you finish. I am desperately trying to eat, but I've got that awful block of unhappiness that sort of settles somewhere at the base of your throat and nothing can push it down, not even food. I am hungry, I know that because my tummy is rumbling, but I also feel hungry in a different way, for love I suppose. Christ, my thoughts are starting to sound like the lyrics to a bad country and western song.

Somehow Nate and I get through the evening. We postpone the wedding, or agree to. I expect that is easier than full on cancellation, it can become that when the great Bitsy wedding train has slowed down. I will allow him to say it was a mutual decision. In the meantime, the emerald ring will go back to the lawyer and I will continue to wear the Tiffany diamond. It has started to feel part of my finger anyway. Nate thinks he is on probation and if he keeps away from Tommy it will be okay, but both of us know that this is just a 'let me down easy' strategy, because he also tells me he wants me to keep the diamond as a present anyway and he's so glad he bought it for me, and then he cries again.

I am not used to seeing a man cry. It seems so heartrending. He looks too big and manly to be sobbing. His tears seem wetter than any tears I've seen. I want really everything to be okay, I want to kiss it better. I feel like his mammy. I gently refuse his request that I spend the night. 'Please, Maggie, please, just this once? I beg you. I promise I won't ask you again.' I am a sucker, I know. I am too far from home. I am in a foreign country and my boyfriend prefers men. But I stay and go to bed with him and have the best sex of our entire relationship. So when I leave next morning I am even more confused than ever. I want my mammy, although she would be utterly useless with this little 'problem'.

19

The station has a visitor, a surprise visitor for me. Sue Lynne hasn't fluffed up her hair and she has forgotten to prop up her little pointy tits, so it must be a woman. It is Lindy. Hallelujah, I believe in God!

'What are you doing here?'

'What a welcome! What am I, chopped liver?'

'I can't believe it!'

'I was in Nashville, and on my way by car to Atlanta so I thought, how about I give little Miss Maggie a call and surprise her. Bilbo here has been so kind and taken me over to Delroy's Diner for breakfast. He is such a doll.'

The doll looks enthralled at the compliment and says, sheepishly, 'It was a real pleasure to be able to do something for such a nice lady.'

To his embarrassment Lindy hugs him, then she turns to me. 'So, what time is this to get into work? We rang your apartment over an hour ago and you had left.'

'I stayed at Nate's.'

'Told you,' Sue Lynne nods satisfied. 'I done got it raaght. She cain't stay away from him.'

I smile grimly and motion to Lindy to come into the office. 'Can you spend the night?'

'Yes ma'am, I intend to. I've booked into the Hilton and you and I are going for dinner. I want to meet Mr Two Rings, your friendly millionaire.'

I say nothing. I feel as if Sue Lynne has the place bugged, but Lindy has to go visit the other stations in town and we arrange that she will meet me after my shift. I am so happy she is here. She is sophisticated and will know what to do. It had occurred to me to call her before now but I was unsure, but fate meant her to know, otherwise why would she land on my doorstep without warning?

Lindy is unequivocal when I recount it all to her over some amazing wine in the restaurant, later. 'Honey, you need to get out, and fast. He sounds mixed up as hell.'

'But I love him.'

'Hell, I love him, who wouldn't love a young, good-looking millionaire?' She has seen photos of him.

'It's going to be crazy cancelling everything.'

'That's an excuse and you know it.'

'I'll have to leave the States. I haven't a visa to get back in, except on holiday, and I want to see my parents and my sisters.'

'So you were only marrying him for a Green Card?' 'A Green Card?'

'Yes, isn't that what you need to stay here? You know, some sharp lawyer can get you one for a couple of thousand dollars. Cheaper than a divorce later on.'

'No, I love him. Do you think he might be queer?'

'Well, having sex with another guy is a bit of a giveaway.'

I tell her about last night and she hears me out, but she thinks that even if he is bisexual I may not be able to cope with it, I haven't lived enough. She says that she had already figured I am not ready to settle down yet.

'Face it, honey, you were dying to screw Bob Templeman at the Seattle gig.'

'I didn't though.'

'I know you didn't, but you two were hanging out of each other like you were gagging for it.'

I feel slightly miffed at this. I thought I had been friendly but not overtly so. People here frequently mistake Irish friendliness for sexual interest. It can be off-putting. The whole country, or at least all the guys in the record business, think everyone is permanently ready for sex. It pisses me off. But maybe Lindy has a point about Bob. I tell her it's just because I know him better than any of the others and therefore I feel more at ease with him.

'Well, it looked like steam was coming out of his ears when you were together. You might need to see a bit of life before you settle down. Marriage USA-style can be a tough business.'

She could be right. I had indeed flirted with Bob, but I was a secure engaged woman then. Not a poor jilted immigrant.

Before Lindy leaves for Atlanta she talks me into taking off my ring. She says it will be more honest, and give me time to clear my head, sort out my feelings. I know Nate will refuse to take it back, so I bring the ring to the bank and they keep it for me. They give me a key to a little box in the back, just like in the movies. It looks lonely sitting in its little box on its own, but I have nothing else of value to put in with it.

213

Now that I'm not getting married and not seeing Nate I need to earn more money. I suppose I will have to start to sell advertising. I never feel more Irish than when I have to go into a shop and start expounding about the benefits of advertising on Q92. Americans are so good at that sort of thing, they don't seem to have the squirm factor. They are so openly enthusiastic about things and love selling. Leroy, the fish guy, is a fine example of American enthusiasm. He has delivered and installed my fish tank. Even though Leroy wasn't making a sale, he spent the hour or so it took to set it up raving on about how fish would change my life. They have already. If it hadn't been for the bloody fish I'd still be engaged.

And I love them, a tank full of lovely little darting rainbows, little angel fish, tiger-fish guppies. It is soporific but calming, better than a TV. Still, I might get one of those next, even though apart from *Saturday Night Live* I think American TV is awful. It would give me something to do in the evenings. I am desperately trying to fill the emptiness in my life, but every day I wake up and I haven't died of a broken heart.

It has been two weeks now, and though I've talked to Nate on the phone, I haven't seen him. I haven't been out much, otherwise I probably would have bumped into him. Priscilla phones and asks if I will go for lunch. I say I will, but we haven't fixed a date yet. I am dreading it really. What will I tell her? More to the point, what has Nate told them? I expect they think I'm some kind of awful bitch.

My parents are surprisingly calm when I tell them I am postponing the wedding. I think they felt we were rushing things. My sisters are merely pissed off that they aren't getting a trip to the USA. My mother wants me to come straight

home, but I tell her I want to fix up a visa before I do. I
don't want to give up the possibility of staying here, not yet.
There's something about the place, for all its flaws, that quite
seduces me. I don't feel so circumscribed, and I feel like I've
been given absolution to reinvent myself, to act out impulses
I've always sat on, and I like being relatively unknown.
Sometimes people recognise my voice – at the gas station,
they'll say something like 'You're her, ain't you? The girl who
talks funny on the radio?'. But mostly I have a sort of blissful
anonymity. And I don't have to wake up to the news of some
ghastly sectarian atrocity each day. Sometimes these make the
front page of the newspaper here, but mostly they are con-
signed to a small paragraph down the side of one of the inside
pages. I like that. It may be cowardly of me, but it means I
don't have to face it all.

20

We're going to Buford's concert, the Maple Syrup Tour. We are promoting it on air even though it's a country gig; God knows what sort of deal Zollie has done with Buford, they seem to have become very pally. I am going to be Bilbo's date. Zollie has some lady friend we are all to meet for the first time. Her name is Shirley, he calls her squirrelly Shirley. Steve, the new DJ, is coming, and of course Sue Lynne and Clarence Lee.

We meet at Zollie's apartment, which is in the same building as mine, and have beer and dips 'n' chips before we go. Zollie also has several drugs to hand. I smoke some dope and pass on the others. Bilbo is driving the Black Box so the rest of us can partake. Shirley is lovely and seems quite taken with Zollie. For some reason, Sue Lynne seems pissed off about this. Clarence is sitting clamped to her, she a vision in pale green polyester, he in light tan. Each time he moves I can hear the crackle of the static, but the dope has made me relaxed and I can cope. I must have been too friendly to her, because when we go to the loo on the way into the concert, she confides in me that Clarence is saving some money so he can buy her a boob job for her birthday. She has to explain what this means. It appears he doesn't think her breasts are big enough – he thinks Dolly Parton the ideal woman – and so she will have silicon implants inserted and end up with a super-large chest. I almost feel sorry for her.

When we worked in Daytona there was a waitress in the next door restaurant who had simply enormous boobs. She used to win the wet T-shirt contest at the Pink Pussycat night club every week. Maureen and Patricia were horrified when they heard this, and so was I. It seemed a bit cheap to us. I expect we all felt morally superior. I was in the loo one night when she came in, and I must have been staring at her in the mirror, when she came over to me.

'Hi, my name is Estelle.'

'Hello, I'm Maggie Lennon, I work next door.'

'I know. I can see you're staring at my boobs.'

'No,' I stammered, 'I'm not.'

'It's okay, I don't mind, I'm used to it. But I've been entering the wet T-shirt contest every week and winning, did you know that?'

'Yes, I did.'

'Well, I have almost saved enough to get a breast reduction when I go home to Cleveland. It's been tough, it isn't easy being a freak. I just want to be like everyone else.'

I looked at her and she seemed on the verge of tears. I felt ashamed that we had all been so quick to judge her. She and I always waved at each other and said hello after that. I am thinking about Estelle when Sue Lynne confides in me. Well, whatever gets you through the night, I think. But I sort of

217

feel sorry for Sue Lynne that she feels it is necessary, and to keep Clarence of all people?

There's a completely different feel to a country and western concert, I find. The crowd seems much more good-natured. It doesn't have the same raw sexual energy about it that a rock concert does. I'd guess quite a few of the audience have smoked a bit of dope, but beer is the drug of choice. They also know all the words to all the songs, and Buford is their main man. They are beside themselves when he sings 'Maple Syrup'. I reappraise him, perhaps I have been a bit harsh on him, he has been kind to me and he most certainly has presence and a way with the crowd – he seems totally different on a big stage with an appreciative audience. When he sings 'Your Cheatin' Heart' I find myself singing along lustily and imagine I am serenading Nate. It is cathartic.

We have backstage passes with *access all areas*, which means we can watch the concert from the wings. We decide to do this. I am getting used to these passes, having had them for Bob Seger, Fleetwood Mac, and a few of the bigger rock groups. It's bullshit, but it gives one a feeling of self-importance, even if in reality the show is best viewed from the auditorium. The truth is that backstage most of the rock groups are burned out from meeting fans, and only say hello and pose for photos out of obligation to the record companies.

Buford is different. He virtually ignores everyone backstage, true fans included, to make a fuss of me, and despite myself I am flattered. Sue Lynne is trying hard to get his attention, pushing her big hair back and wittering on about how he has just 'blown her clean away'. I wish he would.

'Why, Clarence Lee remarked on the tears running down

my cheeks during your tribute to the King, didn't you, baby doll?'

Clarence nods dutifully. 'You done broke her heart. I wiped her eyes throughout.'

But old Buford virtually ignores her and persists in raving on about this wonderful Irish woman, and hugging me like we're the best of chums. 'Isn't she a honey?' he says happily, with his arm round me. I try to free myself from his grasp since he is just a bit sweaty from his performance, but I continue to smile moronically, after all I am fairly stoned. Poor Sue Lynne, I bet she feels like puking and I couldn't blame her, so do I. On the other hand it is nice to be appreciated. It's a distraction and I couldn't have enough of these at the moment.

We all go back to the band's hotel, even Bilbo who is the only one who hasn't been chemically altered. Zollie and Shirley are flying, God only knows what they are on, but she is certainly behaving like squirrelly Shirley. Since I need to ride home with Zollie later I hope they come down off the cloud soon, because Americans aren't into taxis outside New York, and I don't want to be stranded in town. I tell Zollie this and regret it, since he breaks into a chorus of 'Stranded in a Limousine', which he keeps up till we arrive at the Hilton. Sometimes I could choke him, but he has been sweet about my 'postponed' engagement and offered to pay for my family to come out to see me regardless, or as he puts it, 'irregardless'. I have refused, of course, but I appreciate the offer all the same.

The 'down home' country and western guys are not too down home to appreciate their drugs. An ounce of coke is tipped out on the glass coffee table in the suite in the hotel room. I certainly don't want to give Sue Lynne any ammunition, so even though I wouldn't mind a little pop I refuse to do any. She and Clarence refuse piously. I am glad about that too, the idea of Clarence on a coke high going into his shift at the nuclear power plant is not a relaxing one. Zollie and Shirley have no such qualms. The bass guitarist is busy chopping it up to spell *sex and drugs and rock'n'roll*. I suppose sex 'n' drugs 'n' country doesn't have quite the same ring to it. The mood is one of reckless hilarity; I think Zollie and Buford bring out the worst in each other. They are competing line for line. Buford orders champagne and then, to cheers and catcalls, a razor blade from room service as, apparently the coke is too lumpy. I think everyone is flabbergasted when it arrives.

Pretty soon the decibel level has risen dramatically and everyone is talking at each other animatedly about nothing in particular. They all look like characters in a Hieronymus Bosch painting. The three girls in the room, I am unsure who they are with, are giggling like fools; they eventually siphon off to nearby rooms with various band members. I'd love to go home, but it looks unlikely for a while. I am tempted to call Nate, I miss him so much. The dreaded throat lump is back, it won't shift.

What does it matter that he made love to Tommy? I want him now. Finally, Sue Lynne and Clarence can't take any more of the madness and make their excuses. Soon there are only Shirley, Zollie, Bilbo, Buford and me. I give in and do a few lines and get an energy rush. I feel churned up inside still but I start chatting to Buford and he is really quite sweet. He seems really interested in Ireland and my family. Eventually in an effort to slow down we smoke a joint and I find myself telling him about my engagement being off. I don't tell him the reason, in fact I unintentionally give him the impression that Nate has another woman. Zollie and Shirley are not driving me home. They are totally wasted and poor old Bilbo has fallen asleep. We talk for hours, and somehow by the end of the night I find myself agreeing to think over Buford's proposal to marry me so I can get a Green Card.

'Way I see it is this,' he tells me, 'I'd just be helping out a friend. You could go home for a vacation, and you'd have no problems getting back into the country and staying.'

I point out that he has been married three times already. My parents would die. They are strict Catholics.

'Why would you feel the need to tell them? It can be our secret. It can be simply a favour for a friend.'

'It's really sweet of you, but I couldn't let you do that.'

'It would be an honour for me to help out, and then if Nate and you get back together, you guys won't feel no need to rush things. I guess that's what fucked things up for y'all.'

If only he knew the real reason. It's hard for me to keep up the front, but I have promised Nate I will. The truth is I'm too embarrassed to explain it to people anyway. I'm sure his parents just think it's all my fault. I still haven't had lunch with Priscilla, I've been unable to face her.

This idea of having an arranged marriage to get a Green Card sort of sticks in my brain, apparently it's common enough. I do nothing about it, of course, except talk it over with both Sharla and Lindy, who think why not? As Lindy says, 'Make sure it's just a business deal, pay him something, a token.'

Nate and I meet for lunch again and I still can't swallow a bite. He remarks on how thin I am. He's right, I am too thin, there's nothing like pining to take off the pounds. I still love him. I always had a fantasy of what my husband would look like and sound like, and I always had a thing about men

221

with crinkles at the side of their eyes from laughing. He still has those, but his eyes are haunted. I want to rush out of the restaurant and straight out to his house and fall into bed beside him. I want the warmth and closeness of another human being. But there is a stiffness between us, a sort of new formality. I wish I could be sure that I will fall for someone else sometime, but right now it seems impossible. I tell him about Buford's offer.

'I'll marry you,' he says immediately. 'We can go to Las Vegas and do it, we needn't tell my folks.'

'I couldn't marry you, that would mean something. It has to be meaningless.'

'I still love you, Maggie.'

I say nothing, I want to cry. I gulp my water – I have no show on Saturday but I am driving. I wish I had let him pick me up as he had suggested, so I could numb myself with drink. We talk in circles about nothing. What is there left to say?

'Oh Maggie,' he says at one point, 'what will become of us?'

'Have you talked to Tommy?' He is silent. I feel stung. 'You have, haven't you?'

'He's been calling a lot and I guess I got fed up hanging up on him.'

'Are you seeing him again?'

'I have no plans.'

'That's not what I asked you.' I stand up, almost knocking over the chair. 'I need to go,' I tell him. Suddenly I am white with rage. I have to get out of the restaurant before I throw something at him. I hate this passive side of Nate. He's going to let it all just happen to him. He'll let Tommy have him, make him like that all the time, ruin his life. I hate Tommy. I hate Nate Gilmore. I wish I'd never met him.

21

I go into work earlier each day now because it is something to do. It stops me brooding. I am slightly worried that taking a Quaalude every night is not ideal, but I have a prescription for them from a really lovely doctor friend of Zollie's who thinks that if they are not abused they are a good aid to sleeping – he does warn me not to get dependent and to take a half instead of a whole one. I do wish I had enough 'backbone', as the nuns used to say, to get through this emotional maelstrom without the props, but I seem to be on some sort of treadmill, and haven't found the stop button.

Monday morning, I am just in the door when Bilbo tells me there is a call for me, someone from Shine Records is on the line. I rush into the office and grab the phone. It is Rolly Young. I try to sound casual.

'Hey babe, Rolly Young here, just wanted to let you know that "Dogs in the Moonlight" has just gone platinum, and Shine would like to present you with your platinum disc in

LA the weekend after next. Jimmy Farrell will be over from London. Okay?'

'Oh, that's brilliant,' I say. 'I am really delighted.' God why do I sound so gauche! He doesn't seem to notice though.

'Cool. Glad you can make it. I'll have my assistant book a hotel and flights for you and there'll be a limo to meet you. I'll be there myself. We'll party, okay? Oh, my assistant is Jude, she'll call you. Later, babe.' He hangs up.

All thoughts of Nate recede, slightly, I am ecstatic. Zollie is thrilled too, not so much for me as for the station.

'Sheeeit, Maggie, this could put us on the map, we could get reporting status with *Gavin, Billboard* . . . and we could get us some bigass publicity outa this.' He thinks for a moment. 'Wait, let me call Ed, he needs to do another feature on you.'

'No, Zollie, he doesn't. Besides, I haven't had the platinum record yet.'

'You do know, Maggie, that the record will belong to the station.'

'What do you mean?'

'Well, the station played the record. It gits the reward.'

'I played the record. My sister sent it to me. You didn't want me to add it to the playlist, remember?'

'I don't recall stopping you, Maggie.'

'No, but you tried to.'

'Listen, Maggie, stations get gold and platinum records, people don't.'

'Fine, let's wait till it happens.' I am not in the mood to argue with him. But my jollity is ebbing away.

Somehow the rest of the week passes. Rolly's assistant, Jude, calls and takes all the details, apparently this presentation will take place the last night of a radio and records convention. She asks me if I am coming early for that. I say I am not

224

sure, I will speak to Zollie. Zollie is thrilled for me to go for the convention, and seeing as my fare to LA and accommodation is being paid he will fork out for the registration fee. He thinks it will do me good, get me a high profile and above all help Q92. He is eloquent about all the possible giveaways we can scam from the record companies.

Maybellyne is also encouraging. 'This is just what y'all need, honey. You go and meet you a nice boy. I plan to visit LA sometime, I bet it's real glamorous.' Poor Maybellyne. I have her tortured with all my stuff about Nate, and I still haven't told her the real reason. I form the words sometimes but the sound doesn't catch up with them. Nate is homosexual. It makes me feel I am lacking something somehow. Surely I could have done something to fix him? What is wrong with me? Say I had been better in bed? If I was sexier? If I had known more 'things'. Would that have helped?

Next day I call Jude and tell her I will be there for the full four days. She says my tickets will be at the airport. I can't really feel any sense of anticipation. I play 'Ob-la-di Ob-la-da' on the air. I hope Nate is listening. I play Bob Seger 'Still the Same', I play 'You're so Vain', twice. Then I call and register for the record convention. In spite of myself I am beginning to feel excited. I am happening, I tell myself. I am happening.

And then it is time to go. I have spoken to several of my local guys from different labels and they will all be there, and Bob will of course, and Tom and all my new best friends from Seattle. LA, just imagine. Hollywood. I have always wanted to go to California.

I'm booked on an early morning flight and so I will be in LA by lunchtime. I get on the plane and can't find my seat. My ticket says row two, but there is no row two. I am just attempting to eject a fat woman in the second row which is inexplicably called row six, when the stewardess comes to my rescue. 'Ya'll are in first class honey,' she tells me, and leads me out of the economy section, through the curtain, sits me down, and serves me a glass of champagne. The seat is leather, wide and comfortable. I sit back and look out the window. I am happy.

I am met at LAX the other end, by a man with a big sign on a stick saying *MAGGIE LENNON*. He takes my luggage tickets from me and I am whisked away to a waiting limo, which I roll around in, it seems so over the top and unnecessary but I guess by now I'm sort of expecting the weekend to be like this. It is warm and balmy in LA and I gaze in awe through the darkened windows of the limo at the brightness outside as we cruise along the wide streets with familiar names like La Cienaga, and Sunset. There are tall, soaring palm trees, the cover of *Hotel California* made flesh. Finally we stop outside a large, plush hotel in Beverly Hills. The limo driver ushers me into the lobby and puts my bags down. He indicates that I should check in, says goodbye, and leaves.

I feel completely overwhelmed, and slightly nervous that there may be some mistake and I'll be asked for money. I have got some dollars with me, but I don't have a credit card. Then I see Lindy in the lobby talking to a few guys. She breaks away immediately, rushes over and hugs me.

'Hey babe, you look great! It's so good to see you.'

She is completely at home. She marches me up to reception with a wide smile and her insouciance is infectious. I take my lead from her and tell the girl on the desk, as instructed, that I am Maggie Lennon and I am a guest of Shine Records. I am rewarded with a large 'Welcome to LA,' accompanied by an even larger sycophantic beam. Money isn't mentioned, and within seconds a bell hop takes my bags and brings me to a room on the top floor. Lindy tips him a five-dollar bill. There is the slightest hesitation as he checks the denomination, then he closes the door and leaves.

'You look fantastic,' Lindy tells me.

'I feel awful.'

'Hey? Stop that, Maggie May. You're in la-la land now and you're gonna have fun. Okay?'

I nod. 'I hope so.'

'Look, he's a schmuck. Get over him, you're gorgeous. Do you need to shower?' I nod again. 'Right, I'll see you in the lobby bar in twenty minutes.' And she leaves.

I look at the room. It is like being in the movies, it is so posh. I have never stayed in a five-star hotel before. The room in Seattle was nothing like this; there are two sofas, occasional tables and a bed the size of a football pitch. On the table near the window there are flowers and beside them, chilling in an ice bucket, a bottle of Dom Perignon champagne. I suddenly notice a card that has my name on it. *Welcome to LA, Maggie. Rolly Young, Shine Records.* Life is sweet.

I push all thoughts of Nate to the back of my mind as I pull out a change of jeans and a clean T-shirt and throw them on the bed. Then I take a shower. I am just finishing dressing when the phone rings and it is Rolly Young. He is in a suite on the same floor as me and asks if I would like to join him for drinks about six. A limo will be picking us up at seven; we are going to dinner first and then catching Jimmy Farrell in concert at the Roxy. I am feeling a bit tired now, but I guess the excitement will help me keep going. But first I go down to meet Lindy. I need a cup of coffee.

Promptly at six I arrive in Rolly Young's suite. I feel somewhat overawed. It is massive, and full of record people, local

DJs, promotion men, and West Coast types. I am introduced to all of them but I barely recall one name. I see Tom, my local guy, and greet him like we are best friends. He seems as ill at ease here as I do. He comes and joins me on one of the many settees. Tom is from South Carolina, quite a down home type, and he seems in awe of Rolly Young, who is smiling and grinning like a fool, looking cool and Hollywood. I sit beside Tom and pretend to be part of the party. I notice they all go in and out of the bathroom a lot. They talk and chatter a lot, but no one seems to be listening to anyone else. We drink Dom Perignon, which reminds me of Nate. Eventually I need to pee. I move to go into the bathroom. Rolly notices me going in. 'Be sure and powder your nose, baby,' he says.

I am slightly embarrassed; is my nose red or what? Then, while washing my hands, I notice a little glass dish, like my Auntie Martha's salt dish, sitting on top of the vanity. It is full of white powder. There is a tiny little silver spoon in it. It surely couldn't be coke? There is far too much. I know coke comes in grammes. I dip my finger in it and lick it. It makes my tongue numb at once. Yes, it is coke. Oh! I suddenly get it. This is what he means by powdering my nose. I forget that I have told myself I am giving up drugs. I take a spoonful, and snort it. I am not sure if this is okay, but this is what Rolly meant, isn't it? How could anyone notice a spoonful gone anyway, I reason, so I take another. Immediately, it seems, my tiredness goes. I feel cool, part of the jet set. I am flying. I come out and Rolly nods towards me.

'You get some, babe?'

'Yes, thank you. I got some.' I am not sure what to call it. Zollie's term, Colombian marching powder, doesn't seem appropriate – do they refer to it as 'tootski'?

228

'Good, anytime, babe, feel free.'

Lindy comes in, she is with her boss who is obviously a buddy of Rolly's, but she leaves him and comes and sits beside me. I feel better at once. I whisper to her about the coke.

'I'll take a rain check.'

'Oh?'

'Yeah, maybe before we leave. It freaks me out doll, makes me run my mouth.'

The whole deal of being in Los Angeles, and in such a hotel, is what freaks me out. Emboldened now by the coke I look around the room. Apart from two bored-looking model types, there are mostly men in the room. One of them is nice though, his name is Mark. He is quiet and asks me lots of intelligent questions about Ireland. He finds my accent cute. He also, I notice, doesn't 'need to pee' every ten minutes. He is a promotion man for Shine. He works out of Chicago, and like most of the others he has 'come in' for the convention. He doesn't say as much, but I can tell he isn't really a fan of Rolly's. I tell him who I am, and surprisingly he has heard of me and he is extremely complimentary about 'Dogs in the Moonlight', and the fact that I added it without being asked. He asks me how that came about and seems impressed when I explain about Sinead sending it and tell him I talk directly to Abe Goodman, the boss, each week. He says Goodman gives an Ear of the Year award at the convention and that I am nominated, and maybe I will win. He gets me a copy of the convention special of *Sounds Around*, Goodman's tip sheet, and there is my name plain as can be. I can hardly contain my delight. I notice all the other nominees are from places like Minneapolis, Atlanta and Chicago, but at least my name is there.

We don't get the chance to talk much more as a flurry of

limos pick us all up to go to dinner. We end up in some impossibly chic restaurant, but no one has any appetite, except Mark. I know by now that this is a side effect of the coke. It seems so wasteful though, all that expensive food ordered and not eaten; my mother would have a fit. I try to push all thoughts of home out of my head and copy the others while they all rearrange the contents of their plates and drink more champagne. Rolly presses a vial into my hand at one stage, and asks me if I want to freshen up. I do. Everyone else does. It seems most people spend more time going to the loo than eating. Eventually we are herded once more into limos and we arrive at the Roxy. The Roxy! I think of all the groups that played here, The Byrds, The Eagles, Jackson Browne.

I am high, flying, I feel like a rock star. I stay as close to Mark as I can. The concert passes in a mad buzz of music and a haze of champagne and cocaine. Afterwards, we are lined up like school kids and given sticky patches to wear that will enable us to go backstage to meet Jimmy Farrell. He is from Glasgow and seems either shy or bored. Rolly is effusive with him and when it is my turn to meet him he keeps telling him I was the person 'who broke the record wide open'. I nod as if I know what this means. Jimmy doesn't seem to know what it means either. I start to tell him my sister Sinead sent it to me from Belfast when Rolly stops me and tells Jimmy he was 'blown away' by it the very second he heard it, and my enthusiasm only made him work it all the harder. I am appalled that poor Sinead's amazing effort at spotting hits is so cruelly swept away, but before I can utter a word of protest, I am moved along the reception line and Rolly is gushing on about something else to Jimmy. Mark is behind me, I whisper to him 'That's not true, Rolly hadn't even heard of "Dogs in the Moonlight" when I called him.'

230

Mark smiles at me and tells me I will soon learn that the truth has nothing to do with anything in this business. 'And Rolly is *always* the star, baby, you'd better get used to it.'

I don't really care; I can now see that Jimmy Farrell is regarding them all with something close to contempt on his face. Despite their pleading, he is unapologetic; he won't be coming back to the hotel tonight. He will see us tomorrow night. The crowd disperses. Outside, the line of limos await, but I have other lines in mind. I am feeling tired now, and I want to get back to the suite for some more toot. I sit in a daze in the back of the limo on the way home to the hotel.

I feel lonely. Mark has been attentive, and pleasant, but in that almost imperceptible way I think we have both worked out there is no sexual chemistry. He says he is tired and goes to his room, so I go up to the suite alone. The noise level has been jacked up a few notches and there are several more girls, sullen, louche, confident-looking women. I look for Lindy but she has gone. Back at the room my phone is blinking; there is a message from her saying she will see me for breakfast. Paranoia sets in – here I am, my first visit to California, and I am high, alone, and lonely. I think of calling Ireland but I am unsure how much this will cost and decide not to. I would only start blubbing anyway, and then they would think I wasn't having a good time, and I am, am I not?

22

All this chat of Mark's about my possible win has made me self-conscious about my outfit, that it is maybe too Mamie's Modes and not Rodeo Drive enough. The uniform throughout the convention has been jeans and whatever promotional T-shirt you fancy, but apparently this bit is dressy. Lindy comes to the rescue. She thinks we should go to Rodeo Drive to Neiman Marcus and search there. She also suggests that the station should pay for it. I somehow can't imagine Zollie doing a trade-out with Neiman Marcus, but to my surprise when I call him (collect) he agrees to pay half, and says that if I do win, he will pay all, just keep the receipt. I choose a black silk strappy thing with tiny outlines of coloured squares. It is impossibly expensive but it looks the best so I buy it, on Lindy's card. I can't believe Lindy trusts me this much.

In the lobby of the hotel we meet Bob, my smooth-talking, good-looking friend from Atlanta. He is all smiles when he hears we have been shopping. He tells me I am at his table and I am surprised at how relaxed I feel with him after our last meeting in Seattle. I go to my room to get into my gear for the evening. Bob calls and asks if I want him to stop by with some toot, I say yes. It is like fuel for these things, you feel so out of kilter with everyone else without it. I hope I am not getting dependent.

The room is buzzing. We have just watched a new 'hot' group called Sammy and the Mainliners perform their latest offering. Each conference, one or other of the record labels takes it in turn to introduce some new act, hoping of course to break them wide open. Shine is hosting tonight's entertainment. Rolly Young is sitting at the table next to mine looking satisfied with himself. I am beside Tom, Bob and some people I don't know. Afterwards, Jimmy Farrell is to sing 'Dogs in the Moonlight', and then I am to get my platinum disc presented, of course, by Jimmy. I am very nervous. I hope I don't have to speak in case my voice goes weird. Being on the radio is different, you can fool yourself into thinking you are alone, or that no one is really listening. Then suddenly I am up on stage, everyone is clapping and cheering and Jimmy is giving me the disc. It is framed like a picture, it says *Presented to Maggie Lennon for sales of over 1,000,000 records.*

Bob and I sneak out up to his room and do more toot, he wants to do more than toot but I am wearing an expensive dress.

'You're funny,' he says. 'Everyone loved you. You're hot, baby.'

I think it is probably good to be hot, for now anyway. We get back down just as the nominations for my award start. I want to win now, badly. It seems crazy really because two days ago I didn't even know I was nominated. I am certainly getting competitive. I catch Lindy's eye, she is seated at the table next to us. She winks broadly and crosses her fingers.

'And the winner is from Q92 Chattanooga via Ireland, Miss Maggie Lennon.'

I think I am going to faint, but I get up and smile and wobble my way up through a sea of hands to the stage. It feels like the Oscars, and I suppose it is in a way. Abe Goodman, who is surprisingly not much taller than me and like a little leprechaun, hugs me and tells the audience how I was a girl with attitude, I was the sort of programmer they needed in the business, then he hands me the mike. Oh God I feel sick, but I smile even wider and open my mouth.

'Thank you all for voting for me. I can't believe I've won this. Thank you, Abe, for your support.' Abe beams from the front row. 'And I'd like to thank Lindy Konnig for lending me the money to buy this dress. It's such a pity Neiman's don't do trade-outs, because now I'll have to pay you back, or my boss will.'

The audience cheer and laugh at this. They all know about trade-outs. So I get thunderous applause. I make my way back to my seat and plonk the trophy on the table. Everyone hugs me and tells me how wonderful I am. I love it. The trophy is actually a golden ear, it is totally tacky, but I don't care.

Afterwards the suites are really hopping, the music is blasting and everybody seems to love me. I am floating. Bob is marching possessively at my side. I think of 'Hotel California' and realise how on the ball the words are.

In the Shine suite I finally get to talk to Jimmy Farrell. 'This beer is pure piss,' he tells me.

'There's champagne,' I say brightly.

'Ah can't stand it, it's just fizzy piss.' He gestures round the room. 'How can you stick aw' o' this, a wee Irish lassie like you?'

I smile inanely and he shakes his head dolefully. 'Didya ever in yer life think ye would meet so many wankers at once?'

I agree wholeheartedly because I want him to like me, but my words have a hollow ring because I am enjoying the adulation of the wankers very much.

Bob sticks to me like a plaster, all evening. I am trying not to think of Nate, but the buzz is wearing off. Perhaps I will go to bed. I say this to Bob and he smiles at me.

'Want me to escort you to your room?'

'No thanks, I'm really tired, I'll be fine.' And I leave.

My feet are sore anyway as I am wearing my new, very high-heeled shoes, which have wooden soles and a sort of perspex slip-on bit. Lindy has assured me they are 'very LA'. I am walking down the long corridor towards my room when I hear the ping of the other elevator.

'Hey, Maggie baby, gimme some lovin'.' It is Bob.

'You followed me.'

'Well, Maggie, that's what happens if you wear those lil' "follow me, fuck me" shoes.'

'What did you call my new shoes?'

'I believe you heard.' Despite myself, I smile. He takes it as encouragement.

'Shoot, Maggie, you're the star of the show, you can't go to bed early, can you? Why don't we find something to waken you up a little bit?'

I feign ignorance. 'Such as?'

He winks knowingly, and blocks one nostril. 'C'mon,' he says, 'let's go to my room, it's only one floor down, and Miss Sinead ain't here.'

I mean to say no, but somehow I don't, I follow him. His room is not as big as mine. He goes to the little fridge, or mini bar as I have learned it is called, and gets out two beers. We sit at the table. He has a little kit just like Zollie's. I wonder, are they standard issue for record people? He goes through the little chopping thing and lays out lines. We snort a few lines. It is strong. After a few minutes I start to feel a bit shaky. I tell him this and he lights a joint.

'Here, this will help calm you down, hon.'

It doesn't. There is a fast pulse beating in my neck. I am scared. I am going to die of a drug overdose in a strange hotel room in LA with a man I hardly know. My mother will die from the embarrassment of it all. I am about to cry. I tell him I want to go back to my own room. Bob puts his arms round me.

'Maggie, honey, you're just a bit spooked. Look, take this.' He gives me a Quaalude. 'This will work, but let's go back up to your suite and I promise you you'll feel better soon.'

I am so grateful when Bob gently guides me back up to my room, opens the door and says he will put me to bed. I don't even mind that he seems to feel that he is invited too.

He is intent on making love. I tell him I have just broken up with my boyfriend and don't feel ready to be with anyone else, although I am, strangely enough, very attracted to him.

'Never mind,' he says, 'we don't need to have sex, I'll just eat your pussy.'

'But that is sex,' I say in horror, no, make that mild horror, I can't seem to articulate my resistance very well. I should really be screaming, very loudly.

'No, hon,' he tells me, 'I promise you, *eatin' ain't cheatin'*.' He says this with such fervour, almost like it was part of the constitution of the United States, that I give in and have my first experience of oral sex. I am aware that it is extremely

236

intimate and I certainly don't return the favour, but Bob doesn't seem to mind, and it is pleasurable in the extreme. I'm sure it is a double mortal sin, far worse than drugs. I shudder to think what my immortal soul will look like now.

23

Bob and I and a whole posse of Southern record promotion men are on the same flight home, the red eye. The cabin lights are dimmed but we are all wide awake, the steady chopping of coke followed by noisy snorts from the first class loo, can be heard clearly throughout the cabin. The mood is one of hilarity, though everyone looks wrecked. In Atlanta, I say goodbye to Bob. He tells me he will be in touch, but fortunately he is not expecting our 'romance' to continue because, as he confessed when we were on the plane, he actually has a girlfriend in Atlanta. I am surprised at how shallow this makes me feel.

I call Sharla from Atlanta while I am waiting for my next flight and give her the low-down on the convention. I rehash the whole trip. I express misgivings about Bob, and she tells me I have got to stop thinking I need to be in love with every guy I sleep with. I agree with her, although in my gut I don't really believe it. Still, I can live with that philosophy for now. Maybe I have grown up just a bit over the last five days.

Zollie is thrilled to bits with both the platinum disc and the Golden Ear. He is keen for both to remain at the station. I am happy to oblige. In the cold light of day the ear is perfectly ghastly – a large golden ear on a stick. He points out, in his demented way, that I wouldn't have won anyway if he hadn't paid for the dress, so I agree and we are all happy. He gets Ed to do another full page article about me. It is cringingly awful. I sound like a mad leprechaun with golden ears, and the picture of me is vile. The photographer has shot it from below so I look like I have a massive hump on my back and huge nostrils. I send it home anyway; I know my parents will be delighted no matter how I look.

Zollie takes the ear to help with his selling. It is a talisman for him. He brandishes it at possible accounts and tells everyone I am 'flavour of the month'. This means everyone thinks I am wonderful, or says I am even if they don't think it, because other people do and they don't want to look as if they don't know who's happening. I have also made some friends at the convention; Mark calls me all the time now, as does Bob – our little 'escapade' has forged a bond between us. He comes to town to take me for dinner and to work his latest release. He checks into the Hilton. I go to meet him and we do lots of coke and smoke some weed and then we end up in bed. I go into work next morning feeling slightly jittery. I haven't had much sleep. Then, when I am on the air, I suddenly have a massive nosebleed. I put three in a row records on and go outside. Maybellyne follows me into the loo. She presses a cold cloth to my nose and holds it till the bleeding stops. Then she shakes her head and looks me straight in the eye. I am embarrassed at the fierceness of her gaze.

239

'Maggie, honey, this has got to stop.'

'What has?'

'You know what. You look like shit.'

God, this is strong stuff coming from Maybellyne. 'What do you mean?'.

'I mean we are all real worried about you, well, certainly Bilbo and me. How much do you weigh? About ninety pounds?'

'No, about a hundred.'

'It's not enough, and I may be a big ole fat girl, but I'm not dumb. I know what gives people nosebleeds.'

'Maybellyne, I'm sorry, I don't do it very much.'

'Once is too much.'

'I know, but it just helps me forget Nate and besides, everybody in the business does it all the time.'

'You are too intelligent to believe that makes it okay, and last night? Maggie honey, you need to value yourself more.'

I feel ashamed. She is referring to Bob I think. 'I'm sorry,' I mumble.

She strokes my hand. 'You know, baby, you'll be fine, you're already getting over Nate, but you need to ease up on the drugs or you'll forget who you are.'

She's right, of course, but how can I explain how messed up I feel?

'Listen to the words of the song playing right now,' Maybellyne says suddenly. I do, it is Billy Joel singing 'Just The Way You Are'. 'Now that might be real corny but that's how we feel about you.'

I start to cry then and she comforts me. I want my mammy. I want to go home. As Lindy would put it, I need a reality check. But it's impossible. I can't afford a ticket. Maybellyne's words have hit hard though, I have to stop the coke, and I really need to stop obsessing about Nate. But it's not that easy.

Then life intervenes. Sinead rings to tell me my favourite auntie, my Auntie Martha, has cancer and only three months to live. She is our spinster aunt and has been so good to us girls all her life. She also cared for our grandparents till they died, and she is only fifty-eight, it is not fair. I will never forgive myself if she dies and I haven't said goodbye, so I need to get back to Ireland fast. Zollie and Maybellyne agree to loan me the money. I book a flight home, but I want to be sure I can get back into the country, so I call Buford and ask him if he will still agree to marry me. He accepts my proposal with alacrity; I suppose he is an old hand at the marriage game anyway. It is all relatively quick here. You post banns and you can do it in three weeks.

My parents and sisters are thrilled I am coming; mind you, I wouldn't dream of telling my parents how I am suddenly able to sort things out. I have told them my boss has paid for the ticket, and I guess I'll make up a white lie, a sort of venial story about a lawyer getting me a permit. It is far better than admitting the real sin, which by my reckoning my parents would consider major mortal, at least. Hardly an ideal husband, our man Buford. They'd pass out if they knew the truth: a three times married and divorced, overweight country and western singer with one gold tooth, and not even a Catholic. Hell is waiting for me. Well, purgatory, as long as I don't have sex with him, and this certainly is not an option. I'd more or less said that I could only cope with platonic during our chat on the phone, and he'd told me that was cool for now. I suppressed the feeling of alarm at the use of 'for now'.

I am in town at lunch with Buford in Bistro working out some of the details. He seems inordinately happy for a man who is about to be used for visa purposes. Maybe he enjoys the marriage ceremony or something, he obviously isn't too good at the bit after the actual vows are made, but hopefully that won't apply with fake marriages. As I get up to go to the loo I spot Nathan Gilmore in the restaurant. I smile at him and on the way back to my table I stop and talk to him.

'How nice to see you, Maggie, we have missed you so much.'

His words seem so kind and so genuine, I feel touched. He also looks so much like Nate I feel disproportionately familiar. I am about to reply when, to my horror, I burst into tears. He guides me quietly but firmly to the door and out into the sunshine.

'My Lord, I didn't mean to upset you, you poor baby, is everything okay?'

'Yes, it is, I mean it's not really. It's just my Auntie Martha is dying and I have to go home and I am marrying Buford so I can get back into America – it's not a real marriage like it would have been with Nate, just a sort of business deal. I loved Nate, you see, I loved him. Oh, I'm so sorry.' I fall into his big strong hug and sob my heart out. After I wise up and stop, he suggests I come and see him at his office tomorrow.

When I go back in Buford is in a state. He has some poor waitress pinned to the wall accusing her of body-snatching. He didn't see me go outside and consequently he thought I'd collapsed in the loo. When the hapless waitress said I wasn't there he was about to burst in and break down a door. I manage to calm everything down and when Buford introduces me as his fiancée I grimace and don't contradict him. The waitress gets a huge tip by way of apology and Buford and I part amicably with a list of weddingy things for me to do of the form-filling variety. I hope I don't screw up. I guess Buford knows them off by heart.

Lindy is coming down for the mock wedding and then I am returning with her to New York and then home. Zollie is unsure about letting me off the air that long, but I shall only be gone six days, and Maybellyne, Annie Mae and Shirley have all pitched in on my side. I have also just been responsible for 'breaking' a few more hits, and the giveaways are coming thick and fast from the record companies. We are getting free tickets for every major rock concert in Atlanta and Nashville, and we have even been up to Memphis for the Stones' 'Miss You' tour. Zollie loves this high profile and since a lot of it is down to my bullshit and being Irish, I'm still a viable commodity. Anyway, he's a friend now, he is to act as best man at the fake wedding. You need two witnesses even for pretend ones.

I am intrigued by Nathan Gilmore's offer of lunch. He has always made me feel welcome – Bitsy could think what she wanted, but having Nathan on my side meant she toed the line. I also want him not to think less of me. I had given Nate my word that I would not shop him, but something in me wanted to check that I hadn't been painted as the baddie. So during a break at work next morning I phone his office and his secretary puts me straight through. He asks if I have plans for Saturday evening. I say not really, so he says to be prepared for a long day as he would like to introduce me to his favourite restaurant and it might take some time. He offers to send a car, and I am about to say no and then I figure, why not? I might as well have my last dose of luxury.

And luxury it is. I think we are on our way to the golf club, but we only stop there to pick Nathan up and head off to the airport.

'Well, Maggie,' he says as we drive off, 'my favourite restaurant is in Kentucky, my mama was from there. I have a soft spot for the Bluegrass State.'

We drive right to the runway beside the plane. You don't even have to go inside the airport. My God. I try to act nonchalant, but we are flying to Kentucky for lunch. I can't quite take it in, but I have a feeling we're not going there for Kentucky Fried Chicken.

And so I get my first flight in a private jet. It seems incredibly roomy with just the two of us. I am worried that I mightn't be dressed well enough, although I am wearing a nice dress – one of the dresses Nate bought me in Atlanta – and I am thin. Too thin. Then I start to worry that he might be a dirty old man and I may be sending out the wrong signals. My fears are groundless, he is my dream date – affectionate and paternal, and flirtatious in enough measure to make me feel feminine. Another car is waiting for us in Louisville and we are whisked off to a really fancy restaurant. It is obviously a Michelin one, or whatever America's equivalent is. Either Nathan owns it or they think he is God, because I have never been treated so well in my life. The waiters (there seem to be dozens of them) are busy pulling chairs back and anticipating our every whim. My appetite suddenly returns as dish after dish appears before me. Nathan is really good company. I can see why some women prefer older men. He doesn't ask any questions about Nate, just makes a few little remarks that I can nod to, or not. First of all we agree that the lunch will be our secret. Then he says, 'I guess you're upset things didn't work out between you two?'

I nod.

'I know you loved my boy.'

Again I nod. I am not sure how to respond to this. 'Yes, I

love him a lot. I mean, I did . . . I know it all seemed to happen really fast and I'm only twenty-two . . . well, I'm twenty-three now, but—'

'It's not my business, but I'm guessing he screwed up. Now, can things be fixed?'

'I don't think so.'

'Maggie, you know you could have a very comfortable life as Mrs Nate Gilmore?'

'Yes, of course I do, but that's not why I liked him.'

'I know that, but you still have feelings for him?'

'I'm getting over him.'

'You know, not all marriages are made in heaven. If you and Nate like each other and could have a family, make a go of things, well I guess you could both be allowed your "free time" occasionally. You'd have plenty of domestic help.'

I look at him and say nothing. His face is relaxed, but it registers with me then that he *knows* about Nate being queer. They all must guess, even Priscilla. No wonder they were keen on the marriage. Nathan regards me intently.

'I would like you to reconsider. I know Nate wants to marry you. I'm sure he would behave. I think it'd settle him down.'

'I don't think it would work if it wasn't quite real.' I am close to tears.

Nathan is gracious, he knows not to push. Then he says quietly, 'But you are going to marry this singer fella, Buford. Tell me, Maggie, can you trust him?'

'I think so, I mean it's not real either, I won't really be married . . . We aren't going out . . . I won't, eh . . . you know . . .' I am not sure how to put this.

'You mean you won't consummate it?' he says gently.

'No, we won't. He's just doing me a favour. You see, I just

245

don't think I'm ready to leave America for good yet and it's too expensive to get a Green Card from a lawyer.'

'I would be happy to arrange that for you.'

'No, I couldn't let you, but thank you.'

'Okay, here's my final word. If anything goes wrong, I want you to promise me you'll call me and tell me. You hear?'

I promise him I will. And then we have the best lunch of my whole life and the most amazing wine, and I tell him all about Ireland and my mammy and daddy and my sisters and the Christmas tree, and how I felt seeing theirs at Christmas, and he laughs and says Bitsy is just crazy and he'd love to see a higgledy-piggledy tree. He says he's sure I could start a fashion for them.

'I'll bet it's a proper tree, it sure sounds fun with all your little school ornaments hanging on it, not some fancy expensive nonsense. Why, we had a blue tree a year back. I had to put my foot down.' He tells me about growing up with Cora's mammy looking after him and his parents always being away and how he played with Cora's brother because he was the only boy, just like Nate. Then he went away to school and was very lonely. He tells me about taking over the company when his daddy died and how he loves being a granddaddy. We chat endlessly and effortlessly, and he gives me such confidence because he laughs at all my jokes. He also makes me feel important and deserving of all the various people in attendance.

And then, too suddenly, it is five o'clock and it's time for us to leave. The car has waited outside. We fly back and have brandies on the plane. Glenn Gould is playing Bach on the sound system. Nathan says he is the best pianist ever for Bach, and he will send me a recording of him playing the Goldberg variations. I am drunk but happy, and as I get into bed that

246

night I lie awake for a while and think about the unusual day I have just had. Probably one of the best I will have in my whole life, and sadly I realise that I would have done very well as a Gilmore.

But it seems instead I am to be the fourth Mrs Buford McConnell.

'I can't believe I'm going to wear this. I look demented!' I am looking in the mirror at the cowgirl outfit Lindy and Sharla have talked me into wearing.

'Honey, we need to send this up. There has not gotta be one serious moment today. Right, Lindy?'

'Absolutely. Look, doll, it's a *fake* wedding; anyway this is my only chance to go country without losing all my friends.'

Lindy is tying her dark curls with a bandanna, and wriggling into a fringed, suede cowgirl jacket. Sharla and Lindy are my 'bridesmaids'. I am wearing blue jeans, a red and blue checked shirt, cowboy boots and a fringed leather jacket. I also have a cowgirl hat, which I may or not wear. I expect it's the right idea, turning it all into a total farce. Even Buford seems to be playing along, but then he's a cowboy anyway.

The 'ceremony' takes only slightly longer than the driving test, and is easier. At the ring bit Sharla gets a fit of the giggles because the guy who is marrying us is wearing a red wig and Buford's hat brushes it accidentally and knocks it to one side. We are all wasted. Before we came into the 'office', Zollie produced a killer joint. 'Wonderful Wedding Weed' he called it. I need to be stoned to handle this.

We swap rings, kiss and leave with what seems to the poor bewigged notary indecent haste. He just about manages to tell us to 'Hev a reall reall heppy laafe together. Ya heah?' before we leave for Ho Lo's Chinese restaurant in the Big

Black Box, which now has a Pink Floyd *Dark Side of the Moon* prism on the side. Bilbo drives us, of course, I can't believe he doesn't mind chauffeuring loonies around so much. Lindy and Sharla are in the back singing, 'Mama don't let your babies grow up to be cowboys'.

The lunch is, of course, a trade-out. We make our way through a vast menu for eight. The dope has given us the munchies. Zollie is away with the fairies. He keeps saying 'Hullo Ho Lo'. It gets annoying after the twentieth time. Mr Ho Lo, if indeed that is his name, smiles serenely. Personally I think a karate chop in the balls would be a more understandable response. When we get to the fortune cookies – there is unsurprisingly no cake – Zollie stands up.

'I want you all to be the first to know that Shirley and myself have just got ourselves engaged, so the next wedding will be a real one. This here is just a dress rehearsal.'

We all cheer and toast them with Chinese beer. I am genuinely delighted for them. Zollie seems like a different person since he met Shirley. I look around the table: Zollie, Shirley, Bilbo, Maybellyne, Sharla, and Lindy, and Buford of course. I have made some good friends here. I smile to myself. Buford sees me smile and squeezes my arm affectionately.

'Well Mrs Buford McConnell, are you a happy bunny?'

I hear the words out loud and my blood chills. I very nearly throw up the lunch on the spot. What the fuck have I done? Everyone watches as Buford hands me a package, smiles, and declares solemnly, 'I got you something as a memento of the day.'

Shit! I didn't get him anything. I smile, thank him, and take it.

'Go on ahead and open it, baby.'

I open the package slowly and can't believe my eyes. It is

a gun, a fucking gun. Is he crazy or what? But no, everyone is nodding approval. Well, except Lindy, who is trying not to laugh. These people are insane. I know America has a gun culture, I know this is a mock wedding, but how black a sense of humour has he got?

'It's a special ladies thirty-eight; y'all can keep it in your purse. I figured it was the only way you was gonna git your gun in this marriage.'

Oh, so he *has* a sense of humour. I know this is a colloquialism for having an orgasm. Everyone laughs and Zollie pipes up that I was probably missing mine, having to leave it back in gun-toting Ireland.

'Thanks so much, Buford, you shouldn't have.'

I can probably sell it or give it back later. I don't know a thing about guns, even if I am from Northern Ireland. I take a quick look at it and shiver. It looks like a toy. I find it impossible to believe that something this small can end a life. I look at Lindy, her right eyebrow is just passing the top of her forehead. She winks at me and I relax and put it in my bag. I must remember to take it to the safety deposit box tomorrow.

Bilbo has brought a Polaroid camera, which I think is appropriate considering it's an instant wedding. We pose for photos outside in the parking lot. I think we all look absurd but then that's how it should look, and it has been fun. But I have to get home, straighten up my act and get ready for Ireland.

Next morning Lindy and I are on a flight to New York, me with my masses of documentation so that I will be readmitted. I have left my new 'husband' behind without a pang of regret. I hope when I really get married it will be a lot better than this.

★   ★   ★

On the Aer Lingus flight to Dublin, via Shannon, I am sitting beside a priest. It all feels a bit surreal. Maybe the old confessional urge is still in me, because I have to bite my tongue several times to stop myself from confiding in him about my crazy wedding. Now that I am away from the loonies I am starting to come to my senses somewhat. Never mind, I console myself with the fact that we just have to stay married for six months.

The weather is crap the entire six days I am home, but I am not here for the weather. My family are overjoyed to have me back, and I am so happy to see them. There are lots of remarks about my mid-Atlantic accent, which stops after the first day or so when my Belfast nasal has been reabsorbed. My thinness is exclaimed over and worried over by every single family member. Sinead has primed them by implying that it is because of my broken engagement, and I let everyone think that. It is partly the truth – I obviously can't talk about coke. I am managing very well without it though, so I resolve to stay that way. I was getting too dependent, and if I am honest, I don't even enjoy the way it makes me feel. Unfortunately, Sinead has filled their heads full of Nate's wealth and they have seen pictures of him and his house so therefore mingled with all the sympathy is the sense of regret that I won't be elevating the family to millionaire status.

There is a party for me. I have had more to drink in a week here than I would in a month in Tennessee, but of course there are absolutely no drugs. I forgot my birth control pill as well, so I think I might as well stop that for good, or at least till I am in a steady relationship again. My mother seems relieved that I am not getting married yet. She thinks I am not ready for marriage. She is probably right, and she was having awful trouble talking Daddy into going over to that 'godforshaken' country for the wedding.

The day after I arrive I go round to spend a few hours with Auntie Martha. She has a nurse coming twice a day but mostly my mother and her other sisters are taking turns to look after her. She doesn't want to die in hospital if at all possible. She is in the front bedroom propped up with lots of pillows in my granny's big bed. She looks so small and old, I have to stop myself gasping. But she knows I am shocked. After I have hugged her and settled myself on the bed beside her she says, 'Now darlin', I have cancer, so that's my excuse for losing all this weight, what's yours?'

'Well, I expect I didn't feel like eating for a while after I broke up with Nate.'

'But that's been a couple of months now, are you still not over him?'

'I'm not sure. I know it probably wouldn't have worked.'

'Well, with the help of God you'll come home eventually and meet a nice boy here and settle down.'

I am about to say I don't want to when she interrupts. 'I don't mean right away. I know your mammy and daddy would like you home, but this place is in a terrible state now. It's no life for young ones. You have your fun first and get a bit of experience, see a bit more of America. You know you have cousins in Detroit, don't you? You can always visit them.'

'Yes, maybe next year if I'm still there.'

She takes my hand; it's as if she knows everything. She is so wise. 'But don't sell yourself short, and above all don't lose your self-respect. I'll be praying for you.'

Over the next hour I tell her all about my new life, and then I tell her the real reason Nate and I broke up. She doesn't seem shocked.

251

'Don't tell Mammy, please.'

'Sure, why would I? She doesn't need to know, she wouldn't understand. But believe me, love, you did the wise thing. Marriage is hard enough, and them boys are built like that, they can't change. It's very sad.'

I leave feeling heartbroken. Although I say goodbye reluctantly to my family, I leave more certain than ever that I am not yet ready to re-enter the humdrum of this life. I have progressed, I am changed; not necessarily in a better way, but for me in a more dynamic and truthful way. This other Maggie is maybe not so nice a person but is closer to how I feel I really want to be. It is, more importantly, closer to who I am – for now anyway.

24

Back to my crazy life then, but I am not looking forward to getting down to the reality of my bogus marriage to Buford. It makes me uneasy. He spooks me by calling my parents' house twice while I am there. I don't know why on earth I gave him the number, there was absolutely no need. I catch myself laughing to myself about the effect my new marital status would have on all of them if I were to tell. I have had to bite my tongue each time I am alone with either Maeve or Sinead. I hate having this secret, but I have to keep my counsel. My parents would simply freak out. Come to think of it, I am freaking out myself at the idea of what I have done. I am looking forward to my impending divorce which we have agreed will be in six months' time in case we arouse suspicion. Buford had suggested we live together to really fool them, but I'll take my chances, there aren't too many immigration people in Tennessee. I suggest we have a weekly meal together instead, and he settles for that.

The trip back is a pain, delayed flights and storms down the eastern seaboard, and God knows how many changes of plane. I don't know how I manage the drive from the airport, and I am hallucinating by the time I get back. Therefore imagine the shock of opening my apartment door and smelling food cooking and seeing Buford wearing a large plaid apron and wielding a spatula. He immediately calls to mind the nine check teddies from Daytona, except they were a lot prettier.

'Welcome home, baby doll!'

'What are you doing here?'

His face falls when I say this. But I am genuinely puzzled. I remember that I had given him keys because he offered to keep an eye on my apartment during my absence. I had given them to him on our wedding day when I was much the worse for wear and not thinking straight.

'Why, I thought I would surprise you by fixing some dinner. I cook a mean shrimp Creole.'

'I'm not hungry.'

'You will be when you see this meal.'

He gives me a sort of awkward bear hug. I try not to push him away. I expect he's just trying to be sweet, but I have a growing sense of alarm. This is not part of the agreement.

'I've missed you, baby,' he sighs.

'I've only been away a week, why would you miss me?' He ignores this remark. I tell him I need a shower and bed as soon as possible, but then I see the look of disappointment on his face. 'Maybe I'll feel better after a shower. I probably should eat something.'

He accepts this and goes off delightedly to 'fix' rice. Southerners fix everything, nobody here cooks.

I stay in the shower for about thirty minutes. It is blissful. I have missed this water-wasting way to wash while at home.

254

In Ireland our shower is a hand-held rubber tube and barely enough water comes out to wet your hair. Every time you work up a lather, it trickles out and you have to shove your head under the tap to get the soap off. I had to bite my tongue when I was home in case they all thought I had got too jumped-up, but the truth is Americans are spoiled. Life is so much easier here, at least as far as creature comforts are concerned.

Buford is right, he is a good cook. The shrimp Creole is delicious. We have an amicable meal. I tell him all about my trip and about seeing Auntie Martha, and all about my sisters. He has been to Ireland on tour, but never to the North. He says he would like to go with me next time. I say nothing. I can't think of anything I would hate more. I think of how much I was longing to show Nate around Ireland and introduce him to all my friends and I start to feel full of self-pity and begin to cry.

'Why, honey, you're exhausted. C'mon, you get yourself to bed. I'll clear up. Would you like me to spend the night here?'

'No, I'm fine, Buford. And thanks so much for dinner, that was really thoughtful of you. You're so sweet.'

I'd never talk like this in Ireland. It seems so phoney. But I have a split personality now. Buford smiles with pleasure at my words, and I feel like a villain. I can't wait for him to leave. I get into bed and I listen to him thrash around the kitchen for a bit, clearing up. He sticks his head around my bedroom door eventually and says goodbye. It is still early, just about eight-thirty, but I have work tomorrow and I can't wait to be alone. He has left before I remember that I should have asked for my keys back. I fall asleep wishing I was still in Ireland after all, crap showers or not.

I go into the station next day, and nothing has changed,

it's like the song says, 'It feels like I've never been gone'. Zollie is on overdrive and delighted to have me back, we have a lot of work on. Nothing cheers him up more than the prospect of money, and while I was away he has done a deal with one of the largest beer distributors in town. They have bought a huge amount of airtime with us and we are going to be the sponsors of the Roaring River Rafting Trip. We will be sending ten lucky winners and their partners to North Carolina to the Nantahala River for an all-expenses-paid weekend of white water rafting. I have never tried this, but it sounds like it would be fun. There are places for four people from the station as well. I have to cut the commercial and I find the details in my in tray on top of an enormous pile. I am obviously going to have to crowd the airwaves with my voice to make up for lost time.

About two hours after it airs, the phone rings. It is Zollie. I can't make out whether he is laughing or crying.

'Maggie, you have any calls on the giveaway?'

'No, we haven't, it's odd really, isn't it? I thought the phones would be jammed.'

'I 'spect they would be if anybody understood it.'

'What do you mean?'

'Goddammit, Maggie, what kinda language are you speaking? Did you forget all of your American when you were home?'

'I don't know what you're talking about.'

'Hell what does a "wee ring" mean?'

'It means phone us!'

'Not in Tennessee it don't. A wee ring is a small bitty ring, like a pinky ring, Maggie. If you want somebody to phone you, you say CALL US, you got that?'

'Okay, I'll change it.'

'Right, and what in the hell is a crate of beer?'

'You said we had fifty crates of beer to give away.'

'Hell no, I did not! I said CASES of beer; a crate is what you shift furniture in or put a dead body in. Here in America, beer does not come in crates.'

So I change it. I must have picked up all my old habits of speaking while I was home. I preferred the first one though, it sounded less demented.

Priscilla calls just before I am ready to leave the station. I am somewhat jet-lagged, but I've been putting off meeting her for too long. It's sort of now or never, I have run out of excuses. We arrange to meet at the Japanese restaurant near my apartment.

She asks me about my trip home. I am surprised that she knew. I think at first that her father has told her, and I feel betrayed, but she explains that she called the station while I was away. I don't mention the Kentucky lunch, and neither does she. I guess Nathan has kept his word and has not said anything. I still can't quite believe it happened, I have thought about it a lot. I loved that day, it was so unexpected and so grand somehow. I told everyone at home but I juggled the dates and made it before the break up, they were all suitably impressed. It actually made me think at one point that I might have been unbearable if I were rich. I got so much pleasure out of boasting about it. I suppose I had too much hubris. Well, I'm paying for it now.

It takes Priscilla ages to get round to the broken engagement, she is obviously so well brought up. I don't help her; I'm not sure what tack to take on it. She finally shocks the hell out of me by coming out with, 'Did Tommy have anything to do with your break up?'

I can't believe she said that. I practically choke on the

257

rubbery shrimp I am chewing. 'Tommy? What do you mean? Why did you say that?' I squeak.

'Well, I saw him at the airport a few days before you guys split and when I asked Nate why he was here, he couldn't give me a straight answer. In fact, he seemed downright embarrassed. I was puzzled.' I say nothing. 'You know, he's always been totally obsessed with Nate, right from the first day of college. He was like his slave.'

I am not sure how to respond, but she's obviously no fool. So I say, 'Do you think Tommy is a queer?' There, I've said it out loud.

She goes white at once, and for a second I think she will pass out, but she takes a gulp of Perrier and looks directly at me.

'That's not what I meant at all,' she says cautiously. 'He might well be, but he's just real pally with Nate and I guess he prefers him to be a bachelor. I thought maybe he had talked Nate into waiting for a while.'

I look at her and say nothing. I am afraid I might give it all away, but also, I know that in her heart she knows.

'You know, I simply hate the way he is fixated on my brother.' She scowls.

I pause and then say, 'It *was* something to do with Tommy.'
'Oh?'

But I can't bear to tell her what it was so I chicken out. 'I suppose in a way he made things difficult for both of us.'

'You know, Maggie, that is so sad. I know Nate really loves you. He's just plain silly to let Tommy get in the way of that. Maybe in a while y'all can get back together again and I'll get to be your sister-in-law after all.'

Her optimism is touching, but sadly, I fear, unfounded. 'It'd have to be after my divorce,' I say, and I tell her the whole saga about Buford. I ham it up for her benefit. I realise I am laughing without faking it for the first time in ages. I tell her about 'getting my gun', and the absurd wedding lunch at Ho Lo's. We decide to live dangerously and order a pitcher of margaritas. I haven't that far to drive and she says she will spend the night with me. I would nearly marry Nate just to have her in my family, she's just brilliant. She leaves next morning with a thumping hangover and a promise to stay in touch. I hope she means it.

Bloody Buford is seriously getting on my nerves. Three times he has 'dropped by' to see how I am. On the day of our 'month anniversary', he arrives with a bunch of flowers. I thank him profusely and go to the Japanese restaurant with him. Once more I finish a plate of rubbery shrimp. I expect he means well when he comes on all possessive like this, but his behaviour makes me feel powerless and trapped, and deeply beholden to him. On the one hand I can't be rude to him because I have used him shamelessly for my purposes, but he is actually starting to harass me, and I don't like it. He's supposed to be cutting a new album in Muscle Shoals, so why is he in town so much? And I hate the way he touches me all the time, sort of rubs my arm and chucks me under the chin, calls me sugar and lots of irritating stuff like that. Sharla says just to grin and bear it till it's time for the divorce. Only four months to go.

I can't believe I am back from Ireland nearly two months. I haven't talked to Nate or seen him, I am trying my best to dismiss all last traces of love for him, to purge all my soft feelings, to stop my constant longing, but it is really hard. One day, in a fit of abject sentimentality, I go to the bank and take out my ring. I think I will go and throw it at him, and then suddenly I can't bear the thought of losing it. I put it back and decide I have to make an effort to get out more. So I agree to join the gang on Friday night. They have got into the habit of going to La Cantina, one of the downtown bars. Tonight there is a great group on, and one of my record guys, Rick from Warner Brothers, has come into town to hear them. Warner has just signed them. Rick is fun, he knows Bob, and they are buddies. It's a beer and tacos place, but the atmosphere is good and we are in fine form. Zollie and Shirley and Steve have joined us. Little brown bottles are passing from hand to hand, visits to the loo abound, and but I am sticking strictly to the frozen margaritas. I am off the coke, I have promised Maybellyne, and anyway I love margaritas, I get such a buzz from them. Then, on my way back from the loo, I notice Nate. He is standing beside a really good-looking girl. They look as if they are together. Another girl? I can't believe it. But what did I expect? He'd hardly start swanning round town hand in hand with a guy. I am distraught. I go back to the table and within about the next half hour I down an entire pitcher of margaritas.

Sometime later Buford joins us. I look at him smiling and talking bullshit, being really familiar and even worse, groping all over me, and I feel sick. Every few minutes I peer through the crowd to check out Nate and the girl. Who is she? She is looking at him as if the sun shines out of his arse. He is chatting away to her. I hate her. I hate him. Sue Lynne and Clarence arrive and for some reason this puts me over the edge. Next time I go to the loo I take a little brown bottle. Surely Maybellyne would understand, just this once? I need to look bright and breezy, not dull and jaded. I come back and notice that Sue Lynne is flirting outrageously with Buford. He is simpering like an eejit. Good. I am glad she is distracting him from me. She doesn't know about the 'wedding', or if she does she hasn't said. Clarence Lee is sitting nursing a beer and looking dejected.

Sue Lynne manages to get a jibe at me. Obviously the flirting wasn't pissing me off enough. 'I see Nate Gilmore is with Betsy Anne Roberts,' she announces to the table.

I pretend not to hear. She blabbers on. 'You know Roberts, they own the steel company, big time rich, live on Lookout?'

I chat madly away to Rick. My heart rate must be two hundred and forty, but I don't care. I refuse to listen to it. I want it to burst. When will I start feeling normal again? I feel like going over to Nate and asking him about Tommy in front of this Betsy Anne person, but I control myself. There is talk of going to the Hilton where Rick is staying, presumably to do more coke, but I am in a state now and announce I have to go home.

'Maggie honey, there's no way you can drive.' Shirley is concerned.

'I'll take her,' Buford says. 'I need to get an early night anyways. Got to get to Muscle Shoals before ten tomorrow.'

So it is settled. Buford will take me home. Not ideal, but the idea of bed and getting away from here is suddenly appealing, and wasted as I am, I can't help noticing a little moue of disappointment on Sue Lynne's pretty lip-glossed mouth. We push our way to the door past Nate and the girl. He is talking so animatedly to her he doesn't even see me. I am bereft.

I can't remember getting home, but my head is reeling and Buford is 'fixing' me a cup of coffee. I don't want it. I want to be sick. I actually feel as if I want to die, but I am sort of glad he is here. I have done too much bloody coke and my pulse is too fast, after I had meant to give it up for

261

good too. Maybe I will have a heart attack and then Nate will be sorry.

I decide I will take a shower. I stand there crying with the water running down my face and then I get the urge to throw up. I suppose it is practical if you are going to throw up over yourself to get in the shower first. So here I am, wasted, drunk, vomiting, crying, deeply ashamed at myself, and miles from home. If I was any good, I'd sit down and write myself a country and western song.

Buford is in the living room singing to himself and drinking coffee. I pop my head in – there is no door to pop it around – and announce drunkenly that I am going to bed.

'Go right ahead. I'll just stay here till you settle down, honey.' I don't care. I just want oblivion. I take a Quaalude, I adjust the air conditioning unit and get into bed, it used to keep me awake at first but now it sends me to sleep.

I don't know how long I am asleep, or passed out, when I am aware there is someone on top of me, someone heavy and smelling of cigarette smoke and beer. It is Buford. I try to push him off, but the 'lude has knocked me out.

'What are you doing?'

'Honey, I want you so much. I guess despite my heartfelt desire for you we never did consummate that marriage of ours, did we?' He has a wheedling tone in his voice.

'That wasn't part of the deal. Please get off me.'

'Maggie, please let me make love to you, baby. You must know how I feel about you. I thought if I was patient you would come around to me. You don't know how it feels to be me, hopelessly in love with you from the moment I saw you.'

I am pinned beneath him, helpless, and he is naked and aroused. I am afraid, and not afraid. 'Buford, I like you a lot,

262

but as a friend, a good, dear friend,' I stammer. My head is reeling from the margaritas, and the drugs.

'But I lurve you. I want you, baby, just feel.' He whimpers at me, and takes my hand and tries clumsily to make me touch him.

In the end I surrender, and passively allow him to have me. I feel like an empty vessel. It is horrible, but he calms down afterwards, and tries to kiss me. But he doesn't use anything, so if I don't get some god-awful disease I'll get pregnant anyway. I am still off the contraceptives. I tell him I am going to be sick again and I get in the shower for a second time, feeling humiliated and loathing myself. Somehow I get back to sleep in the guest bed. He is snoring loudly in mine.

Next morning I play possum and refuse to wake until he is gone. I lie there listening to him whistle and shower and I feel appalled. I have no control over my life. I seem to have cut the guidelines. My insides churn. I am glad it is Saturday, no work. I call Sharla, no reply. I try Lindy, she answers at once.

'Hey doll, what's up?'

I tell her what happened.

'That's rape!'

'I sort of let him in the end.'

'Well, it was a pity fuck at best. Never mind, Maggie baby, we've all done it, if men only knew. I suppose it's their desperation gets us.'

'Just say I got pregnant?'

'Jesus! You mean he didn't use anything?'

So now I have that to worry about. Plus I have a thumping hangover. Despite the sunshine I stay in the house all day listening to music and feeling sorry for myself. I wish I could lose my memory.

★   ★   ★

263

I haven't answered my home phone for a week. I have a service, call forwarding, which lets my home number ring at the station where Sue Lynne answers it. The pile of pink message slips grows, Buford is my main caller. She hands me a bunch when I come into the station about a week after my encounter with him.

'Why, Maggie, you lil' teaser you! Pore ole Buford has called from Muscle Shoals again. He is just dying to have you return his call,' she simpers at me.

'I am busy, I'll get round to it eventually,' I say tersely.

'He is such a doll, why if I didn't have Clarence Lee for my baby, I would be in lurve with him myself.'

She smiles like a lizard. She has developed this outrageous way of sitting since she got her new boobs; she sort of lies back in the swivel chair and points her nipples at the ceiling. I watch her through the studio window when I am on the air and she is forever tweaking her nipples and rubbing her breasts and rearranging them. They are simply huge now, at least 38DD. She could give Dolly Parton a run for her money. They make her waist seem tiny, and sometimes when I see her mince around the station I get the feeling she will topple over. But she and Clarence Lee are thrilled with them. Zollie finds them a constant source of amusement and butt for his jokes, and poor Bilbo virtually closes his eyes when she passes, so overwhelmed is he by the sheer enormity of them. Yes, Sue Lynne's tits have certainly added a new dimension to life at Q92.

About a week later I am on the air when I see her point to the phone and mouth 'Buford'. I shake my head and she doesn't put it through. I watch her and I see she doesn't hang up, but is pouting and preening and chatting away to him. She can have him. They deserve each other; they both pronounce 'lurve' the same way.

264

The episode with Buford is haunting me. I can't help blaming myself for being so foolish and getting so wasted, and wondering if I have learned anything at all in my year in the States. I have not had a drink since and I have no intention of touching cocaine again. I must be acting too serious though, 'cos after about a week of brooding Maybellyne stops me as I take my coffee break.

'Maggie, honey, what's up?'

'Nothing, nothing.'

'Y'all aren't still fretting over Nate?'

'No, not that, not that at all.'

'You aren't doing that old snorting again?'

'No, I've stopped, for ever.'

'What then?'

I can't say it out loud to Maybellyne, it seems so sordid, and I don't want her to think badly of me, but she teases it out in a sort of yes no quiz, and I tell her all. I can almost feel my body blush as I speak. I want her to absolve me: I have toyed with the idea of going to confession and communion and cleansing my soul, but then I decided it would be hypocritical for me to crave absolution for my misdeeds. I am a grown-up. I need to live with the consequences. Maybellyne is sweet and understanding, and indignant at Buford, but also, she gently reminds me that these things are more likely to happen when our defences are down; in other words when I am wasted.

'He's calling me all the time,' I tell her. 'I won't take his calls.'

'You need to, and tell him he'll have me to deal with if he won't leave you alone. But stay calm, don't get emotional.'

So I finally take Buford's call – we are running out of message slips – and tell him over the phone that I want to go ahead with the divorce. I tell him quietly that I am not in love with him. I say I am scared about being pregnant and he tells me he has had a vasectomy. At least that's one less worry. I tell him I appreciate the fact that he has helped me get a Green Card, but I would not be doing him any favours by encouraging him. I refuse to discuss our 'night of passion' as he calls it, despite his entreaties, and I hope fervently he will get the message. But I am wrong. I think he is living on a different level of consciousness to me. He has talked himself into thinking that if I was to make the effort we could really make a go of our marriage. What fucking marriage? It is like talking to a lunatic. I try to keep calm and talk to him without sounding too desperate – this is Lindy's advice too – but despite my efforts I can't get him to see sense. He is a persistent bastard, and for some reason he has decided that he won't go easily.

25

Fortunately, Buford becomes heavily involved in cutting his new album and is spending most of his time in the studios in Alabama. I am in a sort of routine now. Work is suddenly the most important thing in my life, and I have some good news, Sharla is moving to town. She has got a job here, she is going to sell real estate for Happy Havens. The company builds new developments – a small cluster of houses – and starts up new 'family friendly communities'. I think a job selling real estate would be nightmarish, but the money is good and Sharla is so positive about it all. She thinks she will do well, be a success and own her own home before long. She's probably right. She is charming, and people here like to listen to bullshit. She also looks good and I know that helps in selling, at least Zollie swears it does and he should know. I am just glad she'll be near me, I can use a good friend. One thing I won't do though, even for my closest friend, is move into a Happy Haven development. I have my principles.

The whole thing is dragging on too long. I can't count how many times Sharla and I have analysed Buford's behaviour – it seems so unreasonable. Basically, if I had balls, he would have me by them. Lindy is quite sure it's because I had reacted so badly to his pathetic attempt at lurve-making. It obviously offended his masculine susceptibilities that I didn't swoon with gratitude and desire him intensely for ever more, but what the hell did he expect? I mean you can't just jump the bones of some poor drunken drugged-up female when she has no means to defend herself and call it love, even if you are legally married, can you? I don't think so, especially if the marriage has simply been a dodgy deal in the first place. I don't know. I am going crazy at the idea of having to sue him for divorce. It means I will need a lawyer and they don't come cheap here. Where will I get the money?

I spend a lot of my time now pondering my dilemma, so when Priscilla calls me unexpectedly I am caught off guard and I blurt it all out to her. She is appalled. She is such a kindly soul, but too protected I think, too rich to know what life is all about. At least Nate got out of the house, away from crazy old Bitsy. I am tempted to ask about Nate and the Roberts girl, but I don't. I still think about him all the time. I miss kissing him most of all. He has such a warm friendly mouth. He once told me it hadn't really fitted any mouth but mine so well, and I knew exactly what he meant. These thoughts are flitting through my mind as Priscilla repeats that she thinks I should call Mr Jackson, their family lawyer. Is she out of her mind?

'He's very well regarded, Maggie. Hot Shot Jackson is his nickname,' she says.

'Priscilla, I've only met him once, when I got the engagement ring, and it doesn't seem a good idea to call him now that Nate and I aren't getting married any more. He'll hardly know who I am.'

I pause and before I can stop myself I ask her if Nate is engaged again.

'No, he most certainly is not.'

'Oh? I heard he was dating someone, Betsy Anne Roberts.'

'Betsy Anne?'

'Yes, is he not?' My heart is thumping, I am sorry I asked. What is wrong with me? Why can't I keep my bloody mouth shut?

'No, they are really just friends. Why, she got engaged to Jake Moss, a close friend of Nate's, just last week. I believe Nate took her out for a meal while Jake was away on a business trip just recently.'

For some reason I am flooded with relief. I am so happy I ask her out to dinner next week. My treat, well actually the station's treat. I suggest the Steak House and she agrees. I am glad I have stayed friends with her, it's the last thing I would have expected, but it is consoling in some way.

I am just coming off the air when Nathan Gilmore calls. I am shaking when I answer.

'Hey, Maggie, how're you doing?'

'I'm fine, just fine, I just finished my show, and I am going to go home and have a swim.' I hope I sound scintillating enough.

'Good, well I'll tell you why I'm calling. Cilla told me you were having problems getting yourself extricated from this here marriage of yours. Now don't be mad at her, I quizzed her a bit when she told me y'all had talked and I'd like to help.'

'I don't know what to say.'

269

'Well, let me suggest you say nothing and I have Mr Jackson send him a little letter on your behalf. I think that should take care of things.'

'It's very good of you, but I'm sure he'll agree in the end.'

'Maggie, let me do this for you, please.' And he hangs up. I feel completely overwhelmed.

I get a copy of the letter two days later. It seems fairly straightforward, just informs Buford that Jackson, Buchanan and Jackson will be representing me in our forthcoming divorce which they understand will be a mere formality. I show it to Sharla. She is delighted.

'Honey, you will not see him for dust after this, unless I am greatly mistaken: according to this letter you appear to be a client of the most prestigious law firm in the Southern United States.'

Sharla is not greatly mistaken. Four weeks later and after filling out a lot of forms, and one court appearance lasting five minutes, I am no longer the fourth Mrs Buford McConnell, and he is free to start the hunt for number five.

I enjoy being free. In some way the whole business of going through a fake marriage so soon after I had intended to go through a real one had unsettled me more than I realised it would. And the last few months have virtually pushed me over the edge. I have never even mentioned the episode to my family, they would have gone berserk. So now I won't have to tell them, that's a relief for a start. And the good news is that I have a Green Card. I am now a registered alien. I can move on, I can become a citizen in five years' time if I want. I can't think five years ahead, I am learning to live life as it comes. One thing I do know, I hope I never set eyes on Buford again. I hate the stupid bastard. Zollie is still mates with him, but they haven't been spending too much time

270

together these days. Shirley is taking up a lot of Zollie's time; to Annie Mae's eternal delight, and Zollie's, Shirley is pregnant, and we are all off the drugs. It's official station policy. Buford is still in Alabama trying to record another hit. I hope he misses. Still, maybe I'll get over that eventually too. Lindy says in time I'll see the whole thing as a huge joke. I hope she's right.

26

We are divorced almost six months when Buford finds wife number five. It is Sue Lynne. She has gone and left Clarence Lee, who is allegedly losing his mind with grief. He has just made the last payment on her new boobs. Bad investment. But undoubtedly this is a match made in heaven, she and Buford deserve each other. She is leaving the station and I will suffer through her going away party just to please Zollie. It means I have to see Buford, but I am a big girl now. I have booked a holiday with Lindy and Sharla to the Virgin Islands this fall – I am saying fall instead of autumn. I have reached my twenty-fourth birthday and am still single. I am going to be bridesmaid in September for Zollie and Shirley. I am happy for them, she is so good for Zollie. I think in some way I have found equilibrium.

So this new, mature Maggie goes to Sue Lynne's farewell party. I am feeling cool about it. I know once he is married again I can awaken from the bad dream. I don't even get wound up watching Sue Lynne and Buford eating the faces off each other throughout, I simply wish them well in their new life. She and Buford are moving to Nashville, he is hoping to regain some fame and fortune with the release of this new album. I will be glad to have them out of town. Somehow the conversation gets around to guns – not unusual here. Sue Lynne wants a new one. Why? Did she wear out her old one? I suddenly remember my 'wedding gun'. I say to Buford that I would like to give it back to him, she can have that.

'It was far too generous of you, and I could never use it.' The truth was I had put it into a cupboard in the apartment and forgotten all about it.

'It's a lil' ole lady's gun,' he says, 'too purdy for me to pack, but if you're sure, sugar babe.' He looks at Sue Lynne.

'Oh Buford baby,' she simpers, 'I'd just love to have me a little bitty gun. I could carry it in my purse, for protection. I know just how much you want me to be safe.'

Yes, that's all very well, but how safe are we with idiots like her toting guns about the place?

She nods enthusiastically at the group. 'I just love guns. Whaa', ma daddy has about two dozen. Our family have always had guns.'

'Well,' I say to her, 'you'd better call and pick it up then. I don't want to carry it in the car. I hate the thing. I haven't even touched it ever.'

And tonight, on their way to Nashville, they call to pick it up. They arrive just as I finish my take-away meal. I go to get the gun. I want them all out of here as soon as possible, Sharla is coming round later. Buford looks particularly repulsive tonight and I swear Sue Lynne's tits are getting bigger each time I see her. They sway when she moves. I wonder briefly if they are inflatable. I go to the cupboard to get the

273

thing. I open the box to check it's there and to look, out of curiosity I suppose. It's shiny. I suppose as guns go it is 'pretty' – pretty deadly that is. Then Sue Lynne opens her stupid mouth.

'I guess, Maggie, you're lucky Buford here didn't turn it on you.'

'What are you talking about?'

'Why, the way you was so mean to him, begging him to marry you after Nate Gilmore jilted you, and then two-timing him like that.'

'Two-timing him! What are you talking about?'

'Yes, after all he'd done for y'all.'

I count to ten and grimace. God, give me patience. I feel like screaming. Buford is looking uncomfortable and wants to leave. I don't know what he has told her about us, but I am obviously cast in the role of baddie. I suppose I have to live with that but what in the name of God has he been filling her head with? She is wound up, stoked, she can't stop herself, she is on a roll. All the distaste she has felt for me over the year or so I have known her spills forth like bile. Her lip is quivering with indignation.

'Yew always was a taker, Maggie, not a giver like me. Whaa', I don't know how yew have fooled so many people up till now, yew and that cute aarish accent of yours. Still, I guess they all learn in the end, don't they?' She pauses and smiles her scaly lizard smile. 'Well, Buford and me had better get our asses outa here.'

Go, I think, just get the hell out and leave me alone. But she isn't done yet.

'Oh, and I have some news for you, we're gonna have a lil' baby, what do you think of that? That's all he ast from you and yew couldn't even give him that. Well now he's gonna

274

be real happy and I'm gonna lurve him like he deserves.'

The bastard! He could have got me pregnant, the bloody lying bastard. What a thought! Vasectomy my arse! The gun is in my hand. I suddenly find myself pointing it at her. I pull the trigger. Partly to see what it feels like – it is unloaded of course. There is an enormous bang and Sue Lynne falls down. I guess it wasn't unloaded after all. Then in walks Sharla.

So here I am, waiting for them to come and take me away. What an ignominious end to a blossoming career. I hear the doorbell ring and as if in a trance I buzz them up. Sharla puts a comforting arm round me. 'Don't worry, honey, remember you were preevoked.'

It is like a scene out of a movie. Everything here is in a way. Two paramedics rush in, and with them two policemen. I recognise one of them from the night Nate 'burgled' me. He says hi and smiles in recognition. They seem very friendly for people who have come to incarcerate me.

'I believe y'all have had an incident with a gun?'

I am dumbfounded. I have suddenly lost the power of speech. It all seems to be happening in slow motion. Sharla is explaining something about the gun going off by accident. Buford hasn't said a word yet. It is as if the appearance of the police has rendered him dumb too. The paramedics and the police, in synch, move over to Sue Lynne's body, stretcher at the ready. The paramedic puts a stethoscope to her chest.

'I can't hear a heartbeat,' he declares solemnly.

I feel the room start to spin. I am going, about to lose my grip, when suddenly Sue Lynne sits bolt upright. I scream. I have become a banshee. I scream louder than I have ever screamed in my life. All attention turns to me, I point a shaky finger at Sue Lynne, all eyes follow it. She gets to her feet very slowly. She is clutching herself round the bosom. Her chest is curiously flat. Buford waddles sobbing to her side.

'Oh baby, baby, ma purdy baby I thought yew was a goner.'

Sue Lynne looks dazed. 'Ma boobs seem to have burst or something. Did y'all hear a big ole bang?'

I guess her silicone implants have imploded, and the shock momentarily stunned her. I knew no good could come of those tits. I try to concentrate. One of the policemen is pointing to a hole above the door. There is actually a hole. The bullet has gone into the wall. I sit down, shaking, and finally allow myself the luxury of tears.

Sharla tells them apologetically that it was all just a terrible mistake, we shouldn't have called them at all. I was showing them the gun and it went off by accident. The policeman turns to me and asks if I have a licence for the gun. Buford suddenly finds his voice and tells them he has it and can drop it by the station. They recognise Buford then and spend about ten minutes discussing the merits of country and western music and ask him for his autograph. I wish they would all just go. The bizarre nature of the whole business is too much for me, I just want to sit down and recover. Fortunately, one of the police radios crackles into life and they make to leave. As he is going out the door one of the policemen turns to me and says to me, 'I sure enjoy all of those British groups you play, ma'am. I never miss your show.'

'Thank you,' I manage to croak. I am weak with relief. 'You'll have to drop by the station and I'll give you some albums.'

'Why, that would be real kind of you.'

'No, I'd be happy to, we like to keep our listeners happy.'

'And how's Mr Nate, Mr Gilmore, ma'am?' His tone is respectful.

Of course, my engagement to Nate had been in all the papers, and needless to say we didn't put an announcement in to say we had split. Well this isn't quite the moment to explain the changes.

'He's just fine.' I manage. 'He's doing real good.' I am starting to sound like I am from here.

'You give him my best, ya heah?'

'I certainly will.'

I wonder to myself if that connection had anything to do with how understanding they had been about the whole situation. If it had been Belfast we'd all be in jail by now, or interned.

Buford and Sue Lynne follow them out the door. She is clutching her poor collapsed bosom and weeping quietly. Sharla and I listen as Buford reassures her that he'll pay for the biggest pair of tits in Tennessee. Sue Lynne and Buford *are* the biggest pair of tits in Tennessee. But they are out of my life now, I can move on. Sharla comes in with a pitcher of margaritas and pours us each one. On the radio Joe Walsh is singing 'Life's Been Good To Me So Far'. We drink to that.

277